DEMON SWORDS
IN MAN'S MOST AWESOME WAR

As they came within a hundred yards of the beach many of the Roman soldiers began to glance at each other nervously. The scene on the beach was like nothing they had ever seen before.

A horde of a thousand priests and more were milling along the water's edge, demented, screaming like fiends from the underworld, their hair streaming in the wind, brandishing swords.

Among them were groups of women, seemingly insane, yelling, tearing their breasts, the veritable Furies themselves.

And on the top of the earthworks were the senior Druid magician-priests, their arms upraised to the sky, calling down curses on the approaching fleet . . .

TWILIGHT OF THE SERPENT

THE BOLD NEW EPIC OF ANCIENT SORCERY
BY PETER VALENTINE TIMLETT
AUTHOR OF *THE SEEDBEARERS*

TWILIGHT OF THE SERPENT

PETER VALENTINE TIMLETT

To my parents who, I'm afraid, bear the responsibility of having inflicted me upon an already suffering world . . . and the world upon me, of course.

TWILIGHT OF THE SERPENT
A Bantam Book | February 1977

ISBN 0-553-10081-5

Published simultaneously in the United States and Canada

PRINTED IN THE UNITED STATES OF AMERICA

AUTHOR'S PREFACE

No one knows the etymology of the word
"Britain." The generally accepted answer is that it de-
rives from an old Celtic word "Pretar," or "Pritar,"
meaning "chalk." The old pre-Julian writers referred to
the inhabitants of these islands as the Pretanni, the
chalk-daubed men, and to the islands themselves as
Pretannia, or the Pretannic Isles. The Latin name
"Britannia" was probably a Julian corruption. For the
purpose of this novel I have assumed that prior to the
Claudian invasion in AD 43, and at least up until the
Boudicca rebellion in AD 61, the native inhabitants
would have used the Celtic word "Pretannia," or similar. The latin name "Britannia" would not have been
generally used by non-Romans until well into the post-
conquest Romanization period—but once accepted it
would have been used throughout the remainder of the
400 years of occupation, and Britain it still is today.

The old name for Glastonbury was Glaeston, from
two Celtic words "glaes" meaning "green," and "ton"
meaning "hill"—Glaeston, the Green Hill—and I
have therefore used the name Glaeston throughout this
book.

At the time of the third Roman invasion of
Britain—the Claudian invasion in AD 43—no one referred to dates in terms of AD or BC, for obvious reasons. Throughout the early and middle portions of
this novel I have carefully avoided the mention of
dates as such—the use of the pre-Julian, or even the
Julian calendar would have tended to confuse rather
than clarify the flow of the theme. It is only towards

the end of the novel that I have some of the Christian characters referring to dates in terms of the birth of Christ.

For those interested, however, here is a brief chronology of events expressed in our own Gregorian calendar.

BC 55	—Julius Caesar, first invasion.
BC 54	—Julius Caesar, second invasion.
BC 50–BC 27	—Britain left in peace due to the Roman civil wars. Julius Caesar assassinated in Rome in BC 44. Octavius emerged triumphant and became emperor in BC 27 taking the name of Augustus.
BC 27–AD 39	—Peace owed its continuation to the cautious administration of Augustus (BC 27–AD 14), and subsequently of Tiberius (AD 14–37), which did not include a re-invasion of Britain.
AD 40	—"Little Boots" Caligula (AD 37–41) planned an invasion but had to abandon the idea because of the mutiny of his troops.
AD 43	—Claudius (AD 41–54) successfully invaded Britain with four legions in AD 43 under the command of Aulus Plautius. The Roman army landed in Kent, fought their way northwards, defeated the Catuvellaunni tribe, and established their main base at Camulodunum (Colchester) in 44 AD. From that base they spread out in a systematic campaign of military expansion. By the end of the Plautius governorship in AD 47 the Second Legion held the entire south coast from Kent to Cornwall, the Ninth Legion had established a frontier on the Trent and the Humber in the north, half of the Twentieth Legion held Colchester, and the remaining half of the Twentieth plus the Fourteenth Legion, with Plautius himself in command, had established a frontier against the Welsh

tribes on a line from Gloucester to Wroxeter.

AD 47–52 —Governed by Ostorius Scapula. Continuous warfare with the stubborn Welsh tribes along the frontier. Succeeded in encircling the Silurian tribe in a pincer movement causing their leader, Caratacus (originally the deposed King of the Catuvellaunni) to regroup to the north with the Ordovice tribe. But Scapula finally prevailed and defeated Caratacus and sent him to Rome as a prisoner. But despite this the Silurians and the Ordovices would not give up and guerrilla warfare was continuous. Worn out by the protracted campaign Scapula died in AD 52.

AD 52–57 —Governed by Didius Gallus who, acting on imperial instructions, did not renew the war with the Welsh but merely maintained the frontiers.

AD 57 —Nero became emperor in AD 54 after the murder of Claudius. In AD 57 he withdrew Didius Gallus from Britain and appointed Veranius in his place. Veranius was a strong governor, and although he only served for less than a year before his death he penetrated deep into Silurian territory and laid the groundwork for the subsequent conquest of the Welsh.

AD 58–62 —Governed by Suetonius Paullinus whose stern administration quickly established order. He used the remainder of 58 to completely overrun and subdue the Silurians and the Ordovices, and 59 to overrun the Deceangli in Flintshire. In 60 he made preparations against the island of Mona (Anglesey) and in 61 he attacked and destroyed the remnants of the Druid priesthood utterly.

In his rear Boudicca of the Iceni took to arms in rebellion and sacked Camu-

lodunum (Colchester), Verulamium
(St. Albans) and Londinium (London). Paullinus with 10,000 legionaries and auxiliaries met Boudicca's
horde of 230,000 just north of Towcester and defeated her. 70,000 Britons
were slaughtered for the loss of only
400 Roman lives.

It was against this violent background that the
first Christian church was established in Britain on or
about AD 37, with Druid blessing, and survived not
only the loss of Druid protection when the remnants
of the pagan cult were finally massacred in AD 61, but
survived also against the influx of all the Roman gods,
including the Imperial Cult, and the influx of non-
Roman Mithraism, to become the national religion.

The account in this book of the Roman activities
against the various British tribes, the battles and policies, are historically accurate and can be supported by
evidence from a variety of historians both ancient and
modern. The account of the relationship between the
Druids and the early Christians is mainly fiction. It is
believed by many that a grant of 12 hides of land
(1 hide = 160 acres) was made on or about AD 37 to
12 refugee families originally from Palestine known
collectively as the Culdees led by Joseph of Arimathea.
It is further believed that Joseph had earlier visited
Britain many times on business and had brought the
boy Jesus with him, and that it was the friendship he
established with the Druids during these earlier visits
that caused him later to appeal to them for sanctuary in
Britain for the Culdees during the persecutions in Judea following the Crucifixion. The legend infers that
the reason the Druids granted sanctuary was that they
recognized the Culdees as being the seedbearers to the
New Age, the age of Christianity.

Many who believe the legend state that the grant
of 12 hides of land is mentioned in the Domesday
Book. This is not true. The actual reference in the
Domesday Book is "Glastonbury possesses in its own
ville X11 hides of land that have never paid tax"—

and that is the only reference. There is a later variant of this that refers to Glastonbury as being "The House of God" and "The Secret of the Lord"—and Wm. of Malmesbury states, circa 1130 AD, that he saw the little wattle and daub Christian church at Glastonbury and was told that it had been built by missionaries sent from Gaul by Philip, which missionaries had been disciples of Christ.

There is therefore no real documentary evidence whatsoever to support the story—the whole Culdee/Druid relationship is pure speculation—to believe in the legend is an act of faith. I and many others, however, do believe it, evidence or no evidence. I agree with Tacitus—HAUD SEMPER ERRAT FAMA—Rumor is not always wrong.

And anyway, this book, and the two previous books in the trilogy, THE SEEDBEARERS and THE POWER OF THE SERPENT, were written primarily for entertainment—mine and yours.

P.V.T. 1976

PLACE NAMES
AD 43 –
ROMAN AND MODERN
EQUIVALENTS

Place-Names—Roman and Modern Equipments

Aquae Sulis	– Bath	Isca	– Exeter
Calleva	– Silchester	Dumnoniorum	
Atrebatum		Isca Silurum	– Caerleon
Camulodunum	– Colchester	Lindum	– Lincoln
Corinium	– Cirencester	Londinium	– London
Dubunorum		Luguvallium	– Carlisle
Corstopitum	– Corbridge	Noviomagus	– Chichester
Dubris	– Dover	Ratae	– Leicester
Durnovaria	– Dorchester	Coritanorum	
Durovernum	– Canterbury	Vectis Ins	– Isle of
Eboracum	– York		Wight
Glevum	– Gloucester	Venta Belgarum	– Winchester
Iona (or Mona)	– Anglesey	Venta Silurum	– Caerwent
Insurium	– Aldborough	Verulamium	– St. Albans
Brigantum		Viroconium	– Wroxeter

HAUD SEMPER ERRAT FAMA
Rumor is not always wrong
Tacitus

chapter one

Two score of ghostly figures moved silently and cautiously through the forest, the moonlight glinting on their drawn swords. Slowly and carefully they drew near the outer edge of a small glade and quietly took up their positions. An owl hooted in the distance and more than a few swallowed nervously and glanced about them, their eyes wide to catch even the smallest movement of a leaf. Several of them clutched the amulets that hung around their necks and prayed to Belin, Lord of the Sun, who seemed so distant, so far away, so fearfully absent from this nighttime of the forest. All knew that when Lord Belin was absent from the sky all manner of evil, loathsome things slithered through the darkness of the earth. Some said that in the hours of darkness the very oak trees themselves, given hideous life by the ritual blood that soaked their roots, would stir themselves and grimly stalk the dark forest to do the bidding of their Druid masters. Only the respect they held for their fierce king, and their fear of him, had induced them to follow him into the forest at night—and they took some small comfort from the fact that their chief had been named for the sun god, which should at least give some protection amid this evil darkness.

Cunobelinus himself stood grimly at the edge of the clearing surveying the scene before him. He was a gigantic figure, more youth than man, enormous, powerful and sturdy as a young tree. He held the giant sword of his newly dead father as lightly as though it were a twig. His was not as yet the gnarled and experienced power of older and more mature warriors, but

1

he had all the fearsome, dauntless, impetuous vigor
of youth—yet in addition to the barbaric splendor of
his young strength his eyes were shrewd, intelligent,
even cunning. Here was a man who could not only
fight with the frightening speed and strength of a wolf
but who could also think like a priest—a most dangerous and rare combination.

In the glade a dozen shapes lay huddled asleep beneath skins of fur. A fire burned fitfully in the center,
and beside it a guard nodded, half asleep, unaware of
the gathering force that surrounded them. Cunobelinus
nodded to himself—the reports had been accurate. He
had not believed the tale at first—what stranger would
camp at night with so small a force on the very border
of his kingdom—and yet here they were indeed. Raid-
ers from the Trinovantes, the east coastal kingdom?
Hardly likely—the Trinivantes were ever fearful of
their inland neighbors, the Catuvellauni, and particularly fearful of himself, Cunobelinus, King of the
Catuvellauni. If the Trinovantes ever did dare to raid
his borders then surely they would come in greater
force than a mere dozen.

The Brigantes from the north, from beyond the
River Tees, a fearsome and quarrelsome lot? The Cantiaci from the southeast coast, below the River of the
Med? Again hardly likely—why only a dozen? The
Iceni from the northeast coast? Cunobelinus shook his
head. He had heard that the old king lay near to death,
and Prince Prasutagus of the Iceni was still a boy too
young to plan, let alone launch a raid on the Catuvellauni.

If they were not from any of his neighbor kingdoms then they must be strangers, probably from across
the sea, newly landed at Camulot, the Trinovantian
capital. Whoever they were they had no right to enter
his realm in secret. Their lives were forfeit if only to
demonstrate to his neighbor kings that no one could
secretly enter the Catuvellauni kingdom with impuni-
ty. Twelve corpses on twelve gibbets would make the
message clear.

Cunobelinus raised his sword in signal, but at
that precise moment the guard stirred himself and rose

to tend the fire. The young king shrank back behind a tree and peered through the moonlight, frowning. It *was* a Trinovantian—the way the leggings were wound high around the calf was proof enough of that, a typically Trinovantian method—but still it didn't make sense. Perhaps this dozen was merely the advance party of a larger force close behind—but sense or not it was evidence enough that his kingdom was invaded. He raised his sword again and with a great bellowing roar of challenge he burst from the forest, and with him, from all sides of the glade, came his forty finest warriors, the night air made hideous by their shrieking battle cries.

"Take them alive!" the young king roared. "Leave the guard to me!"

The Trinovantian froze for a few vital seconds in utter shock, then backed away, frantically tugging at his sword. It came clear of the scabbard in time to parry the first blow, but his haste and panic had not put his full strength in his arm, and the blow beat him to his knees. The giant king towered above him, bellowing furiously, his sword raised high aloft. The guard knew that death was upon him. He fell back on the ground on one elbow and raised his sword weakly to fend off the death blow, but the king's sword came down, smashing aside the feeble defense, and the blade bit deep into his skull, the blood and brains bursting clear to soak the ground.

Cunobelinus tugged the sword clear and glared around him. In those few seconds it was all over. A few of the strangers had come bursting from their blankets of fur, only to be seized and pinioned before they could raise their weapons. Most of them had been taken while still asleep.

The young king stalked angrily around his captives. The guard was Trinovantian—or had been—but these obviously were not. "Who is your commander?" he growled.

One of the captives inclined his head, unable pinioned as he was to make any other movement. "We are not warriors—we have no commander—but I lead this party." He drew himself up as best he could. "I am surprised, Prince Cunobelinus, that you do not recognize me—you saw me often enough when you were a boy."

A cloud scudded across the face of the moon, and the glade darkened. The young king peered closely at the prisoner. "You are a stranger here indeed," he growled, "if you call me 'prince.' All know that my father, Tasciovanus, died earlier this year and that I, Cunobelinus, am now King of the Catuvellauni."

A shadow crossed the man's face. "That is sad news—I looked upon him as my friend."

The moon broke clear and Cunobelinus suddenly nodded and snapped his fingers at his guards. "Release him, and all of them—he speaks the truth." He frowned at the speaker. "Very well, but I did not expect to find Joseph Marmore of Arimathea of Judaea skulking at night in secret in my forest. You are fortunate that you were not slain before you could explain."

Joseph bowed. "We were not *skulking,* Cunobelinus, but sleeping peacefully—and I was not aware that we had yet entered your kingdom. I assumed that we were still in Trinovantian territory. We were on our way to see Tasciovanus, your father, and that man," he said, pointing to the dead guard, "was our guide."

"He should have sent a herald on ahead to announce your coming—it is the custom for peaceful travelers."

"Then he has paid a high price for his forgetfulness," said Joseph drily.

Cunobelinus shrugged—the death of a Trinovantian was a small matter to him. "Who are these others?" he grunted.

"Servants of my House—all except this one." He drew forward a young boy, nine or ten years old, no more—robed in white. His manner was calm, and his eyes were grave.

Cunobelinus had noted some minutes earlier that the boy had not shown even a trace of fear when his men had burst upon them. The same could not be said of the others, the servants, who even now were still quaking though they stood released. "Who is he?" he said.

"He is the son of Mary, my niece, of Nazareth,

whose husband is also named Joseph. His name is Jesus."

Cunobelinus circled around and then suddenly bent and thrust his face close to the boy's. The king's hands and sword-blade still reeked of fresh blood, and his wild face could not have been a comforting sight close to, but the boy's expression did not even flicker. Cunobelinus stared into those grave eyes for some long seconds, and then straightened up. "He does not say much," he growled.

"He is not given to idle chatter, true," said the older man, "but already he has confounded the priests of our own land during his discussions with them in the Temple."

The king was intrigued. "He talks with priests?"

"And confounds them."

Cunobelinus frowned. "Is he a priest himself then? He is young to dabble in dark rituals."

Joseph hesitated. "Drucius, your own Druid High Priest at Glaeston, says that he is more than a priest."

The king shrugged. "Who can understand the ways and words of the Druids?" He glanced up at the sky. Above the trees to the east the sky was already beginning to lighten. "Dawn will be with us soon. You will come with us—the rest of my men, and our horses, are a short march from here." He turned and gave instructions to his men and in a few minutes they were on their way, leaving the glade empty save for one sightless face upturned on the grassy dell.

They marched in silence, Cunobelinus himself at the head, a twelve-strong guard to the rear leading the Judaean horses, and flank guards on either side. The strangers from Judaea were bunched together in the middle on foot. Even in his own realm Cunobelinus took no chances when out of reach of his many hill forts. The only thing that puzzled Joseph was that they seemed to be heading south whereas Prae Wood, the Catuvellauni capital, was in the Valley of the Ver northwest of their present position. Soon the party emerged from the forest into broad daylight across open meadowland and Joseph was able to move up alongside the king and ask their destination.

"We left Prae Wood yesterday," said Cunobelinus. "We go south to meet Verica, King of the Belgae, at a tiny hamlet on the River Thamus. He doesn't trust me enough to come to Prae Wood, and I don't trust him enough to go to Calleva—so we meet at London, the least important hamlet on the river border between our two kingdoms. Since you were coming to see my father I assume you have some business to transact. You can come with us back to Prae Wood after I have talked with Verica. It will be safer for you to ride with us than go alone to Prae Wood—these are troubled times and my people are suspicious of strangers."

Joseph nodded. "I thank you. The business I have with the Catuvellauni is simple. Perhaps we can discuss it as we go. I was hoping to purchase some more of your hunting dogs—a hundred if possible. My ship lies at Camulot. I can barter goods for the dogs or pay for them in gold Roman coin, whichever you prefer."

They breasted a hill, and below them a tributary flowed through a tiny valley. Across the stream, on the other side of the valley, a party of men and horses waited. Cunobelinus signaled and saw the raised sword in acknowledgement. "I see no problem," said the king. "One of my chiefs can deliver the dogs to your ship within a week or so and take the payment from your ship-master, in gold I think. My father traded with you many times and I never heard him complain at the bargain he received—I am happy to leave it to your ship-master and my chief to haggle over terms."

Joseph smiled. The instructions he had left with his ship-master would not permit too much haggling. "That is excellent. Once loaded my ship will sail round the coast and meet me in the west, at Glaeston, while I travel overland. Since our business is done—and with your permission—I can take the opportunity to ask Verica for safe conduct through his realm to the western lands."

"As you will." Cunobelinus grunted, and he quickened his pace down the slope and drew ahead of the Judaean.

Joseph shook his head—times had changed. The

old king, Tasciovanus, would have insisted on at least
a week's feasting at Prae Wood in honor of his visit—
would have conducted the bargaining himself—and
would have haggled fiercely down to the last gold coin.
Cunobelinus seemed completely disinterested. This
meeting with Verica must be quite important.

The Catuvellauni mounted their horses, and the
Judaean horses were handed back to the strangers. Within a few minutes the party set off, now a hundred
strong. They rode hard and fast all that day with not
even a single minute's rest, and by the time they edged
the horses down the slope to the River Thamus the
sun was already poised on the brink of the western
horizon. Verica and the Belgae were already there
camped on the south bank. The Catuvellauni dis-
mounted, tended the lathered horses, and set up camp
on the north bank. After a somewhat hasty and even
frugal meal of dried meat and coarse bread Cunobelinus sent an emissary across the river to arrange a
dawn meeting, and with these preparations completed
the Catuvellauni settled down for the night, with guards
posted at every point on the perimeter.

The boy, Jesus, stood alone down by the river
bank staring down into the water as if he could read all
the secrets of the world in their depths. He often spent
hours alone like that apparently deep in contemplation,
and only God knew what grave matters filled the heart
of what to anyone else was merely a young boy. Joseph
was not of the priesthood but considered himself to be
more of a priest than those dogma-ridden fools who
administered the Temple. The Sanhedrin had questioned the boy repeatedly but still they were too blind
to recognize him for what he was. As far as Joseph
knew only three people in all Judaea recognized the
being that was Jesus—his foster father, Mary his mother, and himself.

But curiously there were those outside Judaea who
had glimpsed the truth—one here in Pretannia and
three from the East. Joseph remembered that time two
years ago when the boy was about eight years old—
their last visit to Pretannia in fact. Joseph had presented Jesus at the great Druid college at Glaeston, and

Drucius himself, the Arch-Mage of all Druidry, had talked with the boy in private for a full hour and had then emerged to exact a vow from Joseph to bring the boy again in two years' time—a vow, mark you, not a mere promise, a sworn vow. Even now Joseph could remember the curiously intent expression on the Druid's face when Joseph had described the boy's birth, particularly his description of how three priest-kings from the east had attended what after all was a very humble birth, and in a stable no less, among all the animals. Joseph had not seen the visitors himself— they had departed as mysteriously as they had arrived —but careful questioning of the innkeeper, and others, had established that three strangers from the east had indeed arrived, and wealthy, too, to judge by the description of their raiment—but whether they were priests or kings or both could not be verified, though Joseph himself was quite satisfied as to whom they must have been. Drucius, too, had nodded to himself at the description as though he had expected something of the sort.

Joseph smiled and pulled the furs more closely around his neck. As his eyes closed in sleep he nodded to himself thoughtfully. Only a handful of people had recognized the tremendous event that had taken place, but at this stage a handful was all that was needed.

The Catuvellauni were astir before first light, and so too were the Belgae. The spot chosen for the meeting was an island in the middle of the river, chosen because it could be reached from either bank through shallow water that rose no more than to the flanks of a horse. When the first ray of the sun lanced across the tiny hamlet both kings rode alone down into the water and forded across to the island. Joseph watched them go, his eyes narrowed—a meeting between two such powerful Pretannic kings boded no good for someone.

A hundred yards away, where the tiny wattle and reed-thatched cottages of the hamlet clustered on the north bank, Joseph suddenly noticed the figure of a white-robed Druid priest standing by the water's edge also staring across at the island. Joseph could swear that he had not been there a moment ago. The Judaean picked his way along the bank and as he drew near he recognized the figure. "You are well named, Cranog," he said softly as he came up to him. "Cranog, the heron, standing patiently by a river's edge."

The priest turned to him. His eyes were grave, calm, similar in expression to those of the boy, Jesus —that objective, far-seeing, watchful, analytical expression that Joseph had come to refer to as "the priestly look." It was as though some vast intelligence in an incredibly far-off place was somehow using the priest's eyes to stare upon the world. It was an expression seen in the eyes of only the most advanced priests. Cranog was young to have attained such a mark so soon.

At first the young priest did not recognize him, and then suddenly there was, as it were, a shifting of focus in the depths of the eyes, a change of control, a shift in consciousness, and it was now truly Cranog himself who stared at Joseph as recognition dawned. "Joseph!" he exclaimed softly. "Welcome indeed! How came you to this ill-omened hour?!"

Cranog had been a boy newly initiated into the first degree of Druidism, the blue-robed Bards, when Joseph had first visited Pretannia a decade earlier, and by those strange twists of Karma that some called "coincidence" had been in Pretannia at the time when the boy had taken his initiation into the second degree, the green-robed Ovates, and indeed during his visit two years ago he had attended the ceremony when Cranog took the full Initiation of the White into the third and highest degree of Druidism, and he now wore the White as though he had worn it all his life.

Joseph explained the events of his landing at Camulot some days earlier and his dramatic meeting with Cunobelinus. Then he pointed to the island. "An ill-omened hour, Cranog? You do not feel that they have met to discuss peaceful matters?"

"It may mean a temporary cessation of hostilities between the Belgae and the Catuvellauni themselves," said the priest, "but it is probably stirring an ill wind for others."

"Yes, my own thoughts exactly. I knew Tasciovanus well, and during my visits I came to know the boy, Cunobelinus, but I know little of Verica."

"He is the third of four sons of the dead Commius and no less treacherous than the other three. Commius himself was a friend of Julius Caesar, and although well over fifty years have passed since that cursed Roman withdrew his legions back to Gaul the name of Julius is still reviled by most."

"But not by all."

"True," said the Druid. "Some of the lesser kings still cling to the treaties that Caesar exacted from them, fearful to stand on their own without them, hoping that they will be instrumental in obtaining support from Rome should they be attacked by their more powerful neighbor kings, notably the Belgae, the Catuvellauni, and the Brigantes from the north."

"Faint hope of that since Caesar himself was murdered long, long ago and since no Roman has set foot in Pretannia for fifty years and more."

"And particularly since the present emperor, Augustus Caesar, does not trouble himself to interfere too much in Pretannic matters."

"And for that," said Joseph, "you are presumably thankful. You were telling me about Commius."

"A one-time friend of Julius Caesar," said Cranog, "but he turned against him and joined that magnificent Gallic madman, Vercingetorix, in the great rebellion in Gaul against the Roman occupying power."

"Which was quickly crushed."

"Sadly, yes, and many Gallic Druids were slaughtered in the Roman retribution. Labienus, the Roman, twice tried to have Commius assassinated, but failed. Finally, when Commius abandoned what had become a hopelessly lost cause and voluntarily submitted, it was under certain conditions which the Romans were thankful to grant. One of these conditions permitted him to leave Gaul with his followers and come here to Pretannia where he carved a kingdom by the sword, since known as the Belgae kingdom."

Joseph grunted. "He must have been a fine old warrior to have secured such favorable terms amidst defeat. Tasciovanus always spoke of him with grudging respect. He had four sons, you say?"

"Yes—Tincommius, Eppilus, Verica himself, and Epatticus the youngest. Tincommius succeeded to the kingdom on the death of his father but was ousted and exiled to Rome by his brother, Eppilus. Tincommius appealed to Augustus but to no avail, and Rome recognized the new king and granted the title 'rex' on Eppilus. But in his turn Eppilus was ousted by Verica himself and also exiled to Rome, and again Augustus refused to interfere, and Verica crowned himself King of the Belgae at Calleva, their capital."

"At which the Druid priesthood officiated, I hear."

"True," said Cranog. "Like Augustus himself we Druids accept the reality of what is, and do not waste time and effort bemoaning what might have been. Verica is no worse and no better than the other sons—the Commi filii are all a treacherous, bloodthirsty, and greedy lot."

Joseph smiled to himself at the unconscious use of the Latin language that Cranog presumably detested. "And Epatticus, the fourth son?"

"Yes, Verica there should take care lest he follow the fate of his two elder brothers—Epatticus is no less greedy than the rest of the litter. Verica has sought to solve the problem by officially permitting Epatticus to carve a kingdom for himself along the south bank of the Thamus. Indeed, that land there," he said, pointing across the river, "where Verica is encamped is actually the territory of Epatticus, King of the Atrebates. Verica's own kingdom is now limited to the entire south coast." The young Druid pursed his lips thoughtfully. "In some ways it is a shrewd move—it puts the Atrebates between the Belgae and the Catuvellauni, a sort of buffer kingdom. If the Catuvellauni ever attack south across the Thamus it will be Epatticus who will have to bear the full brunt of it, leaving Verica able to group, deploy, and maneuver in the rear, giving him precious time to prepare should the Atrebates be overwhelmed. In that sense it is a shrewd move, but Epatticus is greedy. He is already slowly and cunningly expanding his territory little by little. Soon he will threaten Calleva itself, the Belgae capital, and *then* we would see a bloody confrontation!"

On the island the meeting had come to a close. Verica's horse was already breasting the shallows across to the south bank, and Cunobelinus came fording to the north. As he came up onto the bank he spotted the two figures and came over to them. "You are Cranog?" he said sourly.

The Druid inclined his head. "Yes. I have been visiting our groves on the east coast and am now returning to Glaeston in the west."

Joseph stepped in quickly. "In that case, and with your permission, Cunobelinus, I and my party will travel with Cranog since we too are bound for Glaeston —if you have no objection," he added, turning to the Druid.

"None at all—you are welcome."

"As you will," said Cunobelinus.

Joseph hesitated, and then said: "How went your meeting?"

"Well enough," said the king.

"New treaties perhaps?"

Cunobelinus frowned, and his eyebrows gathered and darkened above his eyes. "The conversations of kings," he said haughtily, "are not for the ears of peasants, traders, or even Druids! You should take care to curb your curiosity, trader!"

"Yet it is not difficult to guess what you were plotting," said Cranog. "All know that the Catuvellauni under Cunobelinus seek to extend their kingdom yet are hampered by having to keep a large force on the north bank of the Thamus in case of attack by Verica and Epatticus—and the same applies to the Belgae and the Atrebates in case of attack by the Catuvellauni. A truce between you along the entire length of the Thamus would be to both your advantage."

Cunobelinus half drew his sword. "Your tongue could mean your death, Druid!" he snapped.

Cranog shrugged. "Why kill me? The news of your meeting will spread, and as it does so any Druid with half a brain or more will guess what I am guessing now."

The two men glared at each other for some long seconds, and Joseph held his breath, but then suddenly Cunobelinus gave a great bellowing laugh and wheeled his horse around. "I have no quarrel with Druids—or with traders!" and he cantered away back to his men.

Joseph could now breathe with relief. "For a moment there," he said feelingly, "I thought he was going to cut you down—and me to follow!"

Cranog smiled and shook his head. "Fortunately we Druids are still held in some awe, even by kings, though we are not the figures of total authority that we once were. In the ancient days we were as kings to the people, and priests to them also, the true Priest-Kings of old—but sadly those days are no more. Today these so-called kings are nothing more than robber chieftains with little about them that is kingly!"

With a great pounding of hooves the Catuvellauni swept past them up the slope to the north with Cunobelinus at their head. Cranog and Joseph stood watching the dwindling figures until they could be seen no more.

"Come," said the Druid. "Gather your party. Let's get to Glaeston—the air is cleaner there."

* * *

The very first ray of the morning sun skimmed the top of the Hele Stone in the outer circle, lanced through the arch of the great Sarsen Trilithon in the East, and struck the very center of the giant stone circle of Cor Gaur as though it were liquid fire.

Joseph stood stock-still in the center for a few moments bathed in sunlight, and then he sighed and turned to Cranog. "Every time I come to Pretannia I make a point of coming here to see the dawn." He smiled as though slightly embarrassed. "It has become something of a pilgrimage for me," he confessed. "It seems to renew a contact for me, though what that contact is I do not know. For me it is like experiencing 10,000 unbroken priestly years of devotion and service to God in one brief moment of time as that first ray hits me."

"I understand," the Druid said gently. "I know the feeling well."

Joseph smiled. "Yes, of course you do. On my last visit two years ago Drucius was telling me how you Druids believe yourselves to be descended from the migration from the lost city of Atlantis."

"From the Sun Temple of Atlantis on the topmost plateau of the Sacred Mountain that stands on the mighty River Naradek on the Island of Ruta," the young man quoted softly. "Yes, there is a legend that just before the island was destroyed an emigration of the flower of the race was sent forth by the Great Ones, and that after a great many trials and hardships Helios, High Priest of the Sun, and Netziachos, the High Priestess, together with Melchadek, the incarnation of a great inner plane being, arrived on these shores 10,000 years ago."

"It is a beautiful legend," said Joseph. "Drucius also told me another legend about Cor Gaur itself."

"Yes. This great circle and all the other stone circles in Pretannia were built by the ancient Wessex folk 4,000 years ago at about the same time as the great Cheops pyramid in Egypt was built, long before there were any Druids. But about 2,000 years ago, when Druidry was young, the Wessex had degenerated and used Cor Gaur for evil rituals. The legend tells of how Druthin, the then Arch-Mage of all Druidry, and the two great Egyptian priests, Menahotep and Ramin, drove out evil from Cor Gaur and threw down the massive stones as you see them today so that never again could it be put to misuse."*

Joseph looked carefully at the young man beside

---

*For the story of the destruction of Atlantis and the parts played by Helios, Netziachos, and Melchadek, refer to the first novel in this trilogy, THE SEEDBEARERS—and for the story of the building of Cor Gaur (known today as Stonehenge) and of Druthin, Menahotep, and Ramin, refer to the second novel, THE POWER OF THE SERPENT—both novels also published by Corgi Books in London, and Bantam Books in New York.

him. "Do you believe the legends, Cranog—are they true?"

The Druid smiled. "As to the actual events they relate I do not question whethere they are true or not. For me the legends contain great spiritual truths for those with eyes to see and ears to hear. They deal with great human drives, the needs of the human soul. They may be quite literally true, or they may be allegories—it doesn't matter. The real importance of them, and the real truth of them, is the teaching they contain."

"Well, you may be right—I don't know. For me I like to know the actual truth of things."

"Take your own Jewish legends," the Druid said. "Did Moses really hear the physical sound of the voice of God from an actual physical burning bush—or did he see it in his mind's eye as the revelation came to him? Does it really matter which is true? Surely the important thing is the effect it had on Moses himself."

"Ah, yes, but if it was a real burning bush think what a proof that is as to the omnipotence of God Almighty!"

"Joseph, Joseph, is your faith so weak that you need a burning bush to believe in the existence and omnipotence of the Great One? My friend, you disappoint me!"

The Judaean laughed. "Drucius taught you well, my young philosopher! You should have been a Greek—you would have swayed the great Socrates himself with the power of your rhetoric! Come, let's get on to Glaeston—I can hardly wait to see my old friend, Drucius!"

They arrived at the great Druid college at Glaeston during the middle of the afternoon. As the massive gates swung ponderously open they could see the ranks of the Druid priesthood drawn up to meet them. At the rear were the ranks of the Blue, the young initiates of the Bardic Order. In front of them were the Green, the Ovates and the Ovate Druids, and the front ranks comprised the senior priests and priestesses of the White, the Order of Druids, and at their head was Drucius himself. It seemed as if every priest and priestess at Glaeston were there to greet them. It was a great honor and one that had not been granted him on his earlier visit. Joseph was pleased, and as he swung himself down from his horse Drucius stepped forward and embraced him warmly. "Greetings, my friend—you are most welcome—most welcome indeed!"

"Thank you, Drucius, thank you. I am quite overwhelmed by all this. I did not expect such honor."

"There are reasons—special reasons."

"For the boy?"

Drucius hesitated and then stared hard at the Judaean. For a brief moment the Druid's eyes seemed to change focus, and then he smiled and said: "You know more than you pretend, Joseph. Yes, for the boy for reasons that we both seem to know."

Joseph looked round at the serried ranks of priests and priestesses. "Do they know?" he said softly.

The Arch-Mage shook his head. "No, not yet, and it would be an error to reveal the truth too early."

"I agree. Anyway, I *have* brought the boy," he said. "I have kept my vow."

"Yes, and I am grateful. I will not trouble him today but will talk with him tomorrow. For the moment the Mistress of the Blue will look after him—a meal, I think, a wash, and then early to bed—he is, after all else, still a young boy. But for you, Joseph, when you have settled and rested a little after your journey, perhaps you would join me in my private chamber for the evening meal."

The guests were led away to the rooms prepared for them, and the priests and priestesses dispersed. Later Joseph stood by the eastern embrasure in his chamber and stared out at the evening sun. They were strange people, these Druids. They were not a tribe of themselves—their membership was culled from every kingdom in Pretannia. Drucius himself was a Silurian, Cranog came from the Ordovices, Melvina, the High Priestess, came from the Iceni tribe, and if he remembered correctly Morgana, the Mistress of the Blue, had been a sea-dweller from the western isles, a member of the Dumnoni tribe. In addition to these their numbers included members from the Durotriges in the west, and from Verica's own Belgae in the south, and from the Regnenses and Cantiaci in the southeast. There were swarthy-featured priests from the Demetae and the Dobunni and the Cornovii. The Catuvellauni had given their share, and so too had the Coritani and the Trinovantes. From the north had come the young boys and maidens from the fierce and warlike Brigantes, and indeed from the Parisi, and from the wild lands of the far, far north had come those from the tribes of the Novantae and the Selgovae, and those from the Damnonii. Over twenty separate tribes continued to seed the continuing membership of the Druid order, and in addition to these some of the present priests and priestesses had been born within the Druid ranks here at Glaeston or in other groves, and a few came from Gaul and even further afield. But whatever their origin once they became a Druid they threw off all links with what they had been, and from that day forth they did not think of themselves as anything other than Druids. It must be like being born again, thought Joseph—a new beginning, a new life.

A little later, as the evening sun was setting, a young priestess came to escort him to Drucius' chamber. "Ah, Joseph, come in, come in," the Arch-Mage said.

Melvina, the High Priestess, was there, a truly regal, queenly woman robed in silver, who bowed gracefully as Joseph was presented. Morgana, the Mistress of the Blue, responsible under Melvina for the welfare and discipline of the junior Bards, was a magnificently powerful woman, dark and black-haired. Her robe of sea-blue could not quite disguise the litheness of her body. It was said of her that once a year she went to the western isles and there she would plunge naked into the sea and swim out so far that no eye could mark her progress. Some said that she swam to a far dark island and there conferred with the sea-gods and participated in their watery rituals.

Cranog, the heron, was there, and so too was Cerdic, son of Drucius, a small, quiet young man with piercing blue eyes. Kerrin, the Ceremoniarius, was there, responsible under Drucius for all ritual matters at Glaeston including the training and discipline of ritual officers. He was a dark, mysterious, and silent man, a stern disciplinarian.

During the meal they listened politely to his account of the landing at Camulot and his meeting with Cunobelinus. "He is a hungry young man, that one," said Drucius. "Hungry for land, hungry for power, hungry for anything that is not his."

"And hungry for women too by all accounts," said Morgana. "The number of maidens who have gone to feed that appetite is quite remarkable."

"Unwillingly?" said Drucius.

"Oh no, they were willing enough, even eager." Morgana smiled. "He is after all a quite magnificent specimen."

"Enough to tempt a priestess?" said Cerdic.

The Arch-Mage rapped the table. "A poor jest, Cerdic, unworthy of you."

The young man smiled, quite unabashed. "It was said with love, not with malice, but I do apologize if Morgana took hurt from it."

The Mistress of the Blue laughed. "No hurt, Cerdic. I think you are right to remind us that priests and priestesses are still men and women subject to the same basic drives as anyone else. Amongst the Bards in my care there are many who find that human passion is the most difficult trait of all to sublimate to the priesthood."

The Arch-Mage frowned. "If they find it that difficult it may be that they are not suited to our calling. What say you, Melvina?"

The High Priestess was a silent woman, rarely speaking unless addressed, and when she did speak it was usually briefly and bluntly. "My memory reminds me of the hot blood that used to stir my own loins. Has your memory faded so much, Drucius?"

The Arch-Mage continued to frown for a few seconds, and then smiled ruefully. "True enough. It is to my shame that when I was a Bard, newly initiated, I had to do a penance once for creeping secretly down to the river to watch the priestesses bathe." The others laughed. "I had quite forgotten that until Melvina spoke. Yes, Cunobelinus is the archetype of a tribal chieftain—lusty, powerful, indomitable, a bragging, bellowing, bull among men—and highly dangerous."

Kerrin, the dark one, had been standing silent by the embrasure. "But a man that Pretannia will need if ever the Romans come again."

They were all silent for a little. "Yes," sighed Drucius. "That is certainly true." He turned to Joseph. "How goes the Roman rule in Jerusalem?"

The Judaean's eyes grew quite dark. "We bear it because we have to bear it. We are occupied but not conquered. I do not believe that we Jews can ever be conquered in the full sense of the word. Ours is an ancient race with the seeming ability to survive almost anything. We will still be at Jerusalem when the barbarian Roman race has destroyed itself." Joseph's long fingers tapped the table. "But in the meantime we suffer every indignity as best we can. Had we another King David or another Joshua when the Romans came they would not have occupied us so easily. Cunobelinus, Verica, and men like them may not be very priestly—and that's putting it mildly—but as Kerrin says, you will need them if the Romans come again to these islands—and remember, Drucius, the Romans have no love for the Druids."

"Yes indeed, though we have given no cause!" said the Arch-Mage.

"I once read the writings of the infamous Julius Caesar," said Joseph, "and his hatred of Druidry is so deep that he reviles your name with lies. He speaks, for instance, of how Druids commit human sacrifice by stuffing live human beings into a giant wickerwork effigy and burning them alive—and all Rome believes that lie!"

There was an uncomfortable silence around the great table and the Arch-Mage's face expressed an infinite sadness. "It is no lie, Joseph—these vile things do happen in Pretannia, though fortunately they are rare. There is a cult that practice this and other evil rites but they are in no way associated with the true Druid teaching, but sadly they call themselves Druids and so revile our good name. I hold no brief for Julius

Caesar, but in all justice how can I blame the man for not having been able to differentiate between true and false Druidism." He rose from the table and bowed to their guest. "I am sorry to end our evening on so sad a note. If you will excuse us, Joseph—we have our evening meditations to perform and we must sleep so that we are fresh for our usual ritual at dawn."

The weeks passed uneventfully at Glaeston. Joseph visited the Silurians for a week to trade for pearls, and spent a week or more in the Mendips negotiating for lead. His ship arrived at Wirral and had on board a hundred and fifty dogs. "And at a very good price too!" said the shipmaster, rubbing his hands. During all those weeks Jesus spent most of his time in the great college, though he did occasionally accompany Joseph.

Joseph was reluctant to leave—he loved it at Glaeston—but there came a time when he could delay his departure no longer. If he did not sail now the equinoctial gales would prevent him sailing at all and he would be forced to remain all winter. The ship was loaded, the stores on board, the dogs battened down below, and the water casks were brimming. Drucius himself came down to the ship to bid him farewell.

"Joseph, my friend, there is another vow that I have to ask of you." He pointed to where Jesus stood on the poop deck. "Look after the boy. I have told him that when he is a man if he ever wishes to come here to study at our college he will be very welcome, even if he wants or needs to stay for some years. If he wishes to come, will you, Joseph, see to it that he has the facilities to do so?"

"He can have the use of any of my ships at any time," said Joseph, "and I vow that with all my heart. I may perhaps come with him."

"You are always welcome here, Joseph, you know that, but I doubt that it will be I who will greet you. Cranog doesn't know it yet but he will be Arch-Mage after me." He held up his hands. "I know, I know, but I am an old man, Joseph, and my time is near. Do not grieve for me. I am a Druid—death holds no terrors for me." The Arch-Mage grasped his hands. "Farewell,

Joseph. Remember, the boy is very, very special, as we both know." The Druid turned to go. At the gangway he turned again and made a deep obeisance—not to Joseph but to the boy.

As the ship edged away from the jetty out into midstream of the River Parrett the assembled Druids raised their arms in salute, and remained at the salute until they could be seen no more.

Joseph stood at the ship's side for a long time, and there were tears in his eyes. He had met Drucius only a few times in his life but he had come to love the old man and he felt in his heart that he would never see him again.

chapter two

The great central ritual chamber of the Druid college at Glaeston was crowded. Cranog, in the East, was conducting the ceremony as Magus. To his right sat Drucius mediating the Office of the Withdrawn Adept, and by his side was Melvina, the High Priestess. Kerrin, as Ceremoniarius, the Officer responsible for the mediation of the far-off inner plane forces, sat immediately to the left of the Magus. Cerdic took the West, the mediation of Power, Morgana took the South, the mdiation of Love, and Medwenna, a newly initiated priestess of the White, took the North, responsible for the mediation of the forces of the Lodge to the Elemental beings of the Inner Earth. These Officers, together with the remainder of the priests and priestesses of the White, formed the first and innermost circle around the central altar. Those of the Order of the Green, the Ovates and Ovate Druids, formed the second concentric circle behind them, and the outer and third circle comprised those of the Blue, the Bardic Order.

The Eternal Light burned steadily on the altar, and the incense smoke of olibanum and galbanum rose from the thurible. Behind and above the high seats of the Magi hung the geometric symbols of the four Elemental kingdoms—Air in the East, Water in the West, Fire in the South, and Earth in the North. By the side of each of the four senior Officers of the four cardinal points there burned a tall candle. Behind the Throne of the Magus in the East was a highly polished metal mirror. At all other times this was veiled, the black cloth representing the Veil of the Temple, but today at this ceremony of the Vernal Equinox the veil had been removed revealing the reflection of the Lodge in the mirror, symbolizing that at this, the major ceremony of the year, the outer and the inner were as one.

Cranog was coming to the close of the opening section of the ritual. He had already performed the deosil circumambulations, had contacted in turn the great beings at each of the four cardinal points who worked through the physical plane Officers, and had ritually declared the Principles and Virtues under which the ceremony was conducted. Kneeling, facing the East, he had just completed the moving Prayer of Invocation to the Great One. As the last ringing lines faded away Cranog remained kneeling for a few moments of silence and then rose and sat himself again in the East. "Brethren of the Order of Druidry," he said in a powerfully vibrant voice, "I declare that this Lodge is duly contacted on the tides of the Vernal Equinox and that the Light shineth in Darkness. Let all here assembled enter upon their duties, and may the blessing of the Great One be upon you all!"

One of the junior Officers rose and sounded the gong three times, and as the notes died away Cranog said: "Let the Officers extinguish their candles." The Lodge plunged into darkness and Cranog leant across and lightly plucked the sleeve of the Withdrawn Adept's robe. Drucius was an old, old man, more on the inner already than the outer. Cranog knew that he had been clinging desperately to life because of the momentous changes that were to come to Pretannia— but he also knew that the old man had at last given up the struggle. Twenty-seven years had passed since Joseph of Arimathea's last visit, and Drucius had been an old man even then. It was now extremely doubtful that he would last this year's summer. Many changes had taken place in the lands across the sea, but the ripples of those changes had not yet reached these islands. Augustus Caesar was long dead, and Tiberius had ruled as emperor of Rome for twenty-three years and still no Roman had set foot in Pretannia. It was now a total of ninety-two years since last a Roman legion contaminated this land, not since the time of the infamous Julius himself. But news had reached them but a short while ago that Tiberius was dead and that the new emperor was Gaius Caesar, the insane and murderous Caligula.

But the news of Caligula, important though it was, had not made so great an impact on the Druids of Pretannia as the dreadful tidings that they had received four years earlier from Judaea. There was not a Druid in the Temple who had not come to love the gentle, quiet, yet powerful figure of Jesus of Nazareth during the three years that he had dwelt amongst them here at Glaeston. Even Cunobelinus had spoken of him with grudging warmth and respect. It had been a sad day for all of them when he had returned to Palestine to take up his ministry—and yet that sadness was as nothing to the feeling of desolation that had swept throughout Glaeston when the news had come that the Romans had crucified him at Calvary for the apparent crime of sedition.

Cranog leant over and plucked the old man's sleeve again, and Drucius finally stirred himself. "My brethren," he said, and his voice was thin and far away, "instead of our usual equinox address from the inner I wish to speak to you myself from the outer, though indeed the great ones on the inner are close to me as I speak." He paused for a moment in the darkness of the Lodge, and then went on: "My body is old and weak and long past the time when it should have been returned to the earth from whence it came. The time has come when I can no longer hold it together to be with you in Earth, and in order to preserve what little strength I have left this will be the last ritual that I shall attend. For four years now I have been clinging to life waiting for certain events to occur here in Pretannia, and what I am about to say I was going to say at that time, but alas I can hold on no longer. Mark my words well then, brethren, for you will have need of the counsel they contain. The events that I foretell will seem to all Druidry to be the darkness of darkness, and indeed there will be much death and suffering within your ranks—and yet I say to you that amidst that darkness the Light will be born anew."

The incense rose from the thurible and the reflection of the Eternal Light burned steadily in the mirror in the East. "A flower must die in the grip of winter in order to be born again in the fires of spring. A man must die in the grip of old age, and yet the life-force bursts anew in the children he has sired. A sacred oak, though it spreads its arms to the sky for thrice times a hundred years, is still finally stricken by death, and yet the life is carried on anew in the acorns it has borne. All that lives must die, and yet in all that lives the promise of tomorrow's life is contained in the seeds of today's death. As it is in Nature, so it is in the ideas and philosophy of Man. Great ideas are born and flourish, and mankind soars to the heavens on the wings of their truth and beauty, and yet these ideas, these philosophies, must wither and die in order that new life, new ideas, new philosophies can be given the soil in which to flourish.

"Immortality on the inner is the fulfillment of life's vow to all that lives, but attempted immortality on the outer is a crime against Nature, a crime against life itself. Only in death does life renew itself perpetually. Like the sacred oak itself, Druidry must not live forever. It must live out its span of life and then accept death graciously and joyously so that new life can be born anew. Druidry must die in order to fulfill itself, and during its life it must nurture the seeds of tomorrow's life even as the farmer nurtures the seeds of next year's crop. Druidry is not the Light. Druidry is merely one of the lamps that contain the Light, and when that lamp is worn and old it must give way to a new lamp so that the Light can shine more abundantly.

"In old Atlantis the Light shone clearly in the lamp of the Toltec priesthood, but there came a time when that lamp was unfitted for its task and the seed-bearers set forth and so arrived on these shores. For a time the Light shone forth in the new lamp of the old Wessex priesthood who built the great stone circles, but again the lamp became unworthy when the Wessex degenerated into evil, and the Light was transferred to the new lamp of Druidry. For two thousand years has Druidry been a true bearer of the Light, but the time has come when that honor shall be transferred to another, and like the Toltecs and the Wessex before us, Druidry must now face the dissolution of our Order."

The old man paused again. His voice had grown weaker by the minute until it had barely reached the level of a whisper. For some long minutes he remained silent, gathering his small reserves of strength. When he spoke again his voice was a little stronger but still so very weak. "But unlike the Toltecs and the Wessex before us Druidry has not fallen on dishonor. The Toltecs, and the Wessex after them, when their time had come, clung to a power and authority that was no longer theirs. When they could no longer manifest the powers of the Light they aligned themselves with the powers of Darkness and so brought dishonor upon themselves. It is your responsibility to see to it that Druidry does not follow that evil example.

"For two thousand years has Druidry shone with the glory and power of the Light, but those days are now over. For a century and more the inner plane powers have gradually been withdrawn from the Druid priesthood and have been gathered on the inner in readiness for the burst of new life. The new age has already begun in the recent events in Judaea and it is our task to nurture and encourage that new life, and to do all in our power to see to it that the seeds of this new greatness are given the opportunity to grow to full flower.

"Many thousands of years ago the seedbearers set

forth from Atlantis and arrived on these shores, and now again the new seedbearers are due to arrive. Their ways will be different to ours. Their expression of the Light will seem so completely alien to our own mode of priesthood as to cast doubt in your hearts as to their worthiness. But I say to you of my own knowledge that they are the true seedbearers of the Light and that the dissolution of all Druidry, even the deaths of each and every Druid priest and priestess, will not be too great a price to pay to ensure their welfare!"

Drucius rose to his feet and held his arms aloft, and in a burst of sudden strength his voice thundered throughout the Lodge. "Priests and priestesses of the Order of Druidry—I charge you most solemnly and most strictly that it is your task and your honor to succor the seedbearers of the new age against those who will seek to destroy them. Let your guardianship be fulfilled even unto death! In the name of the most holy and omnipotent Great One I lay this task upon you all. Let your duty be fulfilled such that the future races of Man will remember Druidry with honor!" and he turned and strode from the Lodge.

* * *

The sun was hot, and the water was as warm and enveloping as a sensual lover. Morgana dived below the surface and swam down and brushed nakedly and caressingly through the swaying fronds of the river weeds, feeling them trace their loving touch over every surface of her body. Lazily she turned on her back and spread her arms and legs wide and floated to the surface through the intimate caress, arching her back again and again, flexing and reflexing her body as though in the arms of the river god himself. She broke the surface of the river, and her eyes closed and her mouth moved languorously and sensually to take the hot kiss of the sun.

Cranog came down to the river bank and sat by her discarded robe. She came to him through the shallows, the water streaming from her skin, her long black hair clinging wetly and intimately across her breasts.

She came up onto the grass and flung her arms to the sky and stood there as though transfixed by the shaft of the sun's hotness, and then slowly she ran her hands down from her shoulders across her breasts to sensuously caress her thighs. Cranog stepped close to her and lightly kissed each breast in turn, and then slipped her robe over her shoulders. "Ah, Cranog!" she breathed. "What woman has been so caressed by man as I have been by the sun and the river itself!"

Cranog smiled. "I cannot compete with Belin himself as a lover," he said drily, "but there have been moments when you have rolled in my arms with my name upon your lips. I did not hear you cry out to Belin then!"

She looked at him and laughed. "True!" she admitted. "But I am not so sure that even at those times it was not the Lord Belin himself thrusting through you, his priest, to fill me with his warmth!"

He shook his head and grinned but did not argue with her. She was a magnificent woman, Morgana, Mistress of the Blue, and apart from Melvina herself was the most powerful priestess in all Druidry. She had a way of giving herself up totally and utterly and completely to the inner forces of Fire such that her entire being, her body and spirit itself, pulsated with the powers of the life-force, and at those times she radiated the energies of the creative impact as though she was the Sun itself. Drucius once said of her that if every human being vanished from the face of the earth Morgana could repopulate the planet without the aid of man by lying with Belin himself. Of such stuff are legends made.

Cranog remembered her arrival at Glaeston from the western isles some thirty years ago and more. She had been a wildly vibrant, black-haired, vigorously powerful girl whose challenging eyes had struck fire from the loins of every man at Glaeston. Some had said that such abandoned sensuousness had no place in the priesthood, that her vibrancy was that of pure lust —but Drucius had talked with the girl and had subsequently declared that there was no malice in her, no lust in the corrupt sense, but that she was that rare type of priestess in whom the fires of creation burned a hundred times more brightly than in others. Without any training whatsoever Drucius had put her in as the Officer of the Southern Gate in the very next ritual, the Office responsible for the mediation of the inner forces of love and creation, the forces of Fire itself, and even now, thirty-odd years later, the older priests remembered that startling ritual with awe. She, the totally untrained girl, had thrown herself into that ritual with such totally honest and abandoned enthusiasm that she did not just merely radiate the forces of her Office, but became the living creative Fire itself. The effect on all those who attended the ritual was quite devastating. For weeks afterwards the loins of every priest and priestess at Glaeston burned in turmoil, and Drucius was heard to remark, somewhat ruefully: "Well, at least with Morgana at Glaeston the future membership of Druidry is assured!"

Gradually she had learned to control the forces within her and to channel them in the right direction at the right time, but her devastatingly honest abandonment to the forces of creation continued unabated to such an extent that any priest or priestess who felt the stir of sensuousness was said to be touched by "Morgana's Fire."

But of all the young priests at Glaeston it was Cranog who had captured her heart, as much as anyone could in the face of her total dedication to Belin. But even in those early days Cranog had already attained the Third Degree, the Order of the White, and it was obvious that Morgana would soon achieve the same, and there were special rules that governed the mating of priests and priestesses. Those in the lower degrees could mate with whom they liked at their own level. The couple concerned made a formal declaration of intent and from that time forth they were considered more or less as man and wife after the fashion of the peasants. It was rare for those concerned to subsequently attain the Third Degree, for the path to the higher degrees required a dedication that an "avowed" priest could not give. Those of the lower degrees who aspired to the White abstained from mating until their ambition had been achieved. Those of the White, the Third Degree, were not permitted to mate within the lower degrees but only with those of their own level, and the matings in the Third Degree were considered to be of a ritual nature rather than personal, and invariably took place before the altar in the Hall of Ritual, though in private. The only public mating was the once yearly symbolic mating of the High Priest and High Priestess which was an inner ritual that did not require the physical bodies to come together.

Even after thirty years every detail of his first mating with Morgana was still enblazoned within Cranog's memory. He had waited for two years for her to attain the White and had then led her into the Hall of Ritual. He could never remember actually performing the opening section of the mating ritual, though he always supposed he must have done. His memory always began at that point when he turned to face her. In one swift movement she unbuckled and threw off the robe and had stood naked, her arms outstretched, her whole body quivering with expectation. It had been a wild night, and Cranog's fellow priests had joked with him afterwards saying that Glaeston College had been shaken to its very foundations. At dawn Cranog had gone straight to his bed and had slept the sleep of the utterly exhausted, but Morgana had gone down to the river and had swum mile after mile in sheer exuberance.

In successive years Morgana had borne him three children, all girls. Two had died—one from a fever that bad year when the lakes had risen and created a foul swamp of most of the land around Glaeston, and the other in a lone hunting expedition that severe winter a decade ago. They had found the remains of her horse, and the remnants of her bloodied robe, but they had never found her body. It was rare for the wolves to descend from the mountain forests of the north, and even more rare for them to attack a horse and rider. Like the men themselves that winter, the wolves must have been quite desperate with hunger.

Morgana leaned over and touched his lips lightly

with her fingers. "What are you thinking, Cranog—of me I trust?"

He smiled and rumpled her wet hair. "You are too vain to be a priestess—but yes, I was thinking of you, remembering that first time we mated all those years ago."

She chuckled, a low throaty sound. "You were nervous that night, my bold young lover, nervous as a Bard at his first ritual!" She stroked his arm with her long fingers. "I almost had to show you what to do!"

He grunted and fell silent. Presently he said: "I was also thinking of our daughters."

She put her fingers to his lips again. "Shhhh! Don't speak of the dead," she said. "It makes me sad."

Of the three daughters she had borne him only one had taken after her mother, a wild and zestful girl that they had named Zinerva, the white wave. Few priests would go hunting alone in winter, let alone a priestess, and Zinerva's boldness had cost her a bloody and savage death. After the appalling news had been broken to her Morgana had gone away to the western isles to share her grief with the wild seas of her childhood, and on her return she had seemed to most to be the same old Morgana. Only Cranog and Drucius had seen the hurt deep within her eyes.

But their third child had survived and was now a deep and darkly mysterious priestess of the Green, soon to take her initiation into the White. Of the three she had been the one to mostly resemble her father both in looks and in her nature. She was a fair, almost red-haired girl with green eyes. She was a scholar, like her father, but unlike him her studies were not the academic learning of old parchments and rare rituals, her learning was of herbs, and the moon at night, and the still, dark forest. Many a time she had come back to the Temple at dawn, her robe stained with berry juice and crushed grass after a night's ritual under the oak with the elementals of the forest. He had chided her at first, remembering the fate of her sister, but she had said to him: "Look into my eyes, my father. The wolves would not attack me—they would pay me homage," and he had looked into the green depths of her eyes and saw that what she said was true. If Morgana was a child of the sea then her daughter, Gilda, was a child of the forest. Already the other priestesses were beginning to refer to her as the Mistress of the Oak.

"Gilda will take her initiation into the White at the Ritual of Beltane," he said quietly. "Drucius has said that he will attend even though it will take place in the forest in the dark of the moon—but he will never make it."

"How is he?" said Morgana.

Cranog shrugged. "He grows weaker by the hour. How he has lived so long is a mystery to me." He plucked a blade of grass and nibbled it. "Melvina has been in consultation again with the healers but there is nothing further they can do. They say that he should have died many years ago. It is only his fierce grip on the earth plane that has kept the spark alive."

Morgana sat up and shielded her eyes. "Look there!" she said suddenly. "Is that a ship?"

The High Priest rose and stared at the far reaches of the River Parrett. "Yes," he said slowly, "and a seagoing vessel at that." He shaded his eyes against the sun. "Can you make out her markings?"

At forty-five years of age Morgana was still five years his junior and her eyes were better than his. "Yes, some sort of gold symbol on the sail—can't make it out." She rose and stood by his side. "A five-sided star, I think."

"A what?" He grabbed her arm fiercely. "Look again—are you absolutely sure?"

She nodded. "Yes, now that they are rounding the bend, it is quite clear—a gold pentacle." She looked up at him, startled by his expression. "What is it? Who are they?"

He spun her around. "It is them—it must be! By the Lord Belin, it is them! Come, Drucius must hear of this without delay. Let us pray that they have not come too late!"

* * *

Drucius lay on the sleeping couch made comfortable by a dozen skins of fur, but he was barely able to raise his hand in greeting. His skin was so pale as to be translucent, and his arms were like sticks of dead yellow wood. His whole body was so shrunken that he could have weighed no more than a child. But his eyes were still fiercely alive, though withdrawn deep into the caverns of their sockets, and his voice was not yet too frail to speak. "Joseph, Joseph, you nearly left it too late, my friend!"

The Judaean himself was an old man now, though he seemed in the full flower of manhood compared to the shrunken frame of the Druid. He took the thin, dry hands in his own and sat down on the couch. "When I last saw you, Drucius," he said softly, "I did not ever expect to see you again. It is a miracle that you are still alive!"

The Arch-Mage nodded. "So long ago, Joseph—so long ago!"

"Twenty-seven years!"

"And you are now very much the patriarch, like one of your ancient prophets," he smiled. "It suits you, Joseph—very dignified."

The visitor fingered the gray beard that fell across his chest. "In Jerusalem an old man without a beard commands little respect." He had been shocked at Drucius' appearance. It did not seem possible for one so frail to be still alive. He made as if to rise. "But I must not tire you with my gossip—we will talk later."

"No!" The Arch-Mage gripped his hands. "Each day is a battle for me to stay alive, and I cannot fight many more of them. Let us talk now, Joseph—later may be too late." His eyes softened. "Tell us about him, my friend. We have heard naught but travelers' tales, and each tale different to the last. Tell us the truth of what happened."

The others drew nearer to the couch. Cranog and Morgana stood by the foot of the bed, and Melvina, the High Priestess, came to the head. Joseph hesitated, and then smiled. "He spoke of you often, Drucius, and of Glaeston, the green hill. His three years among you all were well spent."

"We were not the only ones so honored," said Drucius.

"True, he spent some years with the Essene community in our own land, and some time in the east, I believe. I like to think that he visited the three priest-kings who attended his birth, though I have no evidence for that at all."

"Did you not ask him?" said Cranog.

Joseph hesitated. "He was not a man you questioned about trivialities. When you were with him there always seemed to be so many more important things to talk about than where he had been, and with whom."

"Tell us about his priesthood, his work for the Great One," said Drucius.

The Judaean spoke for a full hour and answered every question as best he could, though it was Morgana's questions that he found most difficult. Did he never take a woman?" She was quite genuinely puzzled. "Did he never mate with a priestess of your own religion?"

"No, not to my knowledge. Some say that Mary Magdalene was close to his human heart, but I suspect that was simply wishful thinking on her part."

Morgana shook her head. "But all priests mate, those that are capable. Was he not a priest?"

"Well yes, though not in the ordinary sense."

Morgana again shook her head, but the others plied him with more questions and she fell silent. Towards the end of his story their faces darkened as they heard of the betrayal and the trial. "Those who wish to curry favor with our Roman masters," said Joseph bitterly, "are already saying that Pontius Pilate washed his hands of the affair, thus passing the responsibility for his death onto we Jews—but no doubt we shall bear the blame forevermore—but I was there, Drucius, and Pilate did no such thing. Oh, to be sure, he played with the crowd with a politician's skill, seeming to give them choice yet leading them to the choice that he required. Pontius Pilate was more politician than soldier —Tiberius always chose his governors well. Pilate wanted him dead, and Pilate got his wish!"

"But why?" said Melvina. "He was no danger to Rome."

Joseph sighed wearily. "The Romans did not look upon him as a religious leader, or as a prophet, or as a holy man at all. To them he was a political rabble-rouser preaching freedom for all men, and that meant freedom from Roman domination. They suspected him of being a member of the Zealots, and the Zealots were always screaming for the overthrow of Roman rule in Judaea, and still do for that matter."

"And was he?" said Cranog.

The Judaean sighed. "I do not know. He talked with all men in all walks of life. Yes, he will undoubtedly have talked with the Zealots—and yes, he would certainly have had sympathy for their yearning for freedom from Roman domination, who did not? But whether he was an actual member or not I do not know."

"And his disciples?"

"Yes," he said. "One of them at least was a Zealot. Simon the Canaanite was often known as Simon the Zealot."

They fell silent for a few moments, and then Drucius said gently: "And then, Joseph?"

Their visitor visibly sagged at the memory. "I was there," he said simply.

After a few moments' silence Drucius prompted him again. "We have heard that the whole sky grew dark and that the heavens raged in a storm at his passing."

Joseph drew a deep breath. "I know it sounds like a tale to frighten the children with, but it is true—I was there. I have never seen anything like it. At midday it was so dark that you could hardly see his face on the cross."

"And then?" said Drucius.

Joseph shook his head. "None of us can now remember the whole of it. Each of us remembers one tiny incident which has become symbolic of the whole. For me it was his feet." His eyes filled with tears. "Drucius, Drucius, you should have seen his feet! I watched them drive that huge nail through both feet, and I was close enough to hear the bones splinter! And even after they had hoisted the cross aloft I still could not take my eyes away." He buried his face in his hands. "It was his feet! By almighty God, Drucius, you should have seen his feet!"

Great racking sobs shook his body and the Druids fell silent in the presence of such grief. For some long minutes the Judaean wept but at last the sobs died away and he raised his head and wiped his eyes. "I am sorry, my friends—the memory was too much!"

"Go now," said Drucius gently. "Rest a while. We will talk some more tomorrow."

Melvina took the visitor's arm and helped him to the door. "Joseph!" Drucius called, and the Judaean turned. "Tell me, my friend—putting the question in the words of your own religion—do you truly believe that he was the Son of God, the Christ, the anointed one—the Messiah that your own scriptures foretold?"

The entire religious training of his race and their love of religious dogma welled up in Joseph. His every instinct was to question, to analyze, to relate to the Books of the Law and the Prophets, but he thrust them all behind him. "Yes, I do!" he said simply.

"And do you believe that he rose from the dead after three days and appeared to some of the disciples on the road to Emmaus, and subsequently to all the disciples at that last meal together?"

"Yes," he said, "I do!" and he turned and left the chamber.

Even after the door had closed behind him the Druids remained silent, all eyes on Drucius. At last Cranog asked the question that was on all their lips. "Drucius, he has twelve Culdee families with him, some fifty people and more. Are they the ones you have been waiting for—are they the seedbearers?"

Drucius still remained silent for some minutes, and then he looked around at his senior priests and priestesses. "Yes," he said simply. "They are the ones. I am favored above my worth to have been allowed to live to see this day! One more simple task and then I can die in peace!"

* * *

The full moon of the summer solstice rose high in the western sky. Around the outer earthworks of Cor Gaur were a score of fires now allowed to die a little after a late evening meal. The warriors of each tribe gathered with their own kind and peered suspiciously at the neighboring groups. Many of them had never been this close without a sword in their hands. Their fear and distrust and their instinctive urge to fight were only kept in check by the fierce commands of their kings and by their even greater fear and respect of the dreaded Druids who had summoned this tribal gathering. But even so their hands never strayed too far from the hilts of their swords, and each group patroled the perimeter of its allotted area with a dozen guards or more. It was a warm night but instinctively they huddled together around their fires, constantly looking over their shoulders.

Each group comprised exactly one hundred warriors, for this was the figure decreed by Drucius, Arch-Mage of all Druidry, and such was their respect for the Druids that no group had even attempted to bring more. The safety of each group during their journey to Cor Gaur had been guaranteed by the priesthood, and safe conduct back to their homeland had also been assured—and yet each group fingered their swords suspiciously and peered at each other with deep distrust. The tribes had fought amongst themselves since time began and instincts die hard, Druids or no Druids. The priesthood had maintained the same figure for themselves as they enforced on others—Drucius had brought one hundred priests and priestesses only from Glaeston. The priesthood was the only group to go unarmed, for the Druids did not command respect by the sword but by other powers that were only too well known to all.

Around the Bluestone circle were gathered the majority of the priesthood, the green-robed Ovates and those of the White. The tribal kings had each been allotted a space around the circle of great Sarsen Trilithons. At the very center of Cor Gaur a huge fire had been built and the flames from it cast wierdly flickering shadows amongst the giant stones. The fire was tended by Gilda, Priestess of the Green, Mistress of the Oak. Her long fair hair fell to her waist like a copper-hued cascade of reddish gold and several of the tribal kings shuddered as they watched in fascination as she tended the fire. This was Gilda, the witch-maiden, she who could command the wild things of the forest by the power of the green fire in her eyes. All had heard the dark tales that ran in furtive whispers throughout the land, but few had actually seen her. Some said that the wild wolves of the northern hills looked to her as their pack-leader and that she changed her form and ran with the pack through the dark ways of the forest when the moon was high. Others said that the great oaks themselves would solemnly lift their roots and dance ponderously together at her bidding in the dark glades at night, and others said that she lay naked, with the wild things and that the offspring of her matings, half man half animal, ran red-eyed in the deep thickets where few men would dare to tread.

Cranog stepped forward into the firelight and held up his hand. "Mistress of the Oak," he asked solemnly and rituarly, "have all here attended this gathering in accordance with the terms decreed?"

Gilda stared into the fire, and despite themselves the circle of kings stirred apprehensively. It was also said of her that she could read even the deepest and most secret thoughts of a man. The priestess rose and faced the east. "All has been done as commanded," she said quietly, and the kings visibly relaxed.

Cranog nodded. "Then let the matter be stated." He stared round the great Sarsen circle. "You kings of Pretannia have been summoned here to Cor Gaur at the command of Drucius, Arch-Mage of all Druidry, and he thanks you for your loyalty. There are matters of great moment that he wishes to impart to you through me. He asks you to understand why he cannot speak to you himself for he must preserve what little strength he has left. His time is near, as all know."

All eyes turned to where the old Arch-Mage lay weakly on a specially prepared litter. Cunobelinus, King of the Catuvellauni, leaned back against one of

the Sarsen Trilithons. "Our hunters of meat are indebted to the Druids for knowledge of the where-
abouts of game," he growled. "Those of us who farm
are indebted to the Druids for their knowledge of crops.
Our sick and wounded are grateful to your healers for
their recovery. The Druid priesthood comprise our sons
and daughers who chose the priestly way. We would
have come to Glaeston if he had asked us to do so."

Cranog bowed. "We thank you, but it is fitting that
we meet here at Cor Gaur, the once sacred center of
our race. You kings were all crowned here on the King
Stone, as well as in your respective capitals, and it is
here at the King Stone that we will ask you to make
a vow."

Again his eyes swept the circle. The kings of the
western tribes were there, the Dumnonii and the Durotriges. Verica of the Belgae was there, and with him
was Epatticus, King of the Atrebates. The kings of the
Cantiaci and the Cornovii were represented, and there
too was King Boduocus of the Dobunni. The Coritani
were represented, and the Catuvellauni, and there was
the hawk-faced shrewd Venutius, King of the Brigantes.
Fourteen kings in all, a truly royal occasion, though
some were more kingly than others. Of the fourteen
the three most powerful were Venutius of the Brigantes to the north, Cunobelinus of the Catuvellauni of
the middle region, and Verica of the Belgae in the
south. These three would lead the others, though who
could say who the swarthy and dour Silurians would
follow.

"What vow is this?" said Verica.

"A vow that will make this land safe against the
invader," said Cranog. "But first let me make the matter clear." He turned and beckoned the Judaean into
the firelight. "This is Joseph Marmore of Arimathea of
Judaea. In his own land he is a Prince of the House of
David. The royal blood of the ancient kings of Judaea
flows in his veins."

Cunobelinus stepped forward. "I know him. He
is no prince of anything! He is Joseph, the trader. He
used to buy hunting dogs from me a long time ago!"

Verica also stepped forward. "Cunobelinus speaks the truth. I also know him!"

Cranog held up his hands. "Yes, we have known him as Joseph, the trader, but I tell you truly that the blood of kings flows in his veins." He glared round the circle. "But we argue over trivialities, for he is not here as a Prince of the House of David, nor as a trader —he is now Joseph, the refugee, fled from the tyranny of Rome to seek refuge here in Pretannia. Will you be the first, Cunobelinus, to deny him peace among us?"

There was a silence in which only the crackling fire could be heard. Cunobelinus looked up at the black sky pricked with stars. He then stared at the witch-maiden, Gilda. Finally he held up one single finger. "Here we have *one* refugee from Judaea—one! For this you have summoned no fewer than fourteen kings from throughout the land, plus a hundred priests from Glaeston, and put at risk the life of your own Arch-Mage." He glared at the High Priest. "There may be the blood of kings in his veins, but by the Lord Belin, Cranog, his veins would have to flow with liquid gold to make all this worthwhile!"

Cranog smiled briefly. "You are right, of course. He is not alone. He has brought twelve Culdee families, some fifty refugees in all."

Again there was a silence, this time broken by Verica. "I still stand with Cunobelinus—one or fifty, what is this to us?"

Cranog spoke slowly, choosing his words carefully. "They and others in Judaea are the beginning of a new expression of the Light—a new religion if you like. The Druids of Pretannia wish to grant them twelve hides of land on which to build their temple, a tract of land that they can call their own where they can live in peace."**

Cunobelinus shrugged. "If the Druids welcome a rival religion, who are we to oppose the matter—twelve hides are nothing to us."

"They are not a rival religion. We both represent

** 1 hide = 160 acres.

the Great One, though in a different fashion. Their leader was crucified by the Romans at Jerusalem four years ago. You may remember him—Jesus of Nazareth —he studied with us at Glaeston for some years."

Cunobelinus nodded. "Yes, and I also remember him as a boy—a boy without fear."

"He was their Christ, the anointed one, the Messiah promised by their ancient scriptures. Joseph and the other Culdees are all disciples of the new sect called Christians."

"Ah!" Cunobelinus exclaimed. "Now I understand. I hear that the Romans bear little love for these Christians."

"Which is why the Culdees have come here to Pretannia. Glaeston College, the green hill itself, and the hamlet of Wirral, are considered the property of the Druids. We wish to grant them twelve hides of land but we do not have twelve hides to grant. The Durotriges, in whose territory Glaeston lies, is willing to grant twelve hides adjoining Glaeston."

The King of the Durotriges, a grizzled old veteran, nodded. "He speaks the truth—I have so agreed."

"Very well, then what is the difficulty?"

"There is an ancient vow made by the Druids to the Kings of Pretannia," Cranog said, "that the Druids would not seek more land for themselves, nor engage in any land transaction whatsoever, without first obtaining the permission of every king in Pretannia. In the early days of Druidry the warrior chieftains viewed us with suspicion, especially as we had shown ourselves skilled in the use of arms by overthrowing the evil Wessex priesthood in bloody battle. We made the vow to put their doubts at rest, and it was they who insisted that permission had to be sought from every king to prevent the possibility of Druidry aligning themselves with one king against another. It is an ancient vow but we are still bound by it."

Again Cunobelinus shrugged. "I am glad that the Druids respect their vows, no matter how ancient. As far as I am concerned—and I probably speak for all —providing the Culdees remain within the area allotted to them and refrain from interfering in matters that do not concern them, then I see no reason to oppose the matter."

Joseph had so far remained silent, but now he stepped forward. "I swear by all that we Culdees hold holy, and in the presence of you Kings of Pretannia, that we shall remain peacefully in the land granted to us. We seek only the tranquility to follow the teachings of our Lord!"

"Very well—so be it," said Cunobelinus.

"But do you so swear?" said Cranog.

Cunobelinus drew his sword and raised it to his lips. "On my sword I do so solemnly swear—let it turn against me if I am false!" and one by one the other kings rose and swore in like fashion. "But Cranog," said Cunobelinus, "all this is still small note—it could all have been arranged by messenger. I suspect that we have still to come to the main issue of this gathering."

The High Priest smiled. "The King of the Catu-vellauni is shrewd. The arrival of the Culdees does indeed raise a far greater issue, one that threatens us all. Joseph has fled here to Pretannia because of the tyranny of the Roman occupation of Judaea. What if the Romans come to Pretannia? As you have said, Cunobelinus, the Romans bear little love for the Christians and even less for we Druids, and do not let your trade pacts with Rome deceive you into believing Rome to be your friend. If the Romans come to Pretannia we shall all groan under her cruel domination."

Cunobelinus shook his head. "The Romans will not come. Many have tried to sway the emperor in this direction, but failed."

"That is true," said Verica. "My two elder brothers, Tincommius and Eppilus, each in turn fled to Rome when they were justly deposed, but Augustus refused their pleas to interfere."

"And so too did Dubnovellaunus of the Cantiaci when he too fled to Rome, but again Augustus refused to listen. And when Tiberius succeeded Augustus he too maintained this policy of non-interference in Pretannic matters. We have nothing to fear from the Romans."

"But Tiberius is dead," said Cranog. "Gaius Caesar is now Emperor of Rome, and he is an insane and murderous young man. Caligula they call him, 'Little Boots,' and it will not be long before his greedy eyes turn in this direction."

"Well, I know nothing of this Caligula," said Cunobelinus, "but if he is stupid enough to come to Pretannia he will find that we will never tamely submit to occupation."

Cranog shook his head angrily. "If he comes, Cunobelinus, he will not come alone. He could bring five legions with him, thirty thousand men!"

"Thirty thousand! What is that to us? Venutius there of the Brigantes could put one hundred thousand into the field—and so could we Catuvellauni—and so too could Verica of the Belgae. Thirty thousand against one hundred thousand would be no long battle!"

Once again Joseph stepped forward. "You underestimate the power of the Roman army, my friend. With all due respect to the fighting ability of the Pretannic kings, I tell you that the Roman thirty thousand would go through your one hundred thousand like a hot sword through soft cheese! The Roman army is the most highly trained, disciplined, and powerful fighting force that the world has ever seen. You would stand no chance against them—no chance at all!"

"And remember, Cunobelinus," said Cranog, "no Pretannic warrior alive today has ever had knowledge or experience of the Roman army. Ninety-two years have passed since last the Romans were here under the infamous Julius Caesar—even Drucius was a babe in arms at the time."

Cunobelinus was not impressed. "Maybe so, but I tell you that one Catuvellauni warrior is worth ten Roman legionaries!"

Joseph shook his head in despair, and Cranog's voice was sharp with anger as he spoke. "Your arrogance and over-confidence, Cunobelinus, could bring ruin and desolation upon the whole of Pretannia. Joseph is right. If the Romans land with thirty thousand men they will firstly turn to the Belgae kingdom and run through Verica's one hundred thousand while you and the Brigantes sit tight in your own kingdoms and watch. They will then turn to you, Cunobelinus, and run through the Catuvellauni one hundred thousand while Venutius and the Brigantes sit tight. And then it will be the Brigantes' turn. The Romans could take each tribe in turn and defeat them!"

Cunobelinus shrugged. "Even if what you say is true there is nothing I can do about it. I cannot suddenly increase my numbers overnight."

"No, true, but you could cooperate with each other —pool your resources. By your own admission the Catuvellauni, the Brigantes, and the Belgae could put a combined army into the field of three hundred thousand men, and even the Romans would find that a formidable task—and if all fourteen kings were to swear a pact of alliance you could raise half a million warriors between you. Even Caligula would not dare to march against such numbers!"

It was quite obvious that the thought had never occurred to any of them. "Together?" said Cunobelinus. "Impossible!"

"Why?"

"Who would be in overall command? Verica? Venutius? Myself? My warriors would not march under Verica."

"Nor mine under you!" said the Belgae king.

"And if the Romans landed in the south," said Cunobelinus, "do you really think that I would leave my kingdom unguarded while my entire force went south? And even if that could be solved, do you really expect me to give the Brigantes permission to march one hundred thousand warriors through my land? No, Cranog, half a million men is a nice idea in theory but it would not work out in practice."

All night they argued this way and that and Cranog did his best to quell each opposition as it arose, for he knew that the longer they talked the more the idea would take hold. At one point Cunobelinus and Verica nearly came to blows, but finally, just at dawn, Cunobelinus said wearily: "Very well—if the Romans come, *if* they come, we will field the first truly Pretannic army in the history of these islands under the command of the Druid priesthood, though Belin knows that Druids have no experience in war."

"And each king shall be allotted a section of the army to command, and that section shall comprise his own warriors," said Cranog.

"Agreed."

"Then swear it—each of you!"

"Oh very well—yes, yes, yes, I do so swear!"

"Swear on your sword, Cunobelinus, and you Verica, and all of you," and one by one the kings of Pretannia raised their swords and swore the oath of alliance against the Roman threat.

At that moment the first ray of the sun fell on the King Stone at Cor Gaur, and Drucius raised himself up from his litter and walked feebly to the center and raised his arms to the sun. "Let the oath of the Kings of Pretannia be recorded and let the curse of curses fall on he who breaks that vow!"

Despite himself Cunobelinus felt a twinge of fear and apprehension at the solemnity of the dreadful vow to which he was now committed, but then he shrugged and made his way wearily back to his men. "Anyway, it matters not," he muttered to himself. "The Romans will never come!"

chapter three

The stone circle on top of Glaeston, the green hill, was very ancient and now rarely used. The tower, or tor, on the western edge of the plateau was still standing but its stonework was crumbling. Exposed to wind and weather many of the stones lay at drunken angles, and several lay horizontal as though collapsed from exhaustion. In ancient times all the major rituals had taken place on the hill. From there the ancient Druids had called down the Solar Fire, and by the art of their priestly craft had caused the power to flow out through the land along the old trackways, reinforced at each junction by the old stone circles, on and on throughout the land so that to the inner eye the entire network of trackways, circles, cairns, and dolmens glittered like a web of silvery fire, bringing new life, new energy, to all that lived. But alas those days were no more. New priestly ways had been introduced into Druidry and the old rituals were no longer worked except on rare occasions, and the stone circle on the green hill lay abandoned to the nature forces.

But Drucius had a love of the old rituals. It had long been his private opinion that Druidry was all the poorer for their loss. He was quite willing to admit to himself that one of the signs of old age was the complaint that things today were not as good as they used to be—but despite this he was still certain in his heart that Druidry no longer had the priestly power that it once wielded. It was one of the unmistakable signs that Druidry had come to the end of its long and honorable service to the Light. The power had been withdrawn. The new seedbearers had not come before their due time.

The old Arch-Mage had served the great ones all his life since early boyhood, and not once had he ever asked anything for himself, but now, in the extremity of shriveled old age, he asked a favor—to be allowed to terminate this incarnation in the way of the Arch-Mages of old, in the ancient ritual known as the Death of the Adept—and his wish was granted.

In the darkness of pre-dawn the procession as-headdress of fiery green—and Cerdic, son of Drucius, clothed in their finest ritual robes. Cranog, as High Priest, wore a robe of gold with a glittering headdress of red and yellow like the flames of fire. Melvina, as High Priestess, was robed in silver and white—Morgana in the deepest blues and greens of the sea—Kerrin, the dark one, was in midnight black with a headdress of fiery green—and Cerdic, son of Drucius, was swathed in blood-red, the color of the inner earth. The senior Officers took up their positions at the head of the procession. Behind them was the gold-canopied litter bearing the frail Arch-Mage, borne up by six of the youngest and most junior Bards. Next came those of the Order of the White, the senior degree, then those of the Green, and finally the files of the Blue-robed Bards, their youthful exuberance awed into silence by the solemnity of the occasion. Apart from the senior Officers each priest and priestess carried a waxen torch. At a signal from Kerrin, the Ceremoniarius, the procession began and as each filed past the great fire in the center of the courtyard they lit their torches until the procession circling the courtyard became a snake of a hundred glittering scales of fire. When all the torches were lit Kerrin gave another signal and the great gates swung ponderously open, and as Cranog headed the procession through the gates the entire assembly broke into the very moving and very ancient chant from the old Fourth Degree ritual.

> "Helios, Helios, quanto rhopantanek,
> quanto rhopantanek, Helioun!
> Waft thou my soul down the River of Naradek.
> Bring it to Light, and to Life, and to Love."

Close by the gates of Glaeston were the tents of the Culdees. The refugees were astir early to watch the procession. Joseph stood at the opening of his tent. His son, Josue, and his daughter, Anna, stood a little to one side. From another tent Zaacheus came over to talk to Joseph. "What do you make of it, Joseph?" he said quietly. The procession, a hundred strong and more, the waxen torches burning brightly in the darkness of the night, were now clear of the courtyard and heading towards the green hill. "It smacks too much of sorcery to me!"

Joseph shook his head thoughtfully. "They are good people, Zaacheus," he said reprovingly. "They have been servants of the Great One for nearly four thousand years. There is no evil in this."

"The Great One? Is the name of God a stranger

to your lips now, Joseph? Have you already adopted the language of these primitive barbarian priests?"

Joseph smiled in the darkness. "The almighty God is known by many names to many people."

"He is the God of Israel, and we are his Chosen People!"

"God of Israel, yes, but also the God of many other races as well—the father of all humanity, if you like."

"But we are the Chosen Ones."

"Yes, chosen for a particular task, but who is to say that others have not also been chosen for other tasks? Are you so intimate with the mind of God, Zaacheus, that you can declare unreservedly that we are the only race favored by his grace?"

"But he sent his Son to us!"

"And we condoned his crucifixion even if we did not actually carry out the execution. Remember that, Zaacheus, before you condemn the actions of others."

They fell silent, watching the procession. Zaacheus tugged at his beard nervously. "It still smacks of sorcery to me," he said irritably. "And what language is that? It sounds a barbaric and evil tongue!"

"It sounds strange to our ears," Joseph agreed, "but that does not make it evil. The first line is the old Atlantean tongue, so I am told, and the rest is modern Pretannic."

Anna came over to her father. "It sounds beautiful."

He put his arm around her shoulders. "Yes it does—and sad. Drucius, the old man, is due to die today."

She looked puzzled. "I still don't understand how they know—are you sure they won't kill him?"

He laughed gently. "Yes, of course I'm sure. Cranog told me that the healers forecast today as the day, and they will remain up there all day if necessary, and all night and tomorrow until death occurs naturally." He squeezed her shoulders. "I admire them immensely. They look upon the whole of life as one long sacrament. It is no bad attitude to have, despite what Zaacheus might say."

His friend grunted. "A sacrament? Yes, but to what? I just sometimes wonder whether the god they worship is the same as our own true God."

Joseph sighed. Zaacheus was of the old school. It had been hard for him to follow the new way of the Christ, let alone be driven into exile among strangers and strange practices. "There is only one God, Zaacheus—many names but one God."

"The Great One!" said Zaacheus sarcastically, and he spat on the ground.

Joseph rounded on him angrily. "Zaacheus! Remember the old rule—'Thou shalt not blaspheme the name by which another man knoweth God.' When you blaspheme the Great One you blaspheme almighty God himself!"

"They are pagans!" said Zaacheus. "Mark my words well, Joseph—despite your friendship with the Druids it may yet be shown that their so-called Great One is one of the demons of darkness!" and he strode angrily away.

Joseph watched him go and shook his head sadly. "He is a good man, but at times he can be so blind."

Anna looked up at her father. "Are you yourself so certain, Father?" she asked.

He frowned. "Not you as well, Anna! What has come over my people that they can be so unjust? We have been welcomed here as honored guests. It was the Druid priesthood themselves who summoned the Pretannic kings and exacted a vow from them to permit us to worship in peace and to establish our church. Was that the work of evil?"

"No, perhaps not. It is just that . . . oh, I don't know . . . some of the things they do would be called evil in Judaea."

"What things?"

She looked away, suddenly embarrassed. "Don't ask me—I cannot speak of them."

"She means Morgana," said Josue, coming over to them. "And it is she who has stirred Zaacheus to anger against the Druids."

Joseph stared at his son. "What has Morgana to do with this?"

The boy was in his mid-twenties, as yet unmarried. A studious youth, and quiet, not normally given to speaking without being asked. "I was with Zaacheus and others yesterday. We went down to the river to fill our drinking urns with water and for the women to do the washing. Anna was with us."

"And?"

"Morgana was there—swimming. When she saw us she did not seek to hide herself but boldly came up out of the water in front of us all."

"So?"

"But she was naked, Father—completely naked. Zaacheus rebuked her gently but she laughed and flaunted herself at him. He grew red, and very angry, and drove her away. Others have said that they have seen Druid priests and priestesses coupling naked in the fields like animals."

So it had come as Joseph had known it would. The Druid attitude to mating was so alien to Judaean custom. "Drucius explained to me about Morgana," he said carefully. "In their priesthood she represents the fires of creation. For her it would be a sin against her priestly vows to deny the creative fire within her. I admit that in these matters they exhibit a freedom that is totally unknown in our own customs, but that does not necessarily mean that their way is evil."

"Zaacheus said that in Judaea she would be called a whore," said Josue.

"But we are not in Judaea, my son, we are here in Pretannia. We cannot expect the whole world to follow the ways of Judaea."

"A whore is a whore, Father, in any land!"

"If you are going to argue, Josue, then at least get your facts right. A whore is one who exacts payment for the use of her body. Morgana demands no payment, therefore she is not a whore."

"Don't split hairs, Father! Her actions were those of a jezebel!"

Joseph shook his head. "You are quick to condemn."

"Very well, let me then ask you two questions, Father. Would you smile tolerantly and condone the matter if I were to go to Morgana and lay with her? And would you also smile if Anna here removed her raiment and stood naked before your friends?"

Even in the darkness Joseph could see that Anna was overcome with embarrassment. "It is not seemly to discuss these things in the presence of your sister."

"You are right—it is unseemly, but nevertheless it has to be discussed. You spoke of Zaacheus being blind, but what of your own inability to see the growing unrest around you. Many of our people are troubled by these matters and look to you for guidance. What will you tell them?"

Joseph remained silent for some long minutes, and then finally he said: "I would say let not the fish of the sea condemn the birds for flying, and let not the birds of the air condemn the fish for swimming. Let each live out their lives in their allotted custom and seek not to condemn the ways of others. Let those of Judaea remain faithful to Judaean custom, and let those of Druidry remain faithful to Druid custom."

The boy was equally silent, and then he said slowly: "It is a good answer. I only hope it is good enough to bring comfort to troubled hearts."

"And as for you and Anna," said Joseph, "remember that a fish will die in air, and a bird will die in water. It would not be wrong for you to adopt Druid ways, merely unwise. To each their own."

"And Morgana?"

Joseph smiled. "We are people of the Sign of the Fish. She is a bird of the air. Let her fly, Josue, it is her way."

The procession had drawn away and was even then beginning to climb the green hill to the stone circle above. "And seek not to discover the Druid rituals," Joseph added. "They are not evil, but they are not for us."

The boy looked down at the ground. "I am sorry I spoke harshly just now."

"I am glad you did," he said gently. "It is better for these things to be said with honesty than left to fester in secret. Go among the families—tell them what I have said—and let me know who is troubled beyond bearance. Be my ears and eyes, Josue. And remember, we are here to stay, for there is nowhere else for us to go. Let us build our church in peace and seek no quarrel with the Druids. I tell you of my own sure knowledge that though their ways may seem strange they are true priests of the Light, even as we."

The pre-dawn sky grew lighter as the procession wound its way up the hill. It was going to be another fine day, which was just as well for there was no shelter on the hill. It was said of the ancient Druids that it never rained during their open-air rituals because they commanded the weather they required. Cranog never knew how much of the old legends to believe. If the old Druids had indeed known the secret of weather control it was a secret irretrievably lost, for certainly the present Druids were as much at the mercy of wind and rain as anyone else.

Melvina, the High Priestess, walked beside him. She was a strange and silent woman. Despite their close association Cranog had probably exchanged fewer words with her than with the other seniors. But she was a superb ritualist and something of a scholar too. She was one of the few Druids who had taken the trouble to study the priestly ways of other cultures. Cranog had once heard her give a lecture to those of the White on the Mysteries of Dionysius, and it had been quite eerie to hear this calm, matter-of-fact woman describe the blood-stained sexual frenzy of that weird Greek cult. Some said that she was too cold in nature to be a really good priestess and that she could do with a touch of Morgana's Fire to make her more human. But those who said that did not know her. Cranog had once surprised her conducting a lone ritual and she had invited him to join her. Her body was more lean than Morgana's, less voluptuous, but the resultant Ritual of Fire that they had performed had been quite remarkable. At the height of the ritual when Cranog had lain with her in front of the altar it had been as deeply passionate as anything that Morgana had achieved. Afterwards when Cranog was gently washing the ritual oils from her body he had asked her about it. "Morgana is proficient in one aspect of the duties required of a priestess," she had said. "I strive for proficiency in all aspects." Cranog had hoped that she would conceive as a result of their joint ritual but Melvina had avoided the issue by taking the juice of the Netzian berry. "Let them talk," she had said. "Morgana has her way and I have mine."

Morgana walked behind him and even the swish of her robe against her body was an excitingly voluptuous sound. She was no scholar, except where it had reference to her own particular art, but in her one field she was supreme. She could inspire the very stones to bring forth young pebbles if she so desired. She had told him of her meeting with Zaacheus and some of the other Culdees. "He was angry," she had said, "but he will dream of me. He will think it a sin to feel my fires in his loins, but I say it will be a sin if he denies them. They are a strange people, so full of guilt!" Cranog had urged her not to work her craft on the Culdees, and to cover her body when they were near. "Their ways are different to ours. Leave them in peace to practice their priesthood in the way they desire."

Beside her strode Kerrin, the dark one. He was the finest ritualist of them all, hence his appointment to the Office of Ceremoniarius. He was even more silent than Melvina. Many hours of every day he spent with his studies, rarely meeting with his colleagues except at official functions. Cranog had long felt that considerable introspection in a priest produced either a high level beatitude or a dour, inhuman separateness. At the moment Kerrin was neither. Which way he would go was anyone's guess. There was little sign of the serene joy that comes from inner understanding— and yet to be fair there was little sign of any cynicism or sourness either.

Cerdic, son of Drucius, was a pleasant, open young man, but one who had barely made the Order of the White. He was not the priest his father was. It was doubtful whether he would progress much further, but then further progress was not demanded. He was a competent if uninspired ritualist, a willing worker, but would never play a leading role in Druidry, but that assessment was not a condemnation. Each served as best he could at the level he had reached in his personal evolution, and none could ask for more than that.

And finally there was Gilda, daughter of Cranog and Morgana. The witch-maiden the tribal warriors called her, and there was much truth in their unconscious assessment. Gilda would be far more suited to Moon magic than she was to sun-orientated Druidry, but unfortunately Druidry paid little attention to the Mysteries of the Moon. For some time Cranog had been toying with the idea of creating a separate Lodge to study and practice the Magic of the Moon as a complementary balance to their sun rituals. Gilda would be the ideal priestess to head such a Lodge.

And there was himself, soon to be Arch-Mage of all Druidry in succession to Drucius. Cranog had no illusions about himself. He would bear the title of Arch-Mage but he knew in his heart that he was nowhere near the level of advancement of Drucius, to say nothing of the legendary Arch-Mages of old. When Drucius had broached the subject of his succession Cranog had spoken of his doubts. Drucius had said: "It is good that you have assessed yourself accurately, Cranog—there is humility in such self-recognition —but there is no one more suited than you to lead all Druidry in this the last phase of our history. If the end of Druidry comes in your lifetime it will be your particular task to see to it that the dissolution is faced and accepted with courage, dignity, and honor so that no stain shall besmirch the memory of our fair name."

The sky was now quite light. Soon it would be dawn. The torches were doused and the procession wound its way in between the standing stones until the priesthood formed a circle. The litter bearing the Arch-Mage was carried to the western quadrant and the old man was laid gently on the altar stone. Cranog performed the deosil circumambulations and opened the ritual at each of the four cardinal points. This done he knelt beside the old man and took his hand.

The Arch-Mage's eyes fluttered open. "Thank you, Cranog—thank you. You do not know how much it means to me to be allowed to die in the old way. Are the seals on?"

"Yes—all is in readiness."

The old man looked up at the sky. "A thousand times have I passed through the gates of death," he whispered. "It holds no terrors for me, rather is it a gateway to my own true place, to be again with those I love." He gripped Cranog's hand more fiercely. "But there are those now in your care who do not have the advantage of a memory of their past lives. To them death is a fearful prospect, and their knowledge of the inner reality is more an act of faith than a memory of actual experience. When the time comes they will require the strength of your courage to keep their faith firm." He smiled deeply and warmly. "But tell them that I await their coming, each and everyone of them. Tell them that they have the word of Drucius that he will be there to welcome them."

He paused for a moment, but his grip did not loosen. "You are young in spirit, Cranog. Many of the Mysteries are still a mystery to you. But you have a courage and an endurance beyond all others presently in the priesthood. Take care of my children—help them as much as you can. And Cranog, remember, in the darkness of the darkest hour when you are close to despair, visualize me in your mind and I will be truly there."

His eyes closed and his lips moved silently. Cranog bent closer to hear. "Helios, Helios," the Arch-Mage whispered, "waft thou my soul down the River of Naradek. Bring it to Light, and to Life, and to Love." He opened his eyes again. "Farewell, Cranog. Keep faith with the Mysteries!"

Cranog leaned over and brushed his lips against the old man's cheek and then stood up. The Chief Healer came over and examined the frail Arch-Mage. Finally he looked up at Cranog and nodded. "He will go at any moment. It is time for you to go on ahead." The High Priest acknowledged with a gesture and returned to his position in the East. He looked round the circle at the robed brethren. They were still singing the Fourth Degree chant, softly, muted, a whisper of melody in the morning air. He raised his hand and the singing stopped. "Brethren of the Order of Druidry," he said in a firm, ringing voice. "From those on the inner who see the Light face to face, I bring you greetings!"

"Greetings!" came the response.

"To us who as yet are bound by the need to incarnate into the physical world they give the firm assurance that whence they come we may go *if* we be found worthy. They ask us to give them our dedicated loyalty even as they give it to those who are set over them." Cranog paused for a moment. The dawn was just about to break. He felt it in his bones that Drucius would go with the first ray of the sun, a fittingly symbolic end for a Priest of the Sun. It was time to make his own arrangements. "Brethren," he went on, "our beloved Drucius lies close to death. Honorably has he served the Great One throughout his long life, and now he goes to reap the benefits of his just reward. We who must remain will be filled with sadness, but let your grief be tempered with the sure knowledge that beyond the Veil he will await our coming." He glanced round the circle. "Let all here assembled enter upon their duty and may the blessing of the Great One be upon you all."

He signaled the three senior Officers, Melvina, Kerrin, and Morgana, and received their acknowledgements. All four closed their eyes and went into immediate visualization meditation. Cranog visualized the inner plane Lodge with all the clarity and power of his trained mind and mentally gave the password appointed for the epoch. Almost instantaneously there came that familiar shift in consciousness and he found himself standing in the inner Temple. Around him rose a grove of black pillars, polished, symmetrical. The floor was of black and white paving. The black altar stood in the center, the double cube with the Chalice of the Eternal Light upon it. Around the altar were the three Thrones of the High Magi, and in each was seated the awesome and auguste simulacrum of an inner plane adept.

The Lodge was crowded. The majority of those present were not currently in incarnation, but there were a few, like Cranog himself, who were attending by means of an earth-plane ritual. There were representatives there from most of the world's current priesthoods and those from priesthoods no longer seen on earth. There were priests there from ancient Shamballa whose physical plane group and Temple were utterly destroyed a million years ago—and there were those from the later cults of Lemuria, and a strong contingent from the still later priesthood of old Atlantis—and of those from the earth's current priesthoods Cranog could recognize several who had been Druids in their last incarnation. There were priests there from Egypt, and priestesses from the Dionysian cult of Greece, and those who were seers and holy men from the lands around the Middle Sea, and priests from the Fire Temples of Persia, and several of those serene yet forbidding figures from the monasteries of the yellow-robed priesthood of the eastern lands—a hundred priests and priestesses representing a score of different cults that spanned a million years and more of human service to the Great One. To be numbered among the brotherhood of such as these was an honor so great that Cranog could scarcely believe his good fortune. He would sooner be the lowest and humblest brother of such a Fraternity than be king of all the lands on earth.

Melvina came to stand by his side, and Morgana and Kerrin stood behind. All four bowed low to the Thrones, and the center adept of the three acknowledged the salute. "The Officers of Druidry are welcome here," he said. His voice was strong but quiet. He had borne many a famous priestly name in past lives, once an Atlantean High Priest, then a Greek philosopher, then an Egyptian adept, and once long ago he too had worn the White of Druidry. By different names he was a source of inspiration and comfort to a score of cults throughout the world. "To us this is a moment for rejoicing, to welcome our brother known to you as Drucius after yet another life of honor and dedication, though we recognize that for you it is a time of loss and sadness. We beg you to understand our joy even as we understand your sorrow."

Cranog inclined his head. "Drucius will not be lost to those of us who have learned to watch with the inner eye and hear with the inner ear. Our sorrow is already comforted by such knowledge."

"Wisely answered," said the adept. "Your words confirm my hope that the honor of Druidry and this Fraternity is in safe hands. Let us now welcome our brother."

Even as they had been speaking they had been aware of a growing cloud of light gathering in front of the altar. At first it had been a mere wisp of luminescence, a shimmering of light motes, but now it had grown in size and had begun, as it were, to solidify. As the outline became clearer Cranog could see that it was Drucius as he was now, a frail, bent old man, but as they watched they could see the figure growing taller, younger, straightening, the image of years fading rapidly, and as the light faded into form there was the figure of Drucius as he must have been in the full strength of his middle years, a strong, vigorous, yet gentle face and form.

The adept rose and came down to greet him, taking his hands in his own. Cranog had attended the inner Lodge a hundred times during the years of his priesthood, usually with Drucius himself, but this was the first time that he had seen the adept leave his Throne. It was as though by that simple gesture he was demonstrating that Drucius had attained a level equal to his own. The other two adepts also came down to greet him, and Cranog could see the tears of joy in Drucius' eyes.

One by one all those present came to the altar to greet their friend, and then each withdrew into the background and left the Lodge for their own place. Cranog did not see them depart as such, he was merely aware that gradually the Lodge was emptying until even the three seniors bowed and withdrew leaving Drucius with his colleagues.

The erstwhile Arch-Mage spoke to Morgana first, then to Kerrin, hugged Melvina, and then finally he turned to Cranog. "Farewell, my friend. We have already said all that needs be said." He took Cranog's hands. "When you need me," he said simply, "I will be with you."

Cranog could not speak. He gripped the hands fiercely for a moment and then closed his eyes. When he opened them again he was once more seated in the East in the ancient stone circle on top of Glaeston, the Green Hill. The sun was now clear of the horizon, brightly fierce, glaring almost, in a sky devoid of clouds. He saw Kerrin and Melvina open their eyes, revealing momentarily that glazed expression that always accompanied a return from the inner before the mind and eyes could adjust, and then Morgana joined them.

The Chief Healer approached the East. In his hands he carried the Serpent Staff, the symbol of the Office of Arch-Mage, a serpent entwined around a pillar of rock. He placed the staff in Cranog's hands and stepped back. "The Arch-Mage is dead!" he cried in a ringing voice. "Behold Cranog, Arch-Mage of all Druidry!" and as one being the entire assembly intoned the salute. "Hail Cranog—hail!"

* * *

For nearly a quarter of a century Cranog ruled as Arch-Mage, and those years were not easy. The specter of the Druid doom hung over every day of every year. It was the unseen ghastly guest at every ritual, and its forbidding presence was felt in every policy and every decision. Without knowing from which quarter it would come, or in what shape, all Cranog could do was to hold the balance of power in at least some semblance of equilibrium until their final fate chose to manifest itself. The factors needing to be balanced were neither dramatic nor even major—the uneasy equilibrium comprised a myriad of tiny, trivial pressures, each one of which was insignificant in itself yet each capable of being inflated far beyond its importance to threaten the stability of the entire complex set of relationships.

The first tiny pressure to emerge occurred immediately after Drucius' death. Cranog had barely changed from his ritual robe to his mundane robe when Joseph and Zaacheus were announced. After the preliminary courtesies had been exchanged Joseph launched into the reason for his visit. After a few moments Cranog said sharply: "Do I understand you correctly, Joseph—are you saying that some of your people believe that we have just put our own Arch-Mage to death in some sort of ritual slaughter?"

Joseph was embarrassed and apologetic and said that the Culdees did not believe that the Druids could foretell the day of death that accurately, at least not without sorcery.

The expression in Cranog's eyes was very angry. "So if there is no wound on his body we are sorcerers, and if there is we are ritual murderers! What sort of people do you think we are—and what sort of people are you to believe this of your friends who have welcomed you here as honored guests?" He glared at the Culdee. "We have given you freedom of worship—the least you can do is reciprocate with an equal courtesy. I tell you, Culdee, that there is not a Druid in all Pretannia who would not have laid down his own life for Drucius. How dare you bring such accusations against us!"

Again Joseph was full of apology, and while he was speaking Cranog realized that this was the first of so many tests that he would have to undergo. Anger would solve nothing—it would merely drive a wedge between Druidry and the Culdees, the seedbearers. He found himself wishing that these so-called seedbearers were more like the Druid idea of the priesthood—but then he reflected that if the Light required a new form in which to manifest it was hardly surprising that the new form was so different to the old.

So he swallowed his anger and arranged for a selected few Culdees to inspect the body of Drucius so as to allay the suspicion of murder. He then arranged for

certain Culdees to attend the Druid lectures in the Hall
of Learning in an endeavor to teach the Culdees something of Druid beliefs and practices in order to allay
the suspicion of sorcery. This in turn upset some of the
Druids, and Cranog found himself acting as mediator
and peacemaker between what was in danger of becoming two opposing camps.

Then it was discovered that one of the young Culdees had lain with Morgana, and there was an outcry
against that. Some of the Culdee women called Morgana a whore to her face, and she replied that to hold
their men they ought to have fire in their loins, not ice,
and that they could hardly blame the youth since in all
probability she, Morgana, was the first real woman that
he had ever met! The Culdees were angry with Cranog
for not admonishing Morgana—and Morgana was angry with him for not backing her against the Culdees
—but somehow Cranog managed to placate both sides
without seeming to favor either. Over and over again he
found himself saying much the same thing until he was
sick of the sound of it himself. "Be tolerant, their ways
are different to ours." "Your people must understand,
Joseph, that Druid ways are different to yours." "We
both serve the Great One—cannot we agree to differ in
our two respective ways of service?"

But then finally the grant of twelve hides of land
was formalized and all differences were put to one side
in the excitement of building the very first Culdee
church in Pretannia, albeit a crude building of wattle
and daub with a thatch roof. Under Druid law a land
transaction was completed by erecting a standing stone
to mark the new ownership, or the planting of a tree.
Joseph, however, had brought with him two objects
that the Culdees considered as sacred. Both had once
belonged to Jesus of Nazareth. They called them the
Cup and the Staff, and these two objects were often the
center of Culdee worship. To the Druids the former
was a perfectly ordinary household cup made of olive
wood, and the fact that Jesus had used it at that last
meal with his disciples did not, to them, endow it with
any special qualities. The other object was an ordinary
thornwood staff such as any head of a Judaean house

would possess. Certainly it was the symbol of authority of that house, but the fact that it had belonged to Jesus did not endow it with any special spiritual significance. They could not understand why Joseph had gone to such incredible lengths to obtain them from the Judaean authorities on the death of Jesus. There were thousands of such cups in Judaea, and thousands of such staffs—but the Druids shrugged and watched in amusement as the Cup was reverently placed on the new altar in the new church, and the staff was reverently planted in front of the church. The following spring brought intense excitement to the Culdees when it was seen that the staff had budded and promised to come to full flower. "A miracle!" they cried. "A miracle!" The Druids shrugged in perplexity. An old thorn staff, dormant for years, had now begun to grow again when planted in the earth. So what? If it was a miracle it was a miracle of the Earth Spirit, a miracle that was repeated ten million by ten million times every spring. But the Culdees called it the Holy Thorn, and the Druids smiled in amused perplexity.

The delicate balance of relationships at Glaeston would have been enough on their own to keep Cranog busy, but in addition to this the intertribal relationship was as bad as ever despite their vow, and even worsening. As Cunobelinus said: "We vowed to unite against the Romans—*if* they ever come—but we did not swear eternal friendship!" Cranog would have settled for an end to this incessant intertribal warfare and forgone the dream of intertribal friendship, but the suspicions and enmities and spilled blood of centuries did not make ideal overtures for such peaceful co-existence. But each king blamed the other for the continuing warfare, and Cunobelinus particularly blamed Verica.

"If you had refrained from crossing the Thamus and seizing part of Verica's territory," said Cranog sternly, "you may perhaps have found him more ready to cooperate."

"You are strangely misinformed," Cunobelinus snapped. "The territory I now occupy was once ruled by Dubnovellaunus of the Cantiaci."

"Whom Verica of the Belgae overthrew."

"True, but if the territory belonged to Verica by right of conquest then, it now belongs to me by the same right."

Cranog sighed. The logic was inescapable, and in all probability the Cantiaci themselves had seized the territory from some earlier tribe. "I do not wish to argue the rights of the matter, Cunobelinus," he said testily, "I am merely trying to point out that such conquest and reconquest is hardly conducive to intertribal unity if and when the Romans come."

"If, if, if!" the king growled. "Always *if!* Augustus and Tiberius after him were quite adamant in their policy of non-intervention in Pretannic affairs, and this new fellow, Caligula, has been emperor of the Roman Empire for two years now and still there is no move against us."

"But he is certainly interested in this part of the world—he is in Germany right now reconstituting the legions garrisoned on the Rhine."

Cunobelinus pursed his lips. "Is he—now that is interesting. Adminius is in Germany also, apparently."

Cranog studied the king's face—some thought had crossed that shrewd mind. Cunobelinus had three sons —Caratacus, Togodumnus, and Adminius. Caratacus was a wild, headstrong, laughing, highly intelligent youth with flaming red hair, already a fine warrior. Togodumnus was more quietly dour and grim than his brother but his equal with the sword or any other weapon. Both were popular with their people, each in their own way, and it had become a subject of constant speculation as to which of them would succeed on the death of Cunobelinus.

The third son, Adminius, was an entirely different matter—arrogant, cowardly, and greedy. There had never been much love lost between father and youngest son, and when Adminius had gathered a band of ruffians around him and had tried a little empire building on his own, Cunobelinus lost patience with him, defeated his ragged band in a battle that lasted barely an hour, and exiled him from not only the Catuvellauni kingdom but from Pretannia itself.

"Will he go to Caligula?" said Cranog.

Cunobelinus shrugged. "What if he does—there is nothing he can do. Who would listen to such an arrogant, greedy coward!"

But in this matter the normally shrewd Cunobelinus was utterly wrong. Perhaps it was those very defects of character that so appealed to the same traits in Caligula himself, but whatever the reason the news soon came that Adminius had quickly established himself in Caligula's inner circle, and some weeks later came the further news that the legions had left Germany and were massing at Boulogne ready for the push across the Narrow Sea to Pretannia. Cranog immediately put into operation the plan that the Druids had prepared for such a contingency. One hundred priests and fifty priestesses force-marched to the Cantaici territory in the southeast and reached it in three days and there met with Cunobelinus.

"You've heard, obviously," were the first words that Cunobelinus said.

"Yes," said Cranog. "Verica is on his way, I presume."

Cunobelinus shook his head. "No. I have informed him of the situation by runner but have told him to stay where he is until summoned. I am not giving him free entry into this territory until I know it is necessary."

Cranog came as near then to losing his temper as at any time in his life. All night they argued the subject but Cunobelinus was adamant.

"When I see the Roman ships out there about to land," he shouted, "then and only then will I send for Verica, and that's final!" and he stamped angrily away and refused to discuss the matter further.

Cranog was furious. There was nothing he could do to further Pretannic defenses, but he could still put his first plan into operation. Two dozen Druid priests, under the leadership of Kerrin, dressed as Gallic Druids, embarked on a small vessel and set sail for Gaul. It was their task to infiltrate the Roman ranks and sow the seeds of fear and dissension. It was estimated that they would return in a week, but the seventh day came and went, and the eighth, and the ninth, and Cranog was almost beside himself with impatience. Time and again he tried to persuade Cunobelinus to send for Verica but still the King of the Catuvellauni refused. Cranog even threatened to send for Verica himself, but Cunobelinus swore that in that event he would meet the Belgae in full battle and to hell with the Romans, and Cranog had to desist.

Finally on the tenth day the small vessel appeared just after dawn and by noon it had berthed and Cranog was thankful to see all two dozen Druids safe ashore. Kerrin came swiftly to report. At first Cranog was tempted to hear his report in private and keep Cunobelinus in suspense, but he dismissed the thought as too petty. Cranog, the Druid Council including Melvina, Cerdic, and Morgana, together with Cunobelinus, Caratacus and Togodumnus, gathered in Cranog's tent to hear the news.

"You were right, Cranog," said Kerrin wearily. "The Roman legionaries have little love for Caligula and consequently little love for this invasion. They were ready to seize on almost any excuse to mutiny."

"You told them what dreadful people we are?" said Cranog. "Reminded them of the human sacrifices that Julius Caesar wrote about?"

"Yes, and told them of even more frightful horrors that await them, and I think they even half believed them." He turned to Cunobelinus. "I also told them that the Catuvellauni, the Belgae, and also the Brigantes from the north had united and had already amassed a quarter of a million warriors here on the coast to oppose the landing, though I notice," he added bitterly, "that your greed for this territory, Cunobelinus, has prevented you from even bringing the Belgae! The sworn vow of a Pretannic king is obviously worth nothing!"

Cunobelinus jumped forward. "You go too far, Druid!" he bellowed. "We vowed to unite against the Romans, and so we will—but I will *not* be stampeded into any hasty alliance and put this territory at risk. Too much Catuvellauni blood has been shed in gaining this territory to concede it lightly!"

"It will take four or five days for Verica to get here," said Kerrin grimly. "It will take the Romans no more than three days to put you and your Catuvellauni to flight!"

Caratacus also jumped forward, his red hair streaming across his shoulders. "You have obviously never seen the Catuvellauni fight, Druid!" he shouted. "Would you like a demonstration here and now?" and he drew his sword.

Cranog stepped between them. "Put up your sword!" he thundered. "How dare you raise a weapon to one of the priesthood!" He turned to Kerrin. "And whether we disagree with their policy or not we must remember that this territory now belongs to Cunobelinus—we are here as his guests—we have no jurisdiction in a civil matter—and the best reason of all, no amount of recrimination will solve the situation." Kerrin made as if to speak, and then shrugged and stood back. Cranog turned back to Caratacus. The young Prince faced him squarely for some long seconds, and then he too shrugged and put up his sword. "Good," said Cranog. "Now, Kerrin—your operation has obviously been a tremendous success, but have the legions actually mutinied?"

Kerrin nodded. "Yes, they have. The officers are in a fury, and the legates in command are beside themselves with rage at the dishonor. What the insane Caligula thinks of the matter is beyond our conjecture. We can only wait to see what will result from the confrontation."

The Druids and the Catuvellauni did indeed wait —for nearly six weeks. News reached them that the Roman officers both senior and junior pleaded, threatened, cajoled, bribed, but all to no avail. The legions would go anywhere in the far-flung Roman Empire but they would not cross the Ocean to Pretannia—and finally Caligula had no alternative but to abandon the invasion and march the legions back to the garrisons on the Rhine.

Cunobelinus was caustic in his comment. "And if it had been left to you," he said tersely to Cranog, "I would now have 50,000 Belgae warriors on my territory to deal with!" He glared at the High Priest. "So much for Druid prophecy!"

"You were lucky," the Druid said. "Who else but the Druids could have even dreamed that the Roman legions would mutiny? Kerrin was right—if the Romans had come they would have made short work of you, Catuvellauni."

"If, if, if!" he bellowed suddenly. "That's all I hear—*if!* Perhaps now you will believe that the Romans will *never* come to Pretannia—never!"

chapter four

His was a short, tubby body, unlovely to look at even with the eye of love, and few eyes had ever looked upon *him* lovingly. His face was rounded with great, bulbous eyes, and his hair was thinning fast. He was fifty years of age, a half century of grotesque nonentity. Yet for all his ugliness it was his eyes that gave the clue to those who took the trouble to look closely, but few did—gentle, timid eyes, uncertain, and yet lurking in their depths, secretly, furtively, there was a shrewd intelligence. His bearing was similar to the expression in his eyes, furtive, secretive, avoiding company, shuffling silently through the palace, shrinking behind a pillar to avoid a guest or a senator, or more particularly to avoid his licentious wife, Messalina, accepting the salutes of the Praetorian Guard with embarrassment, always bearing himself with self-effacement as though ashamed even to exist. All his life he had been an object of derision because of his infirmity, even from his wife, and even the most junior Praetorian officer found it difficult to hide his contempt for this most un-Roman of Romans. He was the son of Drusus and the brother of Germanicus, both of whom were distinguished generals enriched with great honor in Roman eyes, and yet he himself could not command the respect of even the kitchen servants—and yet he was a man who held the highest position in the greatest empire that the world had ever known, for this was Claudius, Emperor of Rome, having succeeded to the throne some few months earlier after the murder of his nephew, Caligula.

He peered more closely at the mirror, pulling the purple robe more closely about his shoulders. "Cl . . . Cl . . . Claudius," he whispered, "Emperor of Rome!" He regarded his image caustically. "Much of it you owe to the Guard, but some of it you owe to M . . . M . . . Messalina's insatiable appetite for men." He shook his head. "They say that every man deserves the wife he gets—isn't that true?" but the image did not answer. "By Zeus! Whatever d . . . d . . . did I do to deserve Messalina!"

The Empress was a voracious woman whose hunger for men seemingly could not even be dulled let alone satisfied. Claudius knew that she had only married him because it had been possible for him to become Emperor, and she had so ably played her particular part in bringing those pressures to bear that had indeed brought Claudius to the purple. "My poor nephew, Caligula," he whispered. "You n . . . n . . . never stood a chance!" There was talk in Rome that Messalina's sexual exploits would soon lead to further political intrigue that would dispose of Claudius himself leaving Messalina as Empress of the Roman Empire without the encumbrance of an Emperor. Cleopatra had done it in Egypt, why not Messalina in Rome? Claudius shuddered. Caligula had been bad enough but a whore would be far worse. Claudius would kill her himself rather than subject Rome to that fate.

A knock sounded at the door and Silvanus entered. C. Gavius Silvanus, the most able and honored young tribune in the Praetorian Guard. Messalina detested him as she detested all those of ability whom she could not manipulate to her own ends. Claudius, however, liked him. Of all those at the imperial palace he was the only one to whom Claudius could speak freely without embarrassment, simply because Silvanus was one of the few who did not look upon his Emperor with derision. Had the other and more senior dignitaries at the imperial palace known of the conversations that Claudius enjoyed with Silvanus, they would not have considered it seemly for an Emperor to speak so freely to a mere tribune. But Claudius did not care—he had few enough friends in Rome and he was not going to limit his friendship merely because of a difference in rank.

"Come in, tribune," he said. He pointed to the mirror. "Have you ever seen a more unlikely Emperor than this p . . . p . . . poor fellow?"

The boy was tall, fair of face, his blond hair cropped short in the Praetorian fashion. "You do yourself an injustice," he said shortly. His eyes were a quite startling blue, shrewd in expression, and quite fearless. "Like it or not, you are the Emperor of the Roman Empire, and such high position requires a certain attitude of mind to fulfill that function with honor and greatness."

"An attitude I do not have?" said Claudius.

"Not yet, but you will, given time."

And that was another reason for their unlikely friendship. Not only was Silvanus one of the few who did not regard Claudius with contempt, but was also one of the few who did not fawn or grovel to high rank but spoke frankly and fearlessly. Such honesty would not make for a good politician but it certainly did make for a good friend. "Maybe, maybe," said Claudius. "And what brings you here?"

"Aulus Plautius has arrived secretly in Rome from Pannonia and seeks audience with the Emperor."

"Plautius, by Zeus! Now that *is* good news! Bring him to me tonight."

"Shall I inform the Empress?"

Claudius smiled. "Messalina has a lot on her mind. I don't think we need burden her further with this matter. Where is she?"

"In her chamber, I think."

"Alone?" The boy hesitated and Claudius waved his hand. "Never mind, never mind, I do not really wish to know." He cocked an eye at the young tribune. "Palace rumor has it, Silvanus, that you are one of the few who has not yet graced her pillow." He turned back to look in the mirror again. "I want you to know," he said, somewhat bitterly, "that to be a stranger to Messalina's bed is a rare honor, and one that I share only with the very few. I am gl . . . gl . . . gl . . . glad that you are one of those."

The tribune made as if to speak, hesitated, then saluted and withdrew. It was true that so far he had resisted her veiled invitations, pretending not to have understood their import, but sooner or later her invitations would become a command which he could not dare refuse though the prospect filled him with revulsion. If it came to that he hoped that Claudius would understand.

It was past midnight when Silvanus led Aulus Plautius through the palace to Claudius' private chamber. "Welcome, welcome indeed, Plautius!" Claudius said.

Aulus Plautius was a strong, vigorous man in the full flower of his middle years, the most experienced and ablest general in the army. Pannonia had been the most restless of Rome's provinces, seething with rebellion, until Plautius had taken over as governor. His stern administration had quickly reduced the province to good order, for which he had already received the lavish praise of the entire senate and the Roman people. He was too stern a man, too blunt, to be loved in the way that more popular generals were loved, but he commanded immense respect from everyone. He, like Silvanus, was one of the very few who could see in Claudius the qualities so necessary for an Emperor of Rome, but also like Silvanus he knew that Claudius hesitated to use the god-like powers of his high position. He needed to be pressured, to be pushed, to be encouraged to grasp the reins of power firmly and guide the empire of Rome.

"Greetings to the Emperor of Rome," he growled. "With your permission I would like Silvanus to hear what I have to say."

Claudius waved them both to chairs and called

for wine. "Trouble in P . . . P . . . Pannonia?" he asked.

Plautius shook his head. "No, the tribes have learned that not only is resistance to Rome useless but that trade with us will bring them profits. Some of the more farsighted chieftains have already begun to barter."

"Good. You have done well, Plautius. The senate will be pleased. But if everything goes well in P . . . P . . . Pannonia, why come you to Rome, and in secret?"

"As to secrecy, it is simply that I wanted to see you, Claudius, before seeing any of the senate, or the Empress."

Claudius smiled. All Rome knew how much Plautius detested Messalina. "And here you are. What is it you have to say?"

"Britannia!" said Plautius bluntly.

The Emperor frowned. "A barbaric island by all accounts—Pretannia, the natives call it. What about it?"

"The news over the past six months is most encouraging."

"What news? There is any amount of n . . . n . . . news from Britannia, or Pretannia, whatever it's called. People seem to speak of nothing else."

The general leaned forward. "Cunobelinus, their most powerful king, is dead!"

"Yes, I know. That is old news—he died six months ago while Caligula was still Emperor."

"The death of your nephew and your own succession, Claudius, kept Rome too busy to give that news the significance it deserved."

"The Catuvellauni kingdom is now shared by his two sons, Caratacus and Togodumnus," said Silvanus.

"And a kingdom shared is a kingdom weakened," Plautius said.

Claudius pursed his lips. "I don't know about weakened. Caratacus and Togodumnus overran the Belgae kingdom in the south, and Verica fled here to Rome. He has already pestered me several times to restore his kingdom."

"Then why not grant his plea?" said Plautius. "After all, he *is* an ally of Rome. His father signed a treaty with Julius Caesar which the Belgae still honor."

"On paper, yes—but in practice?"

"But the fact that the treaty exists," said Silvanus, "gives you the ideal excuse to back Verica, if you wish to do so."

"A fine point," said Claudius dubiously. "But why should I wish t . . . t . . . to do so? You say that the Catuvellauni are weakened, yet they overran the Belgae. Their kingdom now stretches from the River Ouse in the north to include the whole of the south coast. In their expansion the Catuvellauni have conquered the Iceni tribe and the Trinovantes on the east coast, though admittedly the Iceni still function as a tribe under their own kingship but under dominion of the Catuvellauni—the Dobunni in the west—the Cantiaci in the southeast, and now the Atrebates and the Belgae in the south. Is this a sign of weakness?"

Plautius looked to Silvanus. He was pleased to find his Emperor so well informed. "Yes, it is," said the tribune. "Their forces are now stretched far too thinly. It is one thing to conquer but quite another to occupy successfully, as we Romans know only too well. It requires permanent garrisons to maintain command in the captured territory. Rome has always had the manpower to do this, but the Catuvellauni are numerically too few to achieve similar success—they are stretched far too thinly."

Claudius rose and strode the apartment thoughtfully. "You are speaking of a p . . . p . . . possible invasion," he said suddenly. "You have given me the necessary excuse to do so—now give me the reasons why it would be advantageous to Rome."

Plautius held up his hand and enumerated the points finger by finger. "One—Julius Caesar has already shown that it is possible. Two—failure to honor Rome's treaties is damaging to Roman prestige and causes unrest within the client-kingdoms of other provinces which could lead to a possible resurgence of rebellion. Three—the Caligulan disaster of three years ago caused many of Rome's enemies to wonder whether Rome's greatness is on the decline and we need a fresh show of strength to quell such thoughts. Four—all the general staff preparations necessary for an invasion of Britannia were completed by Caligula's generals and still exist waiting to be used. Five—the island is rich in tin, lead, copper, pearls, and other commodities, and there are undoubted profits to be made from trade. Six —cohorts comprising Britannic warriors would make excellent auxiliary forces for our legions in other parts of the world."

Plautius paused. "And seven," said Silvanus, "did you not receive an impudent demand only last week from Caratacus and Togodumnus for Verica's extradition—do such threats to Rome go unanswered?"

The two men fell silent. "And eight?" said Claudius. "Surely you have a point eight—or have you exhausted your resources?"

"And eight," said Silvanus quickly, "you personally, Claudius, need a triumph to establish yourself truly as Emperor of Rome, to demonstrate that Claudius should be an object of respect and honor and not an object of contempt and derision!"

Plautius drew in his breath sharply. Having spent his time in Pannonia he was not aware of how close Silvanus had come to the Emperor, nor the freedom of comment granted to him.

Claudius stood looking down on them. "I like your point eight," he said finally. "Very well. You have given me the excuse I need, and the reasons I need—now tell me the means by which this can be accomplished."

"You will need four legions of 6,000 men each, plus a further 24,000 in auxiliary cohorts in Britannia itself," said Plautius quickly. "You need one legion of 6,000 men plus a further 4,000 in auxiliary cohorts to be held in reserve. Forty thousand men for the invasion, and ten thousand in reserve."

"You could use the three legions garrisoned in Germany," said Silvanus, "they are the nearest—Legio II Augusta—Legio XIV Gemina—and Legio XX Valeria."

"I could bring Legio IX Hispana from Pannonia," said Plautius.

"And what about Germany?" said Claudius. "I cannot leave it denuded."

"Raise two new legions," said Plautius. "Two would be enough plus a few auxiliaries."

The Emperor nodded. "Yes, I could do that easily enough. As they would be the first legions raised by the new Emperor, I could call them Legio XV Primigenia, and Legio XXII Primigenia pia fidelis. D . . . D . . . Do you know, I'm getting quite excited already!"

"The reserve legion could be Legio VIII Augusta," said Silvanus. "It could be held in reserve at Boulogne."

"But who would I put in command of such a venture?" said Claudius. "He would need to be a distinguished general and a first-rate governor, a man of courage and honor, one personally loyal to myself whom I could trust completely—where could I find such a remarkable man?" but his eyes were twinkling.

Plautius looked down at the ground. "I do not know," he mumbled.

"But I do," said the Emperor. "Would you take overall command for me, Plautius? I can think of no other more suited for the task."

The general smiled and looked up. "Willingly," he said simply, "and I would serve you to my death."

"Let us not speak of death."

"And you?" said Silvanus. "Will you be there?"

"Of course," said Claudius. "I would not miss this for anything."

"No!" said Plautius sharply. "At least, not at the beginning. Let me establish a safe beachhead first—then I will send for you."

Claudius remained silent for a little, and then said: "Oh, very well, but I will want to be present in Britannia at every decisive engagement thereafter."

"Certainly, providing a line of retreat is made for you in case of emergency." He paused for a moment. "May I make a request? I would like Silvanus here to join me—Legio IX Hispana would be honored to welcome such an officer."

The young tribune was embarrassed. "You flatter

me unduly, Plautius. I thank you," he said slowly, "but I would prefer to remain on the Emperor's personal staff—if you will have me."

"Of course, I was hoping you would ask," said Claudius. "If nothing else it will get you away from Messalina's amorous clutches."

Plautius looked down at the ground again, suddenly embarrassed. He was a soldier—palace gossip and intrigue made him feel awkward, especially when the Empress' infidelity was so lightly mentioned by the Emperor himself. "What *of* the Empress?" he muttered. "Will you discuss this with her?"

"Certainly not!" said Claudius firmly. "M . . . M . . . Messalina will have to learn that this is none of her business. It concerns only we three and the senate who will have to vote the funds." He reached for the wineskin. "My friends, let us drink a toast—and in honor of the natives whose fate is about to fall on them let us use their name for their country—I give you Pretannia!"

"Pretannia!"

"Pretannia!"

* * *

Cranog was furious with Caratacus and Togodumnus for having overrun the Belgae, and particularly for having allowed Verica to flee to Rome. "You once had two armies to oppose a Roman invasion, the Belgae and the Catuvellauni, now you have only one."

"But with twice the force," said Togodumnus. "The numbers remain the same."

"If you think that Belgae warriors will fight under a Catuvellauni king, then you are even more naive than I imagined!" Cranog threw up his hands. "And you stupidly allowed Verica himself to escape to Rome where he will undoubtedly plead with the new Emperor, Claudius, for the restoration of his kingdom. Verica is an ally of Rome, don't forget that. The Belgae have a treaty with Rome signed by Julius Caesar himself!"

Togodumnus shrugged. "Tincommius fled to

Rome, and so too did his brother after him, Eppilus. Rome did not listen to them, treaty or no treaty, so why should they now suddenly listen to the third brother, Verica?"

"Perhaps," said Cranog angrily, "because you and Caratacus stupidly sent a threatening note to Rome *demanding* the return of Verica, in chains!"

Caratacus grinned. "We did not think you knew about that note," he admitted cheerfully.

"Since when can you conceal anything from the Druids! Rome does not like threats, nor demands. Your arrogant note may just tip them in favor of honoring their treaty with the Belgae."

"Don't forget, Druid," said Togodumnus, "that the Catuvellauni also have a treaty signed by Julius Caesar, given to our grandfather, Tasciovanus. Would Rome honor one treaty by breaking the other?"

"Haven't you learned the one simple fact that Rome is powerful enough to do what it likes, when it likes, where it likes—and anyway Rome will claim, with some justification, that the treaty with the Catuvellauni is now null and void since it is you who have broken it. One of the clauses in that treaty is that the Catuvellauni will not perpetrate any act of aggression against any other Roman ally—and you *have,* against the Trinovantes, against the Iceni, against the Dobunni, against the Cantiaci, against the Regnenses, against the Atrebates, and now against the Belgae!"

Caratacus shrugged. "Anyway—so what! All our lives Togodumnus and I have been hearing this woman's cry from you Druids—'The Romans are coming! The Romans are coming!'—but so far, nothing! It is now a total of ninety-eight years, nearly a hundred years since last a Roman set foot in Pretannia! How much longer will you Druids tremble at the name of Rome?"

Cranog shook his head. "Oh, what's the use? Your father was just as bad!"

But Caratacus and Togodumnus were not the only problems that Cranog had. In the harsh winter of that year Joseph de Marmore of Arimathea died, coughing his lungs up in the dank and dismal climate. Cranog

was with him at the end. "It is not going as smoothly as
I anticipated," the Judaean whispered. "My people are
suspicious of yours, and yours of mine. Promise me
that whatever happens, Cranog, you won't turn against
the Culdees."

The Arch-Mage took his hands. "I promised the
great ones, I promised Drucius, and now I promise
you—for as long as I am Arch-Mage of all Druidry
the Culdees will be free to practice their religion in
any way they choose."

But it was no easy promise to keep. The moment
Joseph was buried the new leader of the Culdees,
Zaacheus, kept pestering Cranog with a long list of
complaints about the Druids, and the Druids com-
plained bitterly about the unfriendliness and lack of
cooperation from the Culdees. "If these guilt-ridden
fools are the seedbearers to the new age," said Morgana, "then I'm glad I won't live long enough to see
it." Cranog chided her but his heart wasn't in the
rebuke—she merely represented an opinion prevalent
throughout Druidry.

Even Cranog began to wonder whether Drucius
had not made some dreadful mistake, particularly when
Zaacheus refused even to discuss the possibility of
Culdee participation in resistance against a Roman invasion of Pretannia.

"We are a peaceful people," he said. "The Lord
God quite clearly said: 'Thou shalt not kill,' and we
obey His commandments."

"You may change your tune," Cranog said, "when
the Romans burn your precious church and rape your
women!"

"If it is the will of God," the Culdee said pompous-
ly, "we will bear it as best we can."

"I cannot believe, and never will believe," said
Cranog, "that the Great One would deliberately bring
misery to his servers. If your women are raped it will be
by the will of the Romans, not the will of God."

"You do not understand," said Zaacheus.

"I certainly do not understand you Culdees! If you
won't fight then what *will* you do?"

"Survive!" said Zaacheus. "We will bear every indignity heaped upon us without retaliation. We will endure, and we will survive. When every Druid has been put to death for opposing the Romans we Culdees will still be here."

They were silent for a very long time. Then Cranog said heavily: "Forgive me, but try as I may I cannot help but feel contempt for such lack of courage and lack of dignity. The Druids will oppose the enemies of the Great One even if it means the death and mutilation of each and every one of us."

Zaacheus shook his head sadly. "Then truly the Druids do not understand. It takes courage to fight as you do and suffer death—but it takes a different type of courage *not* to fight and live as we do."

It was a theme that echoed and re-echoed throughout the Druid/Culdee relationship—neither understood the other, and never would.

* * *

C. Gavius Silvanus hurried through the palace towards Claudius' private chamber but found the Emperor in consultation with the Empress. "What news?" said Messalina.

Silvanus hesitated. "He has come," said Claudius quickly, "to continue the lessons. He is teaching me the history of Roman military s . . . s . . . s . . . strategy."

The Empress was mollified if not impressed. "Well, at least you are taking *some* interest in imperial affairs," she said waspishly. "But I still want to hear the news from Boulogne."

"The Second, Fourteenth and Twentieth Legions from the garrisons in Germany have arrived at Boulogne and are encamped," said Silvanus. "Plautius and the Ninth Legion have left Pannonia and are on their way to join them. The Eighth Legion, the reserves, are timed to arrive at Boulogne just after the invasion fleet has sailed. We do not want them to arrive earlier and so aggravate an already overcrowded area."

"Any problems?" said Messalina.

"None that I know of."

"And when is the invasion to take place?"

Silvanus hid his annoyance. The Empress should mind her own business—these questions should rightly come from the Emperor. "It is now the Ides of March," the tribune said. "The Narrow Sea is swept by equinoctial gales. We anticipate fairer weather sometime in April."

"The Ides of March," said Claudius. "A solemn portent indeed!"

The Empress rose and headed for the door. "I still say the whole scheme is madness, an irresponsible gamble—and it will take so many of our finest young men away from Rome, perhaps for years."

"We all have to make sacrifices in times of war," Silvanus murmured. Claudius hid his smile but fortunately the Empress had not heard.

Messalina opened the door. "I am seriously displeased with the senate for voting in its favor."

"If it is successful," said Claudius quietly, "it will bring great honor to Rome and to our f . . . f . . . f . . . family."

"If, if, if!" she retorted. "If *not,* how long do you think *you* will remain as Emperor?" and she swept majestically from the chamber.

Claudius sighed. "Mind you, she's right—it *is* a gamble."

Silvanus shrugged. "Nothing in human affairs is certain, everything is a gamble."

"True enough. *Are* there any p . . . p . . . p . . . problems?"

"Yes, a serious one." He hesitated for a moment, and then went on: "We *may* have the whole Caligulan situation all over again—the legions at Boulogne have mutinied."

Claudius stared at him. "Oh no, not again! Why?"

The tribune sighed. "Same reasons as before. Boiling a lot of superstitious nonsense down to its essence, they say that Ocean, separating Gaul from Britannia, marks the proper and known world of mankind. They say that to cross it would be to defy the gods and risk unknown and dreadful hazards."

Claudius' eyes bulged even further. "What absolute n . . . n . . . nonsense!"

"Of course."

The Emperor strode furiously up and down the apartment. "By Zeus! You were right not to reveal this to Messalina. She cannot keep any secret from her pillow—the news would have been all over Rome tomorrow!" He sat down heavily and drummed his fingers on the tabletop. "It is not their real reason," he said suddenly. "It cannot be. They know perfectly well that the illustrious Julius successfully crossed the Narrow Sea to Britannia, not once but twice!" He rose from the table and strode to the embrasure. "Unknown hazards! Rubbish! Roman legions have always been proud of the fact that they have faced and triumphed over unknown hazards a thousand times throughout our history, and these are the most experienced and distinguished legions we have." He smacked one fist into the other. "As for defying the gods, Roman legionaries are a notoriously impious lot—why so suddenly concerned?" He turned back to Silvanus. "There has to be another reason."

"Perhaps there is," said the tribune. "The same reasons were given three years ago but everyone knew that the mutiny was a personal snub to Caligula."

Claudius eyed him thoughtfully. "And you think this is a p . . . p . . . personal snub to me?"

"It is possible."

The Emperor remained silent for some time. "I think you are right," he said finally. "It is the only answer that makes sense—but how are we to deal with it?"

"Tactfully."

Claudius nodded. "You are right again. If I come down on them hard they will simply d . . . d . . . dig their toes in. We have to shame them into abandoning this madness, but tactfully—how?"

"The mutiny was fanned by the Druids—and it is they whom I suspect of having fanned the Caligulan mutiny as well. We caught two Britannic Druids robed as Gallic Druids, infiltrating the Roman encampment spreading lies and rumor. There may have been others."

Claudius shook his head. "It would take more than a couple of Druids to cause three entire legions to mutiny, though they may have seized on the rumors as the ideal excuse."

"Nevertheless, the Druids *are* thought of with awe. We could have these two executed in public at Boulogne to demonstrate that Druids are not magicians, not immortal, and as vulnerable as everyone else."

"G . . . G . . . Good! Do that, and immediately— but something more is needed." He stroked his nose thoughtfully. "I could send a senior member of the senate to address the legions, appeal to their sense of honor, or I could g . . . g . . . go myself, but somehow that doesn't seem to be the right course." Again he was silent for some time. "Ah!" he said finally. "Wait a minute—yes—it might just work, they will appreciate the joke, surely!" He looked up at Silvanus. "I will send Narcissus to address them."

Narcissus was an ex-slave, freed by Claudius himself, a shrewdly intelligent man now holding high administrative post.

"An ex-slave addressing free men—reminding them of their honor!" The tribune was startled. "They'd tear him to pieces!"

"Would they?"

Silvanus thought about it and then began to smile. "If such a man addressed me personally in such a manner I would be very indignant—but the whole idea is so ridiculous that I'm sure I would treat it as a joke."

"P . . . P . . . Precisely."

The younger man began to grin broadly. "It might just work—what a joke!"

But at first the legionaries at Boulogne did not see it as a joke at all. They were hotly indignant when Narcissus climbed onto the platform to address them, and for a moment the situation looked quite ugly, but then some wag in the crowd, planted there deliberately, cried out: "Io Saturnalia! Io Saturnalia!" referring to the annual festival of Saturn when slaves dressed in their masters' clothes and played the role of free men for that one day. "Io Saturnalia!" Others took up the cry and Narcissus, the ex-slave dressed in a free man's clothes, began to look ridiculous. Some began to laugh, and the laughter spread as the humor of the situation took hold. "Io Saturnalia! Io Saturnalia!"

The mutiny was abandoned. Legio IX Hispana arrived from Pannonia, and Aulus Plautius took overall command. All that was needed now was a fair wind for Britannia.

* * *

"Again we have listened to your words, Druid, and again you have been proved wrong!" Caratacus and Togodumnus were furious. "You said the Belgae wouldn't fight under a Catuvellauni king, but here they are, fifty thousand of them—sullen, reluctant, true, but here they are! We have also brought fifty thousand Catuvellauni here to the southeast coast— one hundred thousand men, and now you tell me the invasion won't take place!"

Cranog sighed. "There are three legions at Boulogne—that we know. We *had* to make all preparations for an invasion, but thanks to Druid intervention the legions have again mutinied."

"And we have brought one hundred thousand men across country for nothing!" said Togodumnus.

"No, not for nothing—a necessary precaution."

"Well, I tell you this, Druid," said Caratacus bitterly. "That is the very last time that we will listen to Druid advice. Tomorrow we march back to our capitals —and to hell with the Romans!"

"No!" Cranog came to his feet. "The legions have mutinied, but they are still there at Boulogne. They may yet come."

"The Romans are coming! The Romans are coming!" said Caratacus sarcastically. "That's all we have been hearing for a hundred years! We are sick of it. We march tomorrow—and that is final!"

The argument raged virtually all night but Caratacus and Togodumnus were adamant. At dawn all one hundred thousand warriors marched away leaving the Druids to wait for their colleagues to return from Gaul.

Five days later Kerrin arrived by small vessel with the sad news that two of their number had been caught and executed by the Romans. "And that is not all," said Kerrin grimly. "The mutiny has been abandoned. They are already embarking into the invasion fleet. We escaped only a matter of hours ahead of them. They will be here by tomorrow without fail."

They were all silent for a moment, and it was Melvina who voiced the thought in all their minds. "So if we had not fanned the mutiny the Romans would have sailed weeks ago and would have been met by one hundred thousand Catuvellauni and Belgae warriors."

"Whereas," said Cranog bitterly, "they will land completely unopposed." He shook his head. "How many are coming?"

"Four full legions plus dozens of auxiliary cohorts," said Kerrin grimly. "Some forty thousand in all."

Cranog's face reflected the despair of them all. "Then may the Great One preserve us all!"

chapter five

"I don't believe it!" said Aulus Plautius softly. He stood forward on the leading Roman vessel, a gaudily and lavishly decorated trireme, its three banks of oars sweeping them gracefully and rapidly towards the shore. The sky was quite light—dawn was but a few minutes away.

With Plautius were several of his general staff. His second-in-command, Cn.Sentius Saturninus, pursed his lips. "The beach certainly looks empty enough."

The first wave of the invasion fleet, a score of vessels and more, were within a few hundred yards of the shore. The second wave was still a mile out to sea, and the third wave a mile beyond that.

Hosidius Geta, commander of the Roman cavalry, leaned on the guard-rail studying the beach ahead. "Perhaps they heard that we were coming," he said slowly, "and have fled inland." His division, being the most mobile, would be the first to land.

Plautius shook his head. "Ignorance makes them fearless. They believe that numerical superiority must prevail, and certainly they can put five or six times our number in the field, but they are an undisciplined rabble without any concept of organized and disciplined warfare. No man alive in Pretannia has ever seen a Roman army in action—it is a hundred years since Julius Caesar was here—and they have no idea or experience of how ten trained and disciplined men fighting as one unit can destroy a rabble ten times its own number." He stared thoughtfully at the rapidly lessening gap between ship and shore. "I do not know why they are not there, but it is not because of fear."

"A trap?" said Saturninus.

Hosidius Geta pointed to some woods at the western edge of the beach. "They could be concealed."

Again the commander shook his head. "If so then they present no problem—that wood could only hide two, maybe three thousand men at most. Anyway— we will see."

A few minutes later the first vessel grounded, then another, and another. This was always the weak point in any invasion, it gave too much opportunity for defenders to get in among the invaders before a beachhead could be established, but in this instance there was not an enemy in sight. The first company of cavalry, with Hosidius Geta, were heading inland, fanning out, within minutes. Half an hour later the entire infantry of the first wave were ashore and in their defensive positions on an agreed perimeter two hundred yards from the beach—and Aulus Plautius began to breathe more easily. The cavalry returned from its initial exploration to report. "There is no sign of the enemy for at least two or three miles," shouted Hosidius Geta. His horse was rearing, plunging, difficult to control in the excitement of the noise and bustle of the landing beach. "There is a tiny hamlet there," he shouted, pointing, "about a mile to the north. Richboro, the natives call it—must be the place we call Rutupiae on our maps."

"How many there?"

"A score of terrified villagers, no more," Geta shouted. "But apart from that, nothing for miles around. Britannia is wide open!"

Rutupiae—Richboro! A perfect landfall even after a night at sea. Plautuis was well pleased. "Extend your patrol," he shouted. "Two hours' ride in three directions—return here by noon! If you sight the enemy do not engage—return and report!"

The cavalry commander waved an acknowledgement and wheeled his horse about shouting orders, and Plautius turned to watch the second wave arrive and disembark. Plautius was a cautious and experienced commander, but even he was beginning to think that this was proving to be the easiest campaign of his career. He pushed his perimeter defenses further inland, about half a mile, so as to make room for those still to come, and by noon all three invasion waves were safely ashore, well established and organized. Four full legions with cavalry and auxiliary cohorts, forty thousand men all told. He knew that it would take a half a million native warriors to dislodge him now, and he doubted whether all the Pretannic tribes put together could amass such an opposition. Hosidius Geta returned to report that he had pushed inland to a depth of ten miles and more but still there was no sign of the enemy.

Saturninus slapped his thigh. "By Zeus! Was there ever an invasion as easy as this one?"

Hosidius Geta slid from his horse and joined them. "It takes all the excitement out of soldiering," he grumbled. "They might have at least put up *some* sort of resistance."

Plautius pointed inland. "Don't crow too soon, you roosters," he said firmly. "They are out there—I feel it in my bones—and they will fight and fight fiercely. There will be many a Roman who will not see Rome again, but certainly the Britannic tribes have lost any opportunity they might have had to successfully oppose us, but now it is too late!"

"And our immediate plans?" said Saturninus.

"We will rest here tonight," said Plautius. "It will give time for those with seasickness to recover. We march at dawn—inland to the River Stour, as planned." He turned to Hosidius Geta. "As you said this morning —Britannia is wide open!"

* * *

Way below him Cranog could see the Eternal Light burning steadily on the altar and the tiny figures of the brethren sitting in solemn ritual. He could see his own physical plane body, eyes closed, sitting in trance in the East. Again he felt that curious sense of detachment, remoteness, as though the figures below were puppets, inanimate objects unconnected with himself. It was a feeling he always had when out of his body. When the time came for him to return he knew he would again experience that momentary feeling of rebellion, a fleeting sense of loathing at having to reenter that grotesque body of human flesh with all its limitations and problems. It was a feeling unworthy of a priest, he knew, and he always fought against it sternly. To refuse to reenter would be a form of suicide. Tempting though it was Cranog knew that no problem was ever solved by running away from it. If he did so the same problems, the same wrong attitudes, would come up time and time again in future lives until he had learned to overcome his difficulties. He could of course refuse to incarnate again, and go on refusing, but such continued refusal would lead inevitably not only to the total disintegration of his very soul but also to the total annihilation of his inner self, the divine spark around which his soul was formed. No human problem was ever as serious as that dreadful alternative.

The other senior brethren were obviously having trouble getting out of their bodies. Judging from the parchments in the archives the ancient Druids could all leave their bodies at will, seniors and juniors both, and travel to wherever they wanted, *and* return with full memory of what they had seen and heard. If so then certainly it was a dying art, for today there were barely half a dozen senior members who could get out of their bodies at all, let alone travel and observe, and certainly their subsequent memory was sketchy to say the least.

Melvina and Gilda finally arrived almost simultaneously. Cranog remembered his earth daughter saying that she found it relatively easy to slip from her body during one of her forest rituals in the sacred oak grove, but found it more difficult in the stylized and stereotyped Temple rituals in the Hall of Ritual at Glaeston. Perhaps therefore part of the trouble was that Druidry had been losing direct contact with the nature forces. At one time the majority of Druid rituals were held in the open air, either at one of the stone circles or in one of the forest oak groves, but now the only group ritual to be performed outside Glaeston was the annual ritual of the Vernal Equinox at Cor Gaur. Gilda was the only one to maintain the old oak rituals and hers were private rather than group rituals. Cranog was determined that if and when the Romans were driven from Pretannia he would reintroduce the old nature rituals and try to restore Druidry to its former power and greatness.

Finally Kerrin arrived to join them. All four waited patiently but it was soon apparent that none of the others could achieve their release. Cranog gave the signal and all four rose high above Glaeston College and set out towards the east. In the old days, according to the parchments, any member of the senior Order of the White could achieve instantaneous transfer within the half-world simply by visualizing himself at his destination and willing the transfer to take place——indeed any candidate for the White had to demonstrate his ability to do so at his initiation, for it was held that any junior priest or priestess who lacked this ability was not yet ready for the senior degrees. With the death of Drucius there was now no one in all Druidry, not even Cranog himself, who could demonstrate this ability—— furthermore it was already being mooted by some that no such ability had ever existed and that the parchments were either wrong or were being interpreted incorrectly. With such doubts already being voiced it would not be long, perhaps a generation or two, before all the greatness and power of the ancient Druids would be reduced to the level of fantasy and legend by a world no longer capable of emulating the abilities of their ancestors, particularly if the Druid archives were destroyed.

Cranog had already discussed with his colleagues the possible necessity of having to destroy all the old documents. It was an appalling thought, some of them were more than 2,000 years old—indeed one of them described the method and manner of the building of Cor Gaur itself, complete with diagrams and work methods. The archives contained a body of knowledge that would confer great power on those with the ability to interpret their contents, and under no circumstances could such material be allowed to fall into the hands of the power-hungry Roman barbarians. It had been suggested that the Romans had neither the wit nor the learning to understand their contents, and although possibly and even undoubtedly true they dare not take the risk. It was also suggested that the archives be bequeathed to the Culdees for safekeeping, but it was already known that some of the Culdees, Zaacheus in particular, considered the ancient Druid priestly craft and abilities, if true at all, to be the result of sorcery and evil. With that attitude the Culdees were hardly fitted for the task of guardianship of such knowledge. It was also suggested that they be hidden in such a way that they would not be unearthed for some centuries when the races of Man would or should be more enlightened, but try as they might they could see little evidence that the immediate future would be any less barbaric than it was at present. The final desperate suggestion was that they translate the writings into some sort of code and then destroy the originals. In that way they could remain unmolested until the intelligence of any race rose to a level sufficient to break the code—but Cranog himself pointed out that there was no guarantee whatsoever that a rise of intelligence would occur simultaneously with an equal rise in moral and spiritual responsibility.

Finally the matter was put to the inner planes, and their answer, given through the simulacrum of Drucius, was simple. In the event of a possible dissolution of Druidry at the hands of the Romans, all archives should be destroyed and all evidence of the ancient Druid wisdom be wiped from the face of the earth. In this way the secret knowledge would remain on the inner planes only, safe from the unworthy. If the future priesthood of Man desired such knowledge they would have to develop their spiritual awareness to an extent whereby they could rise to the inner levels, and if they achieved this expansion of consciousness they would be deemed worthy to have the knowledge again, and use it.

They also hinted, however, that the present Druids in earth should not be so vain as to think their hidden knowledge indispensable to spiritual evolution. It may be, they said, that such knowledge was now atavistic, that although it had been necessary at one stage in human development it was now out of date. It was a chastening and humbling thought that all the secret Druid knowledge painstakingly gathered over 4,000 years was now no longer necessary, almost as though the tremendous effort had all been a waste of time—but again it was emphasized that Druidry had served the Great One with honor and distinction but that the evolutionary drive had now shifted to a new phase and that now other knowledge and other practices were necessary for its development. The responsibility of the present Druids in earth was to ensure the destruction of the archives and see to it that the fair name of Druidry was maintained to the very end.

Cranog and the other three seniors sped over the land through the half-world towards the east. They had to determine the extent of the Roman advance and whether the Catuvellauni and the Belgae were putting up any serious opposition. If not it would not be long before the Romans reached the western lands and Glaeston itself. If so then the archives would have to be destroyed now before it was too late.

They arrived at Richboro while it was still dark,

though dawn was not far off. They hovered over the very spot where they themselves had stood just seven days earlier waiting for news of the Roman invasion fleet. When the news had come it had taken them seven whole days at forced-march pace to cover the long physical journey from Richboro to Glaeston, and now they had returned through the half-world in a matter of hours. Cranog was anxious to see what progress the Romans had made in that week.

The beach and the tiny fishing jetties at Richboro were crowded with shipping. The invasion war vessels themselves, the big triremes, lay prow-on to the beach, but surely those other smaller and lighter vessels were store-ships, presumably arrived after the beachhead had been secured. It would seem that Plautius was confident enough to have ordered in provisions and armaments for a prolonged stay. The Romans could have chosen no better place to land, the whole area was one huge natural harbor that could accommodate a hundred vessels if necessary riding safely at anchor, and Richboro itself was situated on a promontory jutting out to sea, a high point that overlooked the surrounding area. No one would be able to take Richboro by surprise either by sea or by land.

Gilda pointed down to a line of fires that stretched in the shape of a crescent some 700 yards long from north to south enclosing the whole Richboro position. This was obviously the defense perimeter. Inside that perimeter a dozen and more wooden storehouses had already been built, and nearby was a huge pile of stones obviously ready to be used in the building of more permanent structures. The Romans had worked fast and well. But as they traversed the whole defense area one fact became disturbingly obvious. To judge from the number of tents and night-fires there could not be above two thousand men in the whole area, and not a single horse, and Plautius was known to have landed with forty thousand men, including cavalry. Where was the body of the main army?

They dropped lower to hover just above the tents. The astro-etheric bodies of the sleeping legionaries were crude, primitive forms that glowed redly and dimly, each hovering above or beside its physical plane counterpart. Only here and there were astral forms sufficiently developed to move away from their physical bodies, and even these were semi-blind, groping entities. Cranog dropped a little lower and contacted several in quick succession, but all he received were crude impressions of the most primitive kind. The Roman army comprised very young souls indeed. The tent of a sleeping centurion, however, yielded something a little better. The astro-etheric form was only marginally more developed but at least it was able to perceive the visitors and recognize them as intruders, for it snarled horribly at their approach. The contact shook Cranog by the sheer bestiality and hatred of the impressions he received, but in the midst of that welter of crudeness he did momentarily receive an impression of a river and a fort. Cranog drew back and conferred with his companions. Probably the River Stour, though they could not explain the fort. They were not worried at having been recognized by the centurion's etheric—the man would wake and remember only that he had had a bad dream about the Druids.

They rose high above the area and set their direction to the northwest, moving as fast as they could. They did not have a great deal of time. Their physical bodies could not remain in a state of trance for very much longer. Soon now they would begin to feel the tug of their withdrawal.

As they came in sight of the River Stour the "air" around them was suddenly crowded with dozens of blind, groping astral forms, but unlike those at Richboro these had no connecting link to any physical body —they were obviously the astro-etheric forms of the newly dead. Under normal circumstances the Druids would have remained to help them over the next stage but they just simply did not have the time. These blind things would find their own way in due course.

The four Druids dropped lower and came upon what had obviously been a fairly large Belgic settlement on the banks of the river. The place was now deserted save for about a hundred or so dead bodies, mostly Belgae and Catuvellauni, though here and there were bodies of Romans who would not see Rome again. They rose higher and followed the river to the north and almost immediately came upon the main bulk of the Roman army encamped at a tiny hamlet called Harbledown. Caratacus and Togodumnus had obviously tried to stop the Romans crossing the River Stour and had failed. But to judge from the number of dead they had seen, the Catuvellauni could only have had a few hundred at their disposal—a mere skirmish rather than a battle—but at least it was heartening that the Catuvellauni were prepared to fight.

The four Druids moved forward cautiously. Below them would be senior Roman officers, and Aulus Plautius himself, and these would presumably be more advanced souls than those they had encountered at Richboro. Also if there were any priests with the army they would be here. The Druids did not want to be recognized by an astral sufficiently advanced to know them for what they were and remember the encounter when their physical bodies awoke. It was highly unlikely that the Roman army could boast of anyone with such skills, but they were not prepared to take the chance.

The army was immense—nearly forty thousand men—and already they had begun to build a fort to secure the river crossing. The Romans had moved with frightening speed and had achieved an astonishing amount of work in only seven days. By cautious probing they quickly ascertained that the camp held no Catuvellauni prisoners. They then rose and headed at full speed to the northwest and in due course came upon the River Medway, and sure enough there were the Catuvellauni encamped on the north bank.

Cranog nodded in satisfaction. This was no skirmishing force, for spread out below them was the entire Catuvellauni horde, some fifty thousand at a rough guess. The main Belgae army, also of fifty thousand warriors, must be still in their own realm to the south. It was a pity that the two had not combined, but the fifty thousand Catuvellauni below would at least give the Romans a hard time. Caratacus was obviously determined to make his main stand on the Medway, and Cranog nodded his approval. The ensuing battle would be of a magnitude unprecedented in Pretannic history.

* * *

Caratacus and Togodumnus emerged from their tent and snuffed the dawn wind. "Are you sure they *will* come?" said Togodumnus.

"Obviously they must," said Caratacus. "They have come to conquer and they cannot conquer by sitting around at Richboro and Canterbury."

"But when?"

Caratacus shrugged. "A few days, a week—who knows? They will not come until they have finished the fort at Harbledown—Plautius will want to secure his line of retreat."

"Then why not attack them now while they are unprepared?"

"They are *not* unprepared—they have merely paused to build a fort. If we attack and are unsuccessful we would be forced to retreat and thus find the Medway at our backs—far too dangerous. I prefer to keep the River Medway between us and them—they will have to cross it to get to us and we will cut them down as they do so."

Togodumnus nodded—it was a good plan. He was glad that Caratacus was making the decisions, his brother had a quicker mind than his own. Togodumnus was good at inter-tribal forays and skirmishes, raids on neighboring tribes to capture women and cattle, but this was something much bigger and he was content to leave matters to Caratacus. "And the Belgae?"

Two days ago they had sent a runner to the Belgae commanding them to join the Catuvellauni at the Medway. "*If* they come we will advance and attack the Romans on the Stour—we would then have one hundred thousand against their forty—but the Belgae will not come."

Togodumnus glanced at his brother. "Why not?"

Caratacus smiled grimly. "They did not exactly enjoy being conquered by we Catuvellauni, nor do they enjoy having to give us allegiance. It would gladden their hearts to see us defeated." He pointed across the river. "And don't forget that Verica, whom we exiled, is at this moment with the Romans. If we Catuvellauni are defeated the Romans will restore Verica so that once again the Belgae will be a kingdom with a king, and no longer subject to Catuvellauni rule."

"But the Belgae will then have to give allegiance to the Romans."

Caratacus shook his head. "I doubt it. I know Verica pretty well. Once restored to his kingdom with fifty thousand warriors at his back, he will turn against the Romans hoping to find them weakened by their struggle with us. If he can defeat the Romans and drive them out, the whole of Pretannia will be his. He is an ambitious man. No—we cannot expect any help from the Belgae." He grinned and slapped Togodumnus on the back. "But take heart, my brother, we are not defeated yet. There are no bridges on the Medway—they will have to swim across and we will cut them down one by one as they come out of the water!"

Togodumnus grinned, and the two brothers walked down to the river's edge to plan how they would line the bank to meet the Roman advance. Sometime later Togodumnus stared thoughtfully across the river. "Ten days ago the Belgae were with us at Richboro—we had a hundred thousand warriors. If we had remained there another three days we could have destroyed the Romans as they came in to land." He looked at his brother. "The Druids were right after all."

* * *

Five days later Aulus Plautius with nearly four full legions advanced on the Medway along the old trackway from Canterbury, the Pilgrims' Way, the natives called it. Plautius had left two thousand men at Richboro and a further two thousand at Harbledown. The remainder, thirty-six thousand men, would be more than enough to deal with the Catuvellauni rabble across the Medway. When they had arrived and encamped, Plautius walked down to the river's edge with Saturninus,

Hosidius Geta, and his own kinsman, T. Plautius Silvanus Aelianus, who was on his general staff. With them were Vespasian, the legate in command of Legio II Augusta and Vespasian's elder brother, T. Flavius Sabinus—also Didius Gallus and that wily old fox, M. Licinius Crassus Frugi.

Across the river they could see the Catuvellauni camp. The whole north bank for half a mile or more was lined with tens of thousands of screaming, near-demented, half-naked tribesmen. In front of the line, right on the river's edge itself, a score of chariots raced up and down, their riders' hair streaming in the wind.

The Romans eyed them calmly. "They are a noisy lot," said Hosidius Geta. "Where is their general's brains in letting them waste their energy like that?" He grinned at Plautius. "It is courteous of them to reveal their entire strength for our inspection and assessment."

Plautius nodded. "The reports were obviously accurate—a great many of them, but ill-disciplined. This should not present too many problems."

Saturninus pointed. "The leading chariot there, the rider with the red hair—that must be Caratacus—he is the only one apparently with any pretense to generalship."

"And the one behind him," said Didius Gallus, "the one with the mane of black hair, that must be his brother, Togodumnus."

"What say you, Crassus?" said Plautius.

The old fox, M. Licinius Crassus Frugi, nodded sourly. "As you say—no problem. Verica's Belgae are not with them, otherwise there would be twice this number. A frontal attack would be too costly, and there is no need to waste several days in constructing pontoon bridges. Outflank them with auxiliary cohorts —establish a beachhead—reinforce with cavalry—and then full attack by infantry. The only way."

"I agree." Plautius signaled Vespasian, and the young legate edged his horse nearer to his commander. "Legate, the German auxiliary cohorts with Legio II— they have been fully trained to swim with full equipment?"

"Yes, commander."

"Very well, then here is what we will do . . ."

Togodumnus was wild with delight at seeing the Romans apparently retreat back behind the hills to the south. "Cowards! Afraid to fight," he bellowed. "So much for the mighty Roman army!"

Caratacus was not so sure, but he had to admit that he was puzzled by the Roman move. "Perhaps they are regrouping."

"Regrouping? Nonsense! They were already perfectly grouped. No, my brother—now that they have seen us in our full strength they are afraid to fight!"

Caratacus shook his head. "No, whatever else they are, the Romans are *not* afraid!" He looked up at the sky. "It is now noon. They probably want a full day for the attack. My guess is that they will camp beyond the hills tonight and return to attack at dawn."

Caratacus was right that the Romans would return, but totally wrong as to the timing. It would not occur to any Catuvellauni warrior, and certainly it did not occur to Caratacus, that any commander would launch a major battle before dawn. The Catuvellauni, like all the tribes in Pretannia, hated to fight at night—who could say what evil, loathsome forms slithered through the darkness of night. But the Romans, unencumbered by such primitive fears, often used a pre-dawn attack.

Four German auxiliary cohorts, two thousand men in all, crept back through the hills a full two hours before dawn and silently approached the river. Once there they split in half and made their way to two separate points half a mile apart and silently began to cross the river. The Catuvellauni had guards posted but they did not see their attackers until they were almost across.

Caratacus came bursting from his tent at the sounds of pandemonium from the river bank. Sword in hand he raced forward bellowing orders as he ran. It was still pitch-dark. "Fires!" he bellowed. "Heap the fires! Give us light!"

There was a mass of struggling men on the river bank, and the Catuvellauni guards were being cut down and driven back as more and more Romans poured from the river. With a great bellowing roar of rage Caratacus leaped into the fray, hacking and cutting his way forward, but there were too many against them and Caratacus and the remnants of the guard were forced to give ground. Behind them the rest of the Catuvellauni camp was in a bewildered uproar. Men ran in all directions. Suddenly the attacking force, five hundred at least with more still coming, veered to one side and began hacking their way along the bank.

Caratacus dropped out of the fight to assess the situation. A further uproar was going on to the north—two attacks obviously. He grabbed Togodumnus as his brother raced by. "Up there! There's another beachhead! Get up there—push them back into the river. Go!" and he gave his brother a shove in the right direction.

Caratacus stared wildly around him. This was ridiculous, an attack in the middle of the night! The sky was only just beginning to turn gray now. A splintering crash brought him spinning round. The chariots! The Romans were in among the chariots! He set off at a run, bellowing orders, and more and more Catuvellauni fell in behind and alongside him. The tide was beginning to turn, now that the main body of the Catuvellauni had begun to realize what was going on. But a great deal of damage had been done. When he arrived at the center he saw that the two Roman wings had joined together. There must be about two thousand of them—a simple matter to deal with. But Caratacus was nearly demented with rage. Of the twenty chariots that he had possessed, more than a dozen lay splintered and broken —and of his herd of forty Arab horses over half lay dead.

The Romans had thrown a crescent ring of shoulder-high shields around their position, their backs to the river. They were defending well but it was only a matter of time before they fell to the screaming onslaught of fifty thousand demented tribesmen. Caratacus saw his brother drive his ax right through a shield and through the Roman who held it. Caratacus sprang into the fray and cut down one of the kneeling defenders, and another. He received a deep slash in his side but he barely noticed it.

Across the river Plautius glanced at Didius Gallus, in overall command of the cavalry, and nodded. Gallus urged his horse forward alongside Hosidius Geta, the cavalry commander. "It is time. Go! The second legion will follow immediately behind you!"

Hosidius Geta saluted, and then raised his arm in signal. As he brought it down the Second and Ninth cavalry divisions moved down into the water and began to swim their horses across.

Plautius nodded to Flavius Sabinus. Flavius moved across and alongside his younger brother, Vespasian, the legate of Legio II. "Well, Vespasian, your time has come. Try not to get killed, you know it would upset your mother!"

Vespasian grinned and signaled his commanders, and the entire second legion infantry began to move down to the river, six thousand men.

Across the river the first of the cavalry were breasting up out of the water onto the river bank. Hosidius Geta, by a pre-arranged plan, waited until half the cavalry were ashore, some two hundred men, and then with a bellowed order the cavalry line plunged forward at full gallop straight at the backs of their own line of defenders. Just when it seemed that they would mow down their own comrades, the German commander of the auxiliary cohorts barked an order and the entire line of defenders flung themselves flat on the ground, their shields covering their bodies against flying hooves, and the cavalry leapt over them and plunged into the thick of the Catuvellauni horde.

The cavalry caused absolute panic in the Catuvellauni ranks. Hacking downwards right and left they cut a swathe right through the densely packed tribesmen and out the other side, from where they began harrying the rear. Meanwhile the line of defenders had picked themselves up and moved forward and gained fifty yards before the confused Catuvellauni could close their ranks against them.

The second half of the cavalry, by the same pre-arranged plan, waited until this maneuver had been completed and then they too charged forward at full gallop. Again the defenders flung themselves flat to allow the galloping horses through, again this second wave cut a swathe through the thick of the Catuvellauni warriors to join Hosidius Geta at the rear, and again the defending line picked themselves up and gained another fifty yards before the Catuvellauni could recover.

There were still only three thousand men this side of the river against fifty thousand Catuvellauni, but so well trained were the Romans, so well rehearsed and disciplined, that the Catuvellauni found themselves harried from all sides. The line of auxiliaries were moving steadily against their front, shields up in a disciplined, unbroken line, swords hacking and slashing in front of them, and at the rear the cavalry were sweeping along their entire line at full gallop.

Vespasian urged his horse through the shallows and up onto the bank, and from there he waved his men to follow. The stolid legionaries were now beginning to arrive, a hundred men, five hundred, a thousand —soon the entire Second legion infantry was ashore. Vespasian gathered his men and the line moved forward. The exhausted German auxiliaries now fell back to the rear to rest and the Second legion infantry took their place in the front line.

Once this maneuver had been completed Plautius gave yet another signal and the Ninth and Fourteenth legions moved down to the river at two points half a mile apart and began to cross. Their task was to attack the Catuvellauni flanks, and once this was achieved the enemy would be surrounded by twenty-five thousand Roman cavalry and infantry—still outnumbered two to one, but there was no doubt in any Roman mind that these odds were more than enough to deal with this ill-organized rabble.

This method of attack would have been suicidal against a well-disciplined enemy—each wave of the attack, heavily outnumbered, would have been cut down and annihilated before the succeeding wave could arrive—but Plautius had found it very successful in the past against a rabble no matter what the size. He had found that an attack made by wave after wave after wave tended to confuse and demoralize an ill-disciplined horde, and so it proved again against the Catuvellauni.

Caratacus had never seen anything like it. Even with his fifty thousand against the cavalry and the one legion commanded by Vespasian the Romans seemed to be everywhere. The Catuvellauni must have lost ten thousand men already and still they were dying by the dozens every second. When Caratacus saw the other two legions begin to cross the river he knew that he was doomed. If he wanted to save anything for the future he would have to get his warriors away to regroup and re-think their strategy. He bellowed his orders and the Catuvellauni began to stream away to the rear, but it was not even easy to run, for at the rear was Hosidius Geta and the cavalry to cut off just such a retreat. But even the Roman cavalry could not stop the entire exodus. They cut down the fleeing tribesmen by the hundreds but half the Catuvellauni made it safely to the wooded area to the rear where the cavalry could not follow.

Vespasian gave a signal and the Second legion came to a halt. He was flushed with excitement. Hosidius Geta came over to him at a gallop and reined his lathered horse. "A fair morning's work!" he shouted.

The young legate looked to the sky. The sun was well up—it must be mid-morning already. A battle that had seemed to last for a mere score of minutes must have lasted for at least several hours. He laughed with the sheer exuberance of it. "We will be in trouble now with our fellow commanders, Hosidius!" he shouted back. "We've left nothing for them!"

Hosidius Geta grinned and urged his horse away to the river. The Ninth and Fourteenth legions were now across, and the Twentieth plus Plautius and the General Staff were just beginning the crossing.

When Plautius arrived, Vespasian and Hosidius Geta reported their casualties. "Approximately fifty cavalry only," said Geta.

Vespasian could not help grinning. "Two hundred auxiliaries lost, and three hundred legionaries."

"And officers?" said Plautius.

"None."

The general nodded thoughtfully. "Five hundred and fifty all told. And the enemy?"

Hosidius Geta looked round the field. "Could be as many as fifteen thousand," he said.

"More like twenty!" said Vespasian, his eyes shining.

Plautius turned to his General Staff. "A successful campaign so far, I think, gentlemen," he said quietly.

"My congratulations," said Saturninus.

"And mine," said Didius Gallus. "The Emperor will be pleased."

"Thank you—thank you," said Plautius. "But our work has only just begun. You will gather the legions, Saturninus, for a steady pursuit of the enemy. The Catuvellauni are to be pushed and harried without rest. The marshlands are to the north, and beyond that is the River Tamesis—the natives call it the Thamus. We will make our camp there."

For three days the Romans pursued the Catuvellauni mercilessly. Groups of stragglers were overtaken and put to death without hesitation. The Romans had neither the time nor the inclination to take and supervise prisoners—nor indeed did they have sufficient provisions to spare for their welfare, their supply line from Richboro was already stretched to breaking point by the rapidity of the advance. The legions themselves were already on survival rations, with little time to forage from the land—and anyway, dead enemies were less bothersome than those kept alive.

But on the third day the pattern of pursuit changed. The rolling woodlands gave way gradually to a treacherous marshland, a full five miles south of the River Tamesis itself. The Catuvellauni knew the marshlands well, and the Romans did not. The survivors now gathered together in groups and began to raid the Roman lines and ambush their patrols, a form of warfare that they much preferred. In the first week in the marshlands the Romans lost on average a hundred legionaries a day, and it was small consolation that the Catuvellauni losses were about the same. The general staff officers urged Plautius time and time again to skirt the marshes and head straight for their goal, the Trinovantian capital of Camulodunum on the northeast coast—but Plautius was adamant. "These people must learn," he said grimly, "that there is no place on earth in which they can safely hide!"

In one particularly fierce skirmish a band of some two hundred Catuvellauni were discovered and surrounded just at nightfall, and rather than risk their being allowed to slip away in the night the Romans attacked at once even though the terrain prevented them from bringing more than five hundred legionaries to the scene. It was a fierce, all-night battle during which the Romans lost over half their force, but when dawn broke not a single Catuvellauni remained alive. Among the dead the Romans were delighted to discover the savagely mutilated body of Togodumnus. The surviving centurion hacked off the head and gleefully carried it to Plautius. The general nodded, partially satisfied, but then he said: "But what of Caratacus?" In the early days of the marshland skirmishing the red-haired giant had been seen time and time again, but try as they might they had not been able to take him—but he had not been seen now for some days. Perhaps he was already dead, his body sunk beneath the marsh, but Plautius was not convinced.

It was during this marshland campaign that emissaries arrived from King Boduocus of the Dobunni tribe away to the west, offering surrender. Plautius knew that the Dobunni were in effect ruled by the Catuvellauni and that Boduocus was "king" in name only. "They must have heard of our victory."

"Apparently not," said Saturninus. "These emissaries set out from Glevum, their capital on the River Avon, some time ago when we were still east of the Medway."

M. Licinius Crassus Frugi smiled sourly. "No doubt they had orders to surrender the Dobunni to us if we won, and to pledge their loyalty to Caratacus if the Catuvellauni won!"

Plautius nodded. "Perhaps you are right, but we cannot altogether blame them. Send them in." Aulus

Plautius received the emissaries courteously, listened to their vow of loyalty to Rome, and then accepted the surrender but instructed them to advise King Boduocus to present himself at Camulodunum as soon as possible to make the surrender official.

The campaign of the marshlands dragged on for weeks but gradually the Romans pushed the Catuvellauni northwards until finally they were forced across the Thamus, as the natives called it, near the hamlet of London, that the Romans renamed Londinium. On the northern bank of the Thamus the Catuvellauni gathered their groups together and made their stand against the Roman advance. The Romans had difficulty at first in finding the fords, but auxiliary troops once more swam across, and others built a temporary bridge upstream. The remnants of the Catuvellauni fought hard but were now too dispirited. After a final battle they fled in disorder northwards, all thoughts of resistance gone. Their only thought now was to return to their own kingdom. Of the fifty thousand Catuvellauni warriors who had marched south to meet the Romans on the Medway, it was doubted whether ten thousand arrived back at Prae Wood, their capital.

Satisfied with the first phase of the Pretannic campaign Aulus Plautius withdrew his forces back over the Thamus and set up permanent camp on the south bank—and sent for Claudius who had been waiting impatiently for this very moment. It was now July. The Emperor arrived in Pretannia in August with the entire Eighth legion, a detachment of the Praetorian Guard under Rufrius Polli and, unexpectedly, an elephant division. The elephants caused some amusement, but the delighted Claudius confessed to Plautius that he had brought them more from a desire to conquer in style than from any real need. With the Praetorian Guard was the young tribune, C. Gavius Silvanus, who greeted Plautius with particular warmth since it was these two who could make some claim as having been the instigators of the entire campaign.

With Claudius and Plautius at their head the five legions pushed on to Camulodunum, which surrendered with barely a fight—and there the Romans accepted the official surrender of no fewer than eleven Britannic tribes, including the Catuvellauni, the Brigantes, the Iceni, the Cornovii, and of course the Dobunni. Verica was officially restored as client-King of a reconstructed Belgic-Atrebatic kingdom—but he did not live long to enjoy his restoration and he was succeeded shortly by his kinsman, Cogidubnus.

Claudius remained in Pretannia for only sixteen days. Leaving orders with Plautius to continue the campaign he crossed the Narrow Sea in early September before the equinoctial gales began and traveled slowly through Gaul and arrived in Rome after an absence of six months, and there celebrated the triumph that the Senate had voted him.

In Pretannia a well-satisfied Plautius now began to plan for the forthcoming military expansion throughout the entire land, using Camulodunum as his main base. But still one question niggled at his mind. It was perfectly obvious to any rational mind, he told himself, that Caratacus must have been killed in those skirmishes in the marshlands, but still the question persisted—where was the red-haired erstwhile King of the Catuvellauni? Where in Zeus' name was Caratacus?

chapter six

The messengers went out from Glaeston to every Druid grove throughout the land, to Men an Tol and Lanyon Quoit in the western lands where the fearful Nine Maidens glowered above Boscawen-Un—and to Kits Coty and Coldrum in the east who had watched from the forest with secret eyes as the Romans had passed on their way from Richboro to Camulot— and to Maes Howe in the far north whose grove contained the ancient runic words—and to Mona, the Misty Isle, in the lands of the Ordovices. To all save one the message was the same—every grove was to be closed down, all parchments without exception were to be destroyed, and each grove was to be obliterated as though it had never existed, though the standing stones were to be left intact. The senior priest of each grove, plus all those skilled in stonework, were to make their way to Glaeston with all speed—all others were to go to Mona.

The message to Mona was different, and was carried personally by Kerrin himself, the dark one. The grove at the Misty Isle was to stand prepared to give shelter to every living Druid in Pretannia. The living quarters were to be doubled, redoubled, and doubled again—earthworks as high as those at Cor Gaur were to be thrown up along the entire eastern shoreline in defense against a sea-borne attack from the mainland of Pretannia—and the armory was to work day and night without ceasing to stockpile as many arms as humanly possible.

"To what limit?" Kerrin asked.

Cranog shook his head. "I wish I knew—I can only leave it to your discretion—but certainly we cannot possibly have too many weapons. The limit, I feel, will be either the supply of raw material or the exhaustion of those who do the work. I leave it to you."

They walked down to the courtyard together, and Kerrin swung himself up onto his horse. "I don't like to leave Glaeston," he said suddenly. He patted the horse's neck soothingly. "Tell me, Cranog, are you *really* sure that all this is necessary?"

There was an emotion in Kerrin's voice quite alien to his usual dour personality. "Yes, I am," said Cranog firmly. "Eleven tribes have surrendered to Plautius at Camulot—or Camulodunum as the Romans call it. I cannot imagine that they will leave it at that." He shook his head grimly. "They came to conquer and to make Pretannia a province of Rome. They cannot do that just sitting at Camulot. They will begin to move out soon, and then it is only a matter of time before they reach Glaeston."

Kerrin sighed. "Yes, you are probably right." He stared round at the great courtyard. "It is strange to think that I may never see all this again." The horse moved restlessly under him and he steadied it with a word. "Parts of the college must be two thousand years old at least—the water-well is nearer four thousand probably."

"True," Cranog nodded, "but better to dismantle it now, stone by stone, than allow it to fall into Roman hands. The very thought of those barbarians tramping through our sacred halls is sickening. I would rather see Glaeston destroyed than profaned!" He looked up at the dark one. "I am relying on you, Kerrin, to make a home in earth at Mona for the whole of Druidry—see to it that it is a fitting place—it may be that the last chapter in our history will unfold at Mona."

"I will not let you down," said Kerrin. "All will be as you have commanded."

Cranog stepped forward and grasped his friend's hand. "Farewell," he said softly. "Safe journey. We will join you in Mona as soon as our work here is completed."

Kerrin wheeled his horse around and urged it at a full gallop through the great gates and on to the trackway to the northwest. Cranog walked to the gate and stared after him until the figure dwindled and vanished in the distance. Cranog's heart was very heavy. Though he had known Kerrin all his life, yet it had only been during these past few months that he had come to understand the value of that dark and silent priest.

A very young Bard, a boy no more than ten or eleven years of age, came to attract his attention. He stammered a little as he spoke—in all his young life he had never before addressed so auguste a personage as the Arch-Mage himself. "The High Priestess bids me inform you," he said gravely and nervously, "that all is in readiness."

Cranog turned to him, hiding the quick smile that sprang unbidden at the sight of so grave a child. "Inform the High Priestess," he said gently and kindly, "that I will come at once." The boy bowed and scampered away. Cranog stared after him, a new thought in his mind. The very young Bards were apprentice priests, true, but still they were children. It was unthinkable that they should have to face the Roman wrath alongside their seniors. He would have to speak to the Council.

The Hall of Learning looked strangely bare, naked almost. The row upon row of shelves, which a week ago were crammed with parchments, were now empty. The line of benches that seated the lecture audiences had been pulled to one side. In the middle of the chamber, on the gray flagstones, a huge brazier burned steadily. The destruction of the archives had been going on for two days. The burning had been meticulously supervised. The Archivist personally checked each parchment and ticked it off on his records before allowing it to be consigned to the flames. Every hour the ash was cleared away in large sacks and dumped in the lake. Of course, they could have disposed of the entire archives in one day with a huge fire outside in the open air, but they dare not risk even a single scrap of uncharred parchment being whisked away by the wind.

Melvina, the High Priestess, was there, and Morgana, and so too were several of the Council. Cranog nodded to them and then walked over to the Archivist. "A sad task, Cadvan," he said quietly.

The Archivist was an old man, a survivor of more than eighty winters. He had been the Archivist for forty years and quite truly knew every parchment in the Hall of Learning. His face was grimy with smoke, and Cranog suspected that his eyes were red-rimmed more from tears than from the heat of the brazier. He looked up at Cranog. "It is like burning your own children," he said briefly.

Cranog patted his arm. "I know—I know," he said gently.

The old man showed him his parchment record. "All the lesser documents have been destroyed. I personally checked every single one myself." He pointed to where a few remained. "There are just the major parchments now."

The Arch-Mage nodded. "Very well—carry on."

The Archivist took a yellowing document, studied

it carefully, ticked his record, and then personally consigned it to the flames. The onlookers watched in grave silence. He took another, studied it, ticked his record, and that too was consumed in silence. He took another, then another—for an hour he worked carefully and meticulously until only one document remained. It was so brittle with age that he could barely unroll it. "It is so old and so precious," said the Archivist, "that no one has been permitted to handle it for a hundred years and more." He carried it over to Cranog. "For forty years I have served as Archivist and this is the first time that I have even touched it. Copies of it, for reference, were among the lesser documents I destroyed earlier." He held it up carefully. "Look!"

The Arch-Mage studied the incredibly ancient yellow parchment. It was the work-plan for the construction of Cor Gaur itself, the sacred center of the race. Cranog stared at the mass of ancient Druid runes and Egyptian hieroglyphics depicting the magic square of the Sun—the complete measurements for every stone and every single alignment—and the precise instructions on how to quarry the giant stones, shape them, transport them, and how to hoist them into position. Meticulously set out were the instructions on the conduct of the very first ritual ever performed at Cor Gaur, nearly four thousand years ago—and the Arch-Mage shook his head in wonderment at the sight of the ancient star-maps and the instructions as to how Cor Gaur could also be used to predict every movement of the stars and planets for tens of thousands of years to come. It was a key to the entire Druid philosophy. Careful study of such a document, coupled with intuitive interpretation, could reveal every single secret of Druid power and thought. Such a document, in the wrong hands, could be used to hold the entire world in abject slavery. Under no circumstances could it ever be allowed to fall into Roman hands.

"Burn it!" said Cranog briefly. The old man hesitated. "Burn it!" the Arch-Mage said harshly, and the Archivist carried it to the glowing brazier. He glanced back, but Cranog's face was set like stone, and the old man cast the parchment into the flames.

They watched in utter silence as the brittle document burst into fire and was consumed. The Archivist held up his record of parchments, every item neatly ticked, and on Cranog's nod that too was destroyed.

Cranog turned to Melvina and the silent Druid Council. "Every single written document here at Glaeston has been destroyed in accordance with inner plane instructions. Soon we will receive confirmation from every grove throughout the land that their documents are also destroyed. When that has been achieved there will no longer be any evidence whatsoever that any documents ever existed." He looked carefully at the council members. "You will instruct the members of all degrees—most strictly—that they must *never* mention the one-time existence of *any* Druid document in the hearing of a non-initiate. I want the Romans and future generations to believe that we Druids did not ever practice the art of hieroglyphics of any type whatsoever. Is that clear?"

They all nodded gravely. "What of the Culdees?" said Melvina. "They may have heard of such matters."

"I am invited to visit Zaacheus at the Culdee Church later today—perhaps you would care to come with me. We may be able to ascertain the extent of their knowledge, if any, without revealing our position."

The Arch-Mage turned to Cadvan. "Thank you for your work," he said gently. "You may feel that your lifetime's service as Archivist is now at an end since the Archives no longer exist." The old man did not reply, but Cranog could see the hurt in his eyes. "But I tell you," Cranog went on, "that in this respect you are now the most important priest here at Glaeston. When you were Archivist you could, if necessary, have been replaced by another—but now you are truly irreplaceable. Your memory contains a hundred times more knowledge of the archives than the rest of us put together—indeed you *are* the Archives now, and we will need to draw upon your memory time and again during the days to come."

The old man brightened. "Thank you," he said simply. "I hope my memory will not fail you."

"I'm sure it won't." He turned to the Council. "There is another matter that I want you to consider most carefully in readiness for a full discussion at the next council meeting. The days to come will be fraught with danger and in all probability a great many will die. Do we take the very junior Bards to Mona to share that danger, or shall we release them from their vows and return them to their parents in their various tribes? And if we return them what shall we do with those who were born here at Glaeston and whose parents are Druid?" He looked round at the council members. "Yes, I can see that the point has not hitherto occurred to you either. Very well—meditate upon the matter. We will discuss it fully later."

Later that day Cranog and Melvina set out to visit the Culdees whose lands adjoined Glaeston. They paused at the great gates to Glaeston College. The stoneworker priests were already at work. The carved stone mountings on top of the portal had already been removed. These were to be broken up, pounded to fragments so that no trace of the carvings remained. Cranog's instructions had been precise on this point. Any piece of stone that bore any carvings whatsoever were to be destroyed utterly. Only the plain blocks of stone were to be kept. Outside the college grounds a piece of land had been leveled and cleared of scrub growth. Here the great stones would be neatly piled, row upon row, ready to be used again.

Melvina sighed heavily. "I can still hardly believe that all this is happening—that everything that is Druid is being destroyed utterly. Four thousand years of a sacred culture being wiped away as though it had never existed!"

"You know the reasons, Melvina—better than most."

"Yes, I know—I know—the old has to die to make way for the new, but still I can hardly believe that it is actually happening."

The Culdee wattle and daub church was tiny. Its

thatched roof and white lime washed walls made it seem more like a peasant's cottage than the sacred center of a new religion. It was picturesque but it had no magnificence, no grandeur. The new phase of human evolution, though Cranog, deserved something more fitting.

Zaacheus, as usual, was suspicious and belligerent in the presence of Druids. His was still the naive attitude that everything Christian was good and that everything non-Christian was evil. Instead of his attitude mellowing with experience it had grown more bitter and distrustful, especially when the death of Joseph had removed the counter-balancing force of tolerance. Cranog's private opinion was that Joseph's son, Josue, would have made a far better leader for the Culdees than the old man, Zaacheus.

"Well, Zaacheus," said Cranog, "you will soon be rid of our contaminating influence. We have begun the work of dismantling Glaeston College, and when that work is completed the entire Druid membership will withdraw to the Isle of Mona to await our fate there."

"You could yet be saved," said Zaacheus piously, "if you would recant your pagan Druid ways and be baptized into the true faith."

Cranog shook his head wearily. "For the hundredth time, Zaacheus, there is little difference in essence between Druidry and Christianity. We both worship the same force, though in a different manner."

"*We* are the children of God!"

Cranog held up his hand. "I am not going into all that old argument yet again," he said irritably. "I merely wish to let you know that you are welcome to the stone that we are leaving behind. There will be thousands of dressed stone blocks suitable for building. You may need them."

"There is nothing we need from you Druids," said Zaacheus ungraciously.

Josue was plainly embarrassed by Zaacheus' obvious hatred for the Druids. "What Zaacheus means," he said quickly, "is that . . ."

"I know what Zaacheus means," said Cranog drily, "but you should not be too proud to accept help even from such pagans as we Druids."

"We do not need your help!" snapped Zaacheus.

"You were not too proud to accept our help when first you arrived in Pretannia as refugees from Judaea," Melvina retorted. The old man's attitude irritated her beyond bearance. "It was only because of Druid influence that you were permitted to remain here at all. And I might remind you that this very land upon which we stand belongs to you Culdees by the grace of we Druids."

"We could have gone elsewhere!"

"Maybe, but you were thankful enough to settle here in Pretannia. We do not expect your thanks or your gratitude," she went on, "but you can at least be a little more gracious in your attitude towards us."

Cranog held up his hand. "Let us not go into all that again. As far as the stone is concerned, the time may come when you wish to use it to build yourself a more fitting place of worship than your present temple."

"It is a church, not a temple," snapped Zaacheus, "and it is perfectly satisfactory."

"No doubt it is, but the time may come when you wish to build a church on more generous lines, and if so then the stone is there for you to use. If not, then leave it where it is. It is of no vital concern to us!"

Josue was obviously still embarrassed and he tried to change the subject. "What of your writings, Cranog —will you take them with you to Mona?"

"What writings?"

The younger man was taken aback. "Have you no writings—records, parchments, that sort of thing?"

Cranog shook his head. "We have no writings whatsoever," he said truthfully. "Why, have you been told that we have?"

"No, no, I just assumed . . ."

"There is an old legend that there were once some parchments filled with Egyptian hieroglyphics that none could understand, but they were lost centuries ago, I believe." Cranog stared at the young man. "I assure you we have no writings whatsoever in any manner, shape, or form." Had there been any doubt at all in the Culdee's eyes Cranog would have seen it, but it was quite obvious that the statement was accepted at face value. The Arch-Mage gave a tiny bow. "And now we must leave. We have much work to supervise. I am truly sorry, Zaacheus, that you think so ill of us."

The old man tried hard to be gracious but it was no small effort for him. "I am concerned for my people and for my God."

"Yes, no doubt you are. Farewell."

Cranog and Melvina were halfway back to Glaeston when Josue caught up with them. "I came to apologize for Zaacheus," he said breathlessly.

Cranog nodded. "It would help him considerably if he could at least learn the art of courtesy. However, it is really of small matter."

The younger man hesitated. "You met and spoke with Jesus of Nazareth, did you not?"

"Yes, many times—so too did Melvina here—indeed every Druid at Glaeston remembers him well."

Josue nodded. "So too do all we Culdees—all except one. You see, Zaacheus never saw him, not even once. He didn't bother with such things. It was only after his death that Zaacheus was drawn into the faith."

Cranog drew in his breath sharply. "Ah!" he said. "I did not know that!"

"Can you imagine what he must feel like," said Josue, "to be the only one in the entire Culdee and Druid company *not* to have met and spoken with the Anointed One?"

"Yes, it explains a great deal."

"He feels a terrible inadequacy because of it and he attempts that deficiency by zealousness." Josue smiled at the two Druids. "You are not the only target for his bitterness—his wrath falls on us as well, but we try to make allowances for him—indeed it must be much harder for him to follow the faith who never met him, than it is for us who did. His is an act of faith —ours is an act of knowledge."

"But in a generation from now," said Melvina, "all who follow the Christian way will have to do so as an act of faith for there will be no one left in earth who actually met and spoke with him."

"Very true," said Josue, "but right now he is the odd one out. In a way he feels himself to be cursed. He had the opportunity but failed to take it."

"Anyway," said Cranog, "I am glad to hear that Zaacheus' opinion of Druidry is not shared by all."

"Our ways are different, and some of our older Culdee members are still shocked by some of your practices, but the majority of us remember what you have done for us and are grateful. You would be surprised," he added, "how often you Druids are mentioned in our prayers," and he bowed and turned away.

Melvina shook her head as she watched Josue stride away. "When will they learn that they have to solve their own problems in earth? The inner plane adepts must grow weary of their constant whining prayers for help on every trivial problem!"

"It is no bad thing to turn to the inner."

"For inspiration, yes—for a statement of spiritual principles, yes—but not to whine to have their problems solved for them."

The weeks passed rapidly at Glaeston. The great gates were removed and burned. The outer wall was largely dismantled and the flagstones of the courtyard prised up. Only the Chalybeate Well was left untouched. Soon they would begin the careful destruction of the College itself. Confirmations had been received from all groves throughout the land concerning the destruction of the parchments and Cranog began to breathe more easily. Senior priests and additional stoneworker priests had begun to arrive at Glaeston and Cranog could see no real problem in dismantling the great College. "It is easier to destroy," he said ruefully, "than it is to create."

Confirmation had also been received from Kerrin at Mona that the work was proceeding rapidly and that already they could accommodate a further hundred priests and priestesses if Cranog wished to send them, indeed Kerrin would welcome the extra help. Cranog sent a message back that as the dismantling work proceeded, and as the accommodation at Glaeston would thus grow less and less, he would release more and more of the priesthood to help with the work at Mona.

Only one problem disturbed them all, and even that was an affirmation of the courage and dedication of even the most junior. The full Council determined that all those below the age of twice seven years would be released from their vows at the forthcoming Autumnal Equinox ritual and returned to their various tribes. For those who had been born at Glaeston, an agreement had been reached whereby they would be received and cared for by the Dumnonii tribe in the western lands. The decision was announced at a full senior ritual and conveyed to the Bardic Order by Morgana, Mistress of the Blue. There then occurred an event unprecedented in the entire history of the Druid priesthood—the Bardic degree flatly refused to accept the decision of the seniors.

At first Cranog was furious and spoke angrily of the Bardic rebellion as being further proof of the dissolution of the Druid Order. A Bard looked upon those of the higher degrees with an awe amounting almost to worship, which was very right and proper—Cranog himself had held such views when he had been a Bard. It was Melvina who put the matter into correct perspective. "The Bards consider you as the representation of Deity itself. In their minds to defy you is tantamount to a defiance of the Great One himself. Their rebellion—if that is the right word for it—is an act of extreme courage and could only have come from the strongest motivation. You should not rule out the possibility that their act has been inspired from the inner. In all justice you should hear their case."

Cranog thought about the matter for some days, and took the problem as his daily meditation subject. To accept Melvina's view required a quite fundamental change in his own thinking. To the junior degrees the decisions of the senior degree, the Order of the White, were law. Druid internal authority was not a rule by majority but an hierarchical system. The decision of the Arch-Mage in any matter was absolute. The inference that an Arch-Mage could be wrong was tantamount to saying that he was unfit for his Office. It was held that senior members of the White, and in particular the Council and the Arch-Mage himself, were in greater rapport with the inner plane adepts than the junior degrees and as such were far more capable of assessing inner plane wishes. To infer that this was not necessarily so was tantamount to heresy.

Finally Cranog agreed that the Bardic case should be presented before the entire assembly. Because the Bards were in too much awe of their seniors and too young to express themselves properly they were permitted to choose two members of the White to speak on their behalf—and they chose Morgana herself, who was responsible to the Arch-Mage for the administration and welfare of the entire Bardic degree, and Cerdic who was the youngest of those of the White and thus closer to their own age.

The assembly gathered in the Hall of Learning. On the rostrum sat Cranog himself, Melvina, and the entire inner council. Though not a ritual as such, it had been decreed that all should wear their full ritual robes. At such assemblies the Bards usually occupied the rear tiers of seats but today they were gathered in the center of the hall before the rostrum. Their young faces were anxious, awed, frightened—many of them were regretting their defiance. As young priests they had been trained to sit quietly, motionless, but such was their anxiety that most of them fidgeted unceasingly. The majority of them were only now beginning to realize the enormity of their defiance. To challenge the authority of the Council and the Arch-Mage himself was no small matter.

When all was ready Cranog intoned the earlier decision of the Council and then said gruffly: "Does the Bardic Degree accept that decision?"

Morgana was seated in the front rank of the Bards. She rose to her feet. "They do not!" she said firmly.

"Are they aware that such defiance of proper authority could lead to expulsion from the priesthood?"

"They are, but since the decision is to expel them from the priesthood anyway, then the point is an academic one."

"The former," said Cranog harshly, "would be a withdrawal with honor since they do but obey their seniors in the priestly hierarchy. The latter, however, would be expulsion in disgrace."

Morgana shook her head. "The honor of a priest is not determined by the opinions of his fellow priests but by whether his thoughts and actions are in accordance with spiritual principle."

"And such principles are determined by the inner plane adepts and manifested on earth through the priestly hierarchy. Obedience to hierarchical authority is one of the prime principles of the priesthood."

"Obedience is a virtue not a principle," said Morgana. "The hierarchical system is not a principle either but merely a system by which spiritual principles are made known in earth."

"A system laid down by the inner planes—are you challenging them as well?"

"The hierarchical system is as good as those who operate it. If the system is operated by perfected beings then the system operates perfectly. But the system is operated by incarnated human souls, and the mere fact that they have had to incarnate yet again is proof that they have not yet reached perfection, and therefore they cannot possibly operate the hierarchical system in any other way than less than perfectly!"

Cranog pursed his lips. "And yet it is a system that has served us well for four thousand years—it has never been proved wrong before."

"It has never been challenged before!" retorted Morgana.

The Arch-Mage sat back and pondered the point. The anxious eyes of the Bards had swung from speaker to speaker. Much of what had been said was way above their heads but some of the older ones had realized that at least the exchange had not been one-sided.

Cranog conferred briefly with the Council and then spoke again. "We accept your point that the possibility of error exists, no matter how improbable, but that is a far cry from being able to demonstrate that an error of judgment has actually occurred. You have yet to prove your case."

"You have yet to prove yours either!" said Morgana firmly.

A subdued gasp rose from the ranks of the senior degrees. Cranog frowned. "The representative of the Bardic claim should demonstrate a little more respect for the ruling council!"

Morgana was quite unabashed. "A statement of fact has nothing to do with respect or any other human attitude of mind. I said that you have not proved your case either—that is neither respectful nor disrespectful —it is a statement of fact. You have made a decision with regard to the Bardic degree and have given no reasons for that decision, nor have you even attempted to demonstrate that it is in accordance with inner plane wishes."

"The Council does not always give reasons for its decisions," said Cranog, "because sometimes those reasons concern abstruse spiritual matters that would not be understood by those in the junior degrees."

"Under normal circumstances, I agree," said Morgana, "but here we have an unprecedented situation wherein a Council decision has been challenged, and I submit that in all justice the Council should reveal their reasons."

Cranog paused and then smiled. "The Mistress of the Blue," he said wryly, "has very cleverly turned this hearing from a trial of the Bards to a trial of the Council. Very well—so be it! The reasons are quite simple. The junior Bards are priests, yet they are still children. The days ahead are fraught with danger. It may be that many Druids will die at the hands of the Romans. We have no right to put a child's life in such danger." He looked down at the anxious faces below. "Our decision was made with love," he said gently, "to keep you safe from such horrors."

Morgana bowed and resumed her seat, and Cerdic rose. "All know that the safety and welfare of the Bards were the prime factors in the Council's decision," he said briskly, "but now that the reasons have been stated in open assembly we can examine them to see whether they are indeed in the best interests of the Bardic degree."

Cranog looked from Morgana to Cerdic and back again. Those two had obviously rehearsed this very well. The Council and indeed himself were being maneuvered very cleverly indeed. "I hope, Cerdic," he said, "that you are not going to argue that it would be in their best interests if they were all slaughtered by the Romans!" He said it with a smile, but Cerdic's expression remained quite serious.

"In a sense I am, yes—at least I am going to argue that the choice is theirs, not ours."

"But they are children!"

"True, but the Council's entire reasoning is based on that one fact, the physical age of the members of the Bardic degree."

Cranog knew what was coming and knew that he would have little defense against the reasoning that would be used. But pure reason—logic, the Greeks called it—should not be the only consideration. "Quite correct, and we have the whole of Nature to support our argument. The smallest bird in the forest will put its own life in danger to protect its fledglings. The wolves and bears hide their young in caves to protect them from predators. We ourselves are born into the complex structure of all Nature, and we violate natural tendencies at our peril. The whole of Nature decrees that the young shall be protected at whatever cost to the parent. The Roman predators are at our gates and we are responding to the call of Nature by hiding our young and seeking to protect them. Is that so very wrong?"

Cerdic looked up at the rostrum. "The members of the Bardic degree are not fledgling birds, wolf-cubs, bear-cubs, or any other form of animal life. They are of the human species, the only form of life whose innermost nature is of the same essence as the Great One himself. I am not saying that we should ignore the laws of Nature, but I am saying that there are other laws that must be considered."

Cranog sighed. "Such as?"

"Birds and animals have but one life as individuals. They do not reincarnate. A two-day-old bird has lived for precisely two days. A ten-year-old boy, however, may house a soul that has incarnated many, many times. The true age of a human being is *not* the total of this present incarnation to date. This, as far as the priesthood is concerned, is a statement of the obvious."

"But the personality of a ten-year-old boy may not be able to express the wishes of the soul that indwells him."

"That is obviously true of non-initiates, the farmers and tribal warriors, but we are speaking of priests. The souls that indwell the bodies of the junior Bards must have a fair measure of control of the young personalities, otherwise they would not have been guided to the priesthood."

"But not enough control to make decisions of this nature. To terminate an incarnation so early is a waste."

"With respect, Arch-Mage, we are not deciding whether or not to terminate the incarnation, but simply whether or not the junior priesthood shall share with us the dangers of our calling."

"I still say they are too young!"

"Again, with all the respect that I can muster, I must point out that the initiation ritual into the Bardic degree states quite categorically that the indwelling soul of the Candidate is expressing itself sufficiently through the young personality for us to exact quite far-reaching priestly vows. Such vows will affect them quite dramatically for many lives to come. If they are considered sufficiently developed to make a major decision affecting many of their future incarnations, then surely they must be competent to make a decision affecting this one life only." Cerdic paused, and then went on: "Forget that they are so far only children in this incarnation—look at them with the inner eyes and see them for what they truly are, well-developed souls dedicated to the priesthood." Cerdic waved his arm to encompass all the youthful faces that stared anxiously up at the rostrum. "They say that you do not have the right to banish them from the priesthood merely because they came into this incarnation but a few short years ago. They demand that they be treated as priests, not children, treated with respect and honor, and they demand that they be allowed to remain among us no matter what danger may be ahead!"

Cerdic resumed his seat and an utter silence pervaded the hall. Morgana rose to her feet. "May I put one very personal question to you, Arch-Mage?"

Cranog nodded. "Very well."

"I, and some others here, remember you as a boy, Cranog. I used to go swimming with you when you were indeed ten years of age. You were then a member of the Bardic degree even as these are now. Do you remember?"

"I remember."

"If this situation had obtained then, and if you had been banished from the priesthood for reasons of safety—what would your feelings have been?"

Cranog shook his head. "That is very unfair, Morgana!"

"It is perfectly fair—it is asking you to remember what it was like to be a dedicated ten-year-old priest."

The Arch-Mage was silent for some time, and then he said slowly: "I would have felt shamed. I would have felt that I had been considered unworthy." Again a silence stilled the chamber. Finally Cranog pointed to one of the young Bards in the front rank. "Stand up, boy," he said kindly. "How old are you?"

The boy rose slowly to his feet. "Twelve years, my Lord," he stammered.

"And what is your name?"

"Zelta, my Lord."

Zelta! Cranog shook his head—was everything conspiring against him today? Zelta had been the name of the young Druid boy-priest who, according to legend, had suffered a martyr's death two thousand years ago. "Did you understand what has been said today, Zelta?"

The boy blinked nervously. "Yes, my Lord—most of it."

"Do you and the others really understand that if you come with us to Mona you may very well die a bloody and ferocious death with a Roman sword in your belly?"

"Yes, my Lord."

Cranog leaned forward. "Tell me this, Zelta—*why* do you wish to share this horror with us?"

The boy licked his lips nervously. "Because I am a priest, and because I want to do as you do."

Cranog drew in his breath sharply. A memory came into his mind as clear and sharp as ice, a memory of Drucius speaking to him when he, Cranog, had just been initiated into the White. "The prime function of a Priest of the White is to set an example of spiritual honor for all to follow," Drucius had said, "and one of the prime evils that a Priest of the White can commit is to deny initiation to those worthy of it."

Cranog waved the boy to his seat and conferred with the Council. Finally he rose and said: "It goes against every instinct of Nature to put children in danger, but we cannot deny the force of the reasoning put before the Council today. We find that those of the Bardic degree must be considered primarily as priests rather than children, otherwise their initiation into the priesthood is a mockery. As you know, when a priest demands a new experience, whether it be a new experience in life or a chance to take an initiation into a higher degree, then no one, not even the highest, is permitted to deny that demand. Therefore we of the Council are not permitted to deny the right of the Bardic degree to follow the priestly way if they so choose, no matter how dangerous that path may be. The Council therefore withdraws its instruction—the Bardic degree will accompany us to Mona!"

The Bards themselves could scarcely contain their excitement—they had not really believed that a Council decision could be reversed. Their faces were wreathed in grins and they could hardly wait to get out of the hall to discuss the prospect among themselves. Morgana, too, was smiling, and Cerdic, and so too were many of the senior priests and priestesses.

Cranog stepped down from the rostrum and came to stand in front of the Bards. He bowed low, his arms spread wide. "I consider it an honor to be numbered among such company," he said simply, and strode from the hall.

chapter seven

Gilda, the Witch-Maiden, sat patiently on the forest trail waiting for the Lord of Day, Belin, to sink to his rest beyond the western horizon. His departure would signal the advent of her goddess, the Queen of Night, and for her purpose the presence of the Moon was imperative.

Nearby, beyond the forest's edge, lay a Roman marching camp. She had watched it each day for nine days from first light to last waiting for the opportunity she needed. Her plans required that one lone legionary should enter the forest, but always they hunted in pairs or in groups of three or more, never alone. But since there were no Pretannic warriors within a day's march she knew the Romans would grow careless, and on the ninth day a young and beardless legionary had entered the forest alone at midday to hunt. She had followed him a little way to make sure of his purpose and had then retraced her path to the glade near the forest's edge to make her preparations for his return.

As the Lord Belin had eased beyond the zenith towards the west, the trees had grown shadows that hour by hour had crept inexorably across the forest floor until they grew less discernible in the waning light. The time of night was approaching, and soon the young Roman, too, would approach the nightfall of his years.

A sound reached her ears, the rustle as if of large game, and she permitted herself a smile of anticipation as the Roman came clumsily along the trail and into the glade. His face was flushed and his tunic torn. He was hot and tired, and the absence of any trophy at his belt suggested that his sport had been unsuccessful. They were no woodsmen or hunters, these Romans.

His hair was a startling blond—no true son of Rome was this, the spawn of some dalliance with a woman of northern climes—and his eyes were as blue as ice. But no matter what his racial heritage he was Roman enough for her purpose.

He stopped in sudden shock at the sight of the girl and stared wildly around the glade, tugging his sword clear, but then quickly realized that the glade was empty save for the native woman. Gilda stared at him in pretended shock, frozen as if in sudden fear. She turned as if to escape and pretended to stumble, sprawling full-length on the forest floor.

The Roman took a couple of paces towards her. "Wait!" he called. "Don't be frightened!"

She scrambled to her feet and ran into the forest, but the fool did not pursue her. Again she pretended to stumble, and again she measured her length on the ground. This time she pretended to be stunned and lay there on her back, her limbs flung aside. Beneath her lashes she could see him approaching.

"Wait!" he called. "I won't hurt you!" He came up to where she lay and stood staring down at her. "By Zeus, but you're a magnificent specimen!" He knelt beside her and tentatively reached out a hand to touch her body.

She rolled to one side, sprang to her feet, and raced deeper into the forest—and this time she could hear him stumbling after her. Dodging through the trees, occasionally pretending to stumble, she kept just ahead of him, and led him deeper and deeper into the darkening forest. At one point his outstretched fingers grasped her robe, but she wriggled free and raced on. Her body was glistening with sweat. Her face, as she glanced again and again over her shoulder, was a mask of pretended terror, but inwardly she was laughing a paean of triumph.

At last she reached the glade that she had been aiming for, and burst into the clearing a scant few feet ahead of him. The glade was dominated by an enormous oak tree whose lower branches were so huge and gnarled that they reached out and sagged by their own weight to almost brush the ground. The massive bole was ominously stained, and among the clumps of mistletoe that festooned the lower branches were hung certain grisly objects that would have given the Roman pause had he noticed them—but he had eyes only for the girl. She faked a trip on a protruding root and went sprawling headlong and lay still, pretending to have smashed her head on a stone. Her right hand, however, beneath her body, grasped the hilt of her knife in readiness. By her side, partially concealed in the grass, was a running noose of vine-rope. The rope ran for a few feet through the grass and then to the end of a branch that almost brushed the ground. Had the Roman been more observant he would have seen another rope attached to the branch, strained taut, running down to a protruding root a few inches from the girl's fallen body.

He came up with a rush and knelt beside the girl, putting one foot into the prepared noose. Gilda's right hand, grasping the knife, flashed out and sliced through the other rope holding the branch, which whipped into the air back to its normal position. The noose snapped close round his ankle and the Roman's body was snatched into the air to dangle helplessly, his fingertips a few inches above the ground.

Gilda stepped clear, watching the Roman closely, recovering her poise. The trap had been a makeshift affair and all sorts of things could have gone wrong. She shuddered to think what would have happened to her at this Roman's hands had the trap failed.

His body was jerking furiously in his desperate attempts to free himself. Already he had strained upwards and had grasped the rope above his feet and was trying to pull himself up to the branch above. If she delayed by even a few more seconds he would be free. She picked up a club of wood that she had previously hidden and moved closer to the struggling body. She dared not get too close or those strong hands would grasp at her. Gilda positioned herself carefully and then smashed the club against his head. The force of the blow jerked his hands free, and once more he dangled helplessly full-length. The blood flowed from his head, but still he was not unconscious. Again she smashed the club against his head, and again, and at last the body hung still. She threw the club away and hastily cut him down. She slipped the coils of rope from the branch, tied his wrists together, and bound both arms behind his back. Thus secured she began to drag him towards the tree, and in a matter of minutes she had him bound tightly to the enormous trunk.

His whole body was covered in blood and still it poured from the head wounds, but already she could detect a lessening in the flow. From a further hiding-place she brought out her ox-hide carrying bag and emptied the contents onto the grass. She took the bowl and made her way through the forest for a hundred yards or so to where a small stream gurgled through the trees. When she returned she found that the boy had recovered consciousness and was moaning hideously from the pain in his head. With a gentleness curiously at odds with her previous violence she began to wash his body free of blood. That done she then began to bathe his wounds, and the boy's moans rose to shrieks and she had to hold his head still by grasping his hair. The blood began to flow again but soon died to a trickle. She then took up a paste of certain herbs that she had prepared earlier and began to smear his wounds. "Bear it for a few moments longer," she said softly in crude Latin. "It is an ointment known only to we Druids. Soon the pain will subside, and in a few minutes it will be gone."

Her task finished she glanced up at the sky. Belin had long since sunk to his rest, and the twilight was already deepening into night. At this time of the year, however, it would be two hours or more before the Queen would appear.

"Why don't you kill me?" the boy burst out.

She nodded. "Perhaps I will, but first you must join me in a Moon ritual, and since the Queen will not appear for some time we must amuse ourselves as best we can." She looked at him thoughtfully. "For the purpose of the ritual it is necessary that you know who I am, and so know you that I am Gilda, Mistress of the Oak."

He stiffened at the sound of her name. Gilda—
Gilda, the Witch-Maiden! The natives spoke of her
with awe and dread. The legends attached to her name
were so bizarre that few Romans believed she existed
at all. If only half the things they said of her were
true, then death would indeed be a merciful release.

"I see you know my name," she said drily. "Do
not believe all you hear of me."

"Blood sacrifices," he said venomously, "and
other foul acts!"

"Sacrifices! You, a Roman, dare speak to me of
sacrifices! How many of my people have you already
sacrificed to the so-called glory of Rome—and how
many in other lands? Don't speak to me of blood—
your own hands reek of it!"

The forest was now quite dark. She struck a spark
to a pile of dry leaves and twigs that she had gathered
earlier that day, and fed the flames with larger pieces
of branch. Soon the boy could feel the welcome heat
on his face. She then prepared a meal of dried meats
washed down with water from the forest stream. At
first he refused the food but then reluctantly accepted
the morsels from her hand. The meal finished, she fed
the fire again and settled down to wait.

"What is your name, Roman?" she said softly.

He did not answer at first, and then said curtly:
"Flavius—and I warn you now, Witch-Maiden, that
my commander will by now have been informed of my
disappearance. Soon they will come to seek me, and
when they do your life will not be worth a dried fig!"

She shook her head. "They will not leave their
camp at night, especially for one of junior rank. I will
see to it," she added ominously, "that they find you at
dawn."

He tried to accept the apparent finality of her
statement stoically, but despite himself he shivered at
the prospect.

"We all have to die sometime," she said gently,
seeing the shiver. "It is not certain yet whether you
will die tonight, but if you do, and if you meet your
death with courage, you will have redeemed much of
your guilt."

"Guilt!" he burst out suddenly, straining against his bonds. "What guilt?"

The gentleness fled from her eyes and they grew stony with resolve. "How many of my people have you personally murdered?" she said harshly.

"I have murdered no one!" he shouted. "A few killed in battle, that's all!"

"When a highly developed and powerful nation wages war on those weaker than themselves," she said angrily, "such killings are murder. You cannot absolve such guilt by calling it something else!"

Again they fell silent, and she stirred the fire with a stick. "Eight years ago you Romans landed at Richboro to conquer our realm and murdered thirty thousand of the Catuvellauni tribe at the Battle of the Med, and more during your march northwards across the Thamus to establish your main base at Camulot—Camulodunum you called it." The flames leapt up and threw her angry face into bitter highlights. "Forty thousand Pretannic warriors died during those first few months," she said quietly. "Forty thousand murders!"

The boy remained silent. He had been eleven years old at the time, living with his family in Rome. He could still remember the excitement in his own heart, and the pride in his father's eyes, when they heard the news of that magnificent campaign. The Witch-Maiden obviously had different memories of those stupendous events.

All that first winter Aulus Plautius had driven his men hard, building a fortress at Camulodunum large enough to accommodate two whole legions. At the same time he established a military supply port nearby at Fingringhoe at the mouth of the River Colne so that he could be supplied by sea direct from the Roman garrisons on the Rhine in Germany, yet still maintaining Richboro in the southeast as a secondary supply port fed from Boulogne. It had been a textbook campaign—a bold landing in force, the demoralization of the enemy with an early battle victory, and then the strengthening of beachhead and supply lines before commencing further expansion.

"And then the following year," said Gilda bitterly, "like some monstrous disease you Romans began to spread across the land—and a further one thousand of our people died!"

Flavius nodded. That first spring after the invasion, Legio IX, Hispana, had marched inland, skirted the fen country, and had struck north establishing forts a day's march apart at Chelmsford, Cambridge, Godmanchester, Water Newton, Great Casterton, Ancaster, and finally at Lincoln.

Gilda stirred the fire and then sat with her legs drawn up, her chin resting on her knees. "But at Lincoln the advance ended—Lindum you called it—because beyond the Trent to the west, and beyond the Humber to the north, were the Brigantes, a tribe as fierce and war-like as the Catuvellauni had been, and your Aulus Plautius was fearful of tangling with *them!*"

"Not *fearful,*" said the boy coldly, "merely establishing a frontier line." Flavius remembered the report. Hard on the heels of Legio IX had gone the Roman road-builders, and before the end of that first year they had completed Ermine Street as far as Lindum. Plautius had quite rightly believed in good lines of communication. "Is this a history lesson, Witch-Maiden?" he said sneeringly. "For if so then I am probably better informed than you.

"At the same time as Legio IX went north to Lindum," he went on, "Legio II, Augusta, with Vespasian as its legate, struck south, back over the Tamesis and the Med down to the south coast, with Verica giving them free passage through the newly reconstituted Belgic-Atrebatic kingdom." The boy's face lit up as he recalled the stirring lessons of history that had been drummed into him. "But as Vespasian began to move westward he began to encounter fierce opposition. From Chichester—Noviomagus as Vespasian renamed it—he launched an onslaught against the Isle of Wight, and after one of the bloodiest battles of his career he finally overran it. Using the island as a base, he then began to land supplies at various points along the coast to support the legion's westward march. While Legio IX was having a relatively easy time at Lincoln, Legio II under Vespasian had to fight battle after battle throughout that long year, and throughout the year to follow."

Flavius forgot the possibility of his impending death in the excitement of his memory. "I know all this, Witch-Maiden, because when Vespasian later came to Rome he visited my father's house and I was permitted to sit with the men and listen to him recount his Britannic campaigns." He shook his head admiringly. "He told us that in those two years he had to fight thirty major battles and scores of lesser skirmishes, and had to take no fewer than twenty Pretannic hill-forts by long-range ballista fire, driving the defenders from the ramparts, before he finally subdued firstly the Durotriges and subsequently the Dumnonii tribe and established his most westerly fort at Bodmin!"

"A truly great man," said Gilda sarcastically, "to have caused such death and destruction!"

"It is to the honor of your people," said the boy coldly, "that Vespasian rates the Pretannic warriors as the most fierce and courageous enemy that he has ever faced."

Gilda snorted. "We are honored by such distinction!" she said bitterly.

The boy's face grew thoughtful. "There was one curious thing, however," he said slowly. "Vespasian said that throughout his entire western campaign he had not encountered so much as a single Druid. The legendary Druid college at Glaeston simply did not exist. Glaeston could boast no more than a pile of stones, and a tiny and obscure religious cult who called themselves Culdees. They gave him no trouble, and indeed seemed anxious to appease the legionaries. Vespasian reported to Plautius that the so-called Druid power and influence must be pure legend." He paused for a moment, and then said: "Indeed you are the first Druid that I have ever encountered. Where are the Druids, Witch-Maiden? Did you flee like cowards into the mountains?"

Gilda smiled. "You Romans would give much to know the answer to that question. You will see us when it is time."

Flavius shrugged. "Keep your ridiculous secrets if

it pleases you," he retorted. "It matters not to us whether you show yourselves or not. But let us continue with the lesson."

"While Legio IX had been establishing itself in the north," the boy went on, "and Legio II in the south, Aulus Plautius himself with Legio XIV, Gemina, and half of Legio XX, Valeria—leaving the other half to maintain the base at Camulodunum—pushed directly westward into the middle lands, into the realm of the Catuvellauni, and established forts at their erstwhile capital, Prae Wood, which we renamed Verulamium—and also at Dunstable, Towcester, High Cross, and finally at Leicester, which we renamed Ratae Coritanorum. They then struck south, crossed the River Avon, and established a main base at Cirencester, which we renamed Corinium Dubunorum, and established his western frontier line on the River Severn."

"With good reason," said Gilda, "for beyond the Severn are the Silurians and the Ordovices—*they* will never tamely submit to Roman domination."

Very true, thought Flavius, which was why Plautius had to establish his lines of communication before tackling those Welsh tribes. In addition to Ermine Street, which Flavius knew was planned to run eventually from London to Lincoln, Plautius had begun construction on both Watling Street and the Fosse Way, which Flavius knew were planned to run from London to Wroxeter and from Exeter to Lincoln, thus laying the foundation of what in due course would be a network of interconnecting roads that would cover the entire province. These primitive tribes seemed totally unable to comprehend the necessity of good lines of communication.

"He was a great man, Aulus Plautius," mused Flavius, "and a great military governor. At the end of three short years his forces held Lincoln in the north, the entire middle lands, the entire southeast coast, and the entire southern and southwestern reaches."

The Druid priestess remained silent.

"I was nearly fifteen," Flavius went on, "when Plautius' term of office came to an end and he returned to Rome to celebrate an ovation voted to him unanimously by the entire senate."

"Three, nearly four years of slaughter!" said Gilda angrily.

"Three years of military brilliance!" retorted the boy.

"So brilliant," said the priestess contemptuously, "that he never did discover that Caratacus had survived the Battle of the Med and had joined King Arviragus and the Silurians."

The boy shrugged. "*That* did not remain a secret for very long."

So brilliant had Plautius and Vespasian been, thought Gilda, that neither of them had even begun to suspect that the famed Glaeston College had been deliberately dismantled to prevent it from being profaned. Any man with any pretense to intelligence ought to have realized that such fame could not have sprung from mere legend.

She glanced at the boy and smiled to herself. The boy's commander, and Scapula himself, would give a great deal to know that every Druid priest and priestess had been withdrawn to Mona. They would discover the situation for themselves sooner or later, but the longer that fact remained concealed the better.

Also the so-called brilliant Roman commanders had been particularly obtuse for not having realized the true identity of the Culdees. To them they were merely an obscure religious cult of little military or social interest. She wondered what the boy would say if she told him that the term of office of his hero Plautius had come to an end in the forty-seventh year after the birth of the Culdee's spiritual Lord, Jesus of Nazareth. The boy would gain instant promotion if he could carry *that* news to Scapula. The Romans had no love for Christians.

"You can sneer at our commanders if you must," said Flavius, "but the fact remains that we Romans have defeated no fewer than twelve Pretannic tribes, or have accepted their submission—the Coritani, the Cornovii, the Dobunni, the Catuvellauni, the Iceni, the Trinivantes, the Cantiaci, the Regnenses, the Atrebates, the Belgae, the Durotriges, and the Dumnonii. Only five tribes stand against us—the Brigantes and the Parisi in the north, and the three Welsh tribes of the Demetae, the Silurians, and the Ordovices—and of course you Druids. Resistance will continue but the result is inevitable."

"Really! That's what they thought in Rome five years ago when your Emperor appointed P. Ostorius Scapula to take over from Plautius. Scapula came thinking that it was going to be easy, but after five years of continuous warfare the situation is still exactly the same as when he arrived. The result, my friend, is far from inevitable!"

True enough, thought Flavius grimly. To observers in far-away Rome it had indeed seemed as though Plautius had broken the back of Pretannic resistance and that the campaign was virtually over. But when Scapula arrived he had found the entire frontier line of the Fosse Way in flames from end to end and his officers tired to the point of exhaustion from continuous warfare with the stubborn Welsh tribes. "It is true," he admitted reluctantly, "that the Welsh remain undefeated, but Scapula certainly has many achievements to his credit."

"Such as?" she said contemptuously.

"The promulgation of the Roman law *Lex julia de vi publica* for one."

She smiled. "A stupid law. Boiling it down it simply means that non-Romans are not permitted to carry arms except for the purpose of hunting or self-defense. Anyone found carrying arms can simply plead that he is going hunting, or has just returned from the hunt." She shrugged. "Far from keeping the tribes subdued, it actually incited the Iceni to rebel."

"True," said the boy, "and in dealing with it Scapula showed himself to be just as brilliant as Plautius."

King Prasutagus of the Iceni had been a very sick man—and still was for that matter. His wife, Queen Boudicca, allowed herself to be persuaded by young King Cori of the Coritani tribe to mount a rebellion. The news reached Scapula in the west that the Iceni, the Coritani, and the remnants of the Catuvellauni, were massing at Cambridge and already numbered thirty thousand with more arriving every day. Scapula had not dared withdraw any of his four legions from their existing positions, but what he did do was to withdraw from each legion the non-Roman Batavian and Thracian auxiliary cohorts. This gave him a force of some five thousand men. With himself at the head— and against the heated advice from his entire general staff—he marched on Cambridge and scattered the rebels far and wide.

"A brilliant maneuver," said Flavius.

Scapula could have exacted the most dreadful revenge on Boudicca and the Iceni, but he let the matter drop, deeming that they would have learned the lesson that rebellion was useless. Anyway, he needed the goodwill of the client-kingdoms for a particular project he had in mind.

"What you people do not understand," said Flavius, "is that we Romans are not interested in destroying your people utterly. We want to establish a lasting peace under a civilian administration so that trade between Rome and Pretannia can commence. You cannot remain as savages forever. For the sake of generations to come you must abandon your primitive and barbaric ways and become part of the civilized world."

"Our experience to date of you Romans," she said sarcastically, "has not led to any great burning desire on our part to adopt Roman ways! We see no moves towards peace, and little evidence that you wish to share your so-called civilization with us. Deaths by the tens of thousands have been the only gifts from Rome to Pretannia!"

Flavius knew that the Senate and the Emperor in Rome, and indeed Scapula himself, were ever mindful of the need to bring the province to a civil administration as soon as possible. The governor was also ever mindful of the fact that he still had only half a legion at Camulodunum to police the entire middle lands, and that the further westward he pushed into Wales the greater would be the area in his rear to be administered. To cover this weakness he had sought and obtained permission from Rome to establish a "colonia" at Camulodunum, a system whereby veteran legionaries newly discharged from active service were settled in and around Camulodunum with grants of land. Such private Roman estates would be far closer to the people than the active legionaries at the fort, and thus would be able to more accurately gauge the temper of the populace and so provide an early warning of any possible insurrection. As the number of estates grew they would provide at least some sort of military substitute.

Scapula, being as much a politician as a soldier, was aware that the "colonia," as well as being a military substitute, was also the first step in the civilizing process. Shrewdly he lost no time in taking the second step by declaring the old Catuvellauni capital of Prae Wood, renamed Verulamium, as a "municipium civitas," the first Roman civilian town in Pretannia. Certain Pretannic nobles from a variety of tribes in the area were offered Roman citizenship, a share in the administration of the town, a share of the profits to be made from civilian trade with Rome, and as the greatest inducement of all Scapula dangled the carrot of the possibility of future self-government.

"What about Verulamium, the municipium civitas?" said Flavius. "Isn't that evidence of our long-term plans for a shared Pretannic civilization?"

Gilda laughed rudely and derisively. "You Romans do have this naive attitude that the nature of a thing can be changed by giving it a different name! You can call it a 'municipium civitas' as much as you like, but it does not alter the fact that it is a town based firmly on the master-slave principle. The vast majority of us would rather die by the sword than live under such conditions!"

Flavius shook his head. She might be right. Certainly there was no evidence of any lessening of resistance. The Welsh tribes were particularly obdurate, as he knew from personal experience. Three years ago—a year after the unsuccessful Iceni rebellion—Flavius had come out to Pretannia as part of a detachment of reinforcements for Legio XIV under Scapula himself at his newest fortress at Glevum situated at the juncture of the rivers Avon and Severn, thus poised to push into Silurian territory itself.

Scapula's plan had been simple. In the north he pushed westward from Ratae Coritanorum into the territory of the Cornovii, occupied it, overran the Deceangli tribe in North Wales, built a fort at Kinvaston and a legion-sized fortress at Wroxeter which he renamed Viroconium. From Wroxeter in the north, and Glevum in the south, slowly and with great patience, Scapula began to move into Wales in a pincer movement.

The campaign would have undoubtedly been short and successful had it not been for one man—Caratacus! The erstwhile King of the Catuvellauni had fled to Wales after the battle of the Med, and the aged King Arviragus of the Silurians had shrewdly made him his battle-commander, putting aside inter-tribal differences in the face of the common enemy.

Because of Caratacus it became a long, cruel, and bitter campaign. Scapula soon found that if he moved too quickly his advance guard would be ambushed and slaughtered before the main body could arrive. Every mile of mountain, hill, and forest had to be taken slowly and doggedly, and then consolidated before a further advance could be made—and all the time he had to keep his lines of communication to the rear open and defended, otherwise he knew that he might be cut off, and if that happened there was a good chance that no Roman would get out of Wales alive.

All that spring and all that summer the two arms of the Roman pincer had crept painstakingly forward. The Silurians never rested, never gave up, they contested every inch of ground, and sometimes it took a week of the most cruel fighting to gain even a mile. The Roman losses grew steadily day by day, and the only comfort to Scapula had been the knowledge that the Silurian losses were marginally greater.

By late autumn the two arms of the pincer had advanced westward sufficiently to be able to turn inwards to close the gap, but when the first light snows began to fall the Romans had no alternative but to halt the advance and dig themselves in to endure the appalling prospect of a long, hard winter in the Welsh hills.

All through those long ice-cold months the Romans fought desperately to keep their lines of communication open. There was insufficient food to be had from the harsh winter terrain, and the bulk of their supplies still had to be brought through from Viroconium and Glevum. If those lines were closed the Romans would either have to starve or retreat, and Scapula knew that if the Romans retreated now from Wales they would never return.

When the snows at last began to melt the Romans began their advance again, but they soon discovered that Caratacus had taken half the Silurian force through the gap in the pincer, marching his men through the trackless mountain reaches, and had circled round to the north to join up with the Ordovices. That maneuver came close to destroying the Roman spirit. With Caratacus now in the north to his rear, Scapula knew that Viroconium itself was threatened. Wearily he swung his half of the Roman force northwards in pursuit of the elusive Caratacus, and instructed the Roman forces in the south to abandon the pincer movement and to dig in and hold the territory that they had gained. The young legate in command of the southern forces did his best to comply, but now that Scapula was moving away the remaining Silurians under Arviragus could concentrate all their attention in the south, and the Romans found themselves being pushed back mile after mile until finally they were driven across the Severn estuary where it had all began.

Meanwhile Scapula was faring much better in the north in the mountain fastness of Snowdonia, and all that spring and summer Caratacus found himself being driven deeper and deeper into the mountains. So far the Silurians and the Ordovices had avoided a set battle with the Romans, preferring the art of the running skirmish, but now they had no choice if they were to prevent their forces from being scattered far and wide by such relentless pursuit. Caratacus chose what bade fair to be an impregnable position near Caersius, a position among steep hills with a river running across their front and the flank approaches defended by piled stones. It was there that the two forces met.

The Romans came up to the position in the late evening and Scapula himself went down to the river's edge to assess the terrain. Caratacus saw him come, and he too went down to the river. Scapula, in full Roman armor, looked across the water at the giant, half-naked, red-haired Pretannic King. For some long minutes the two men stared at each other, and then slowly, almost ritually, Scapula raised his sword in salute, and Caratacus nodded grimly and raised his own sword in response.

The Romans attacked at dawn. Scapula had no alternative but to go for the direct frontal assault across the river and into the screaming, near-demented horde that faced them. In all his career Scapula had never met such resistance. The Roman dead piled the far bank and the river ran red with Roman blood, but still the defending line would not break. Caratacus himself was everywhere, hacking, cutting, and thrusting at the Roman wall coming up out of the river. Soon the Roman attackers were having to scramble over their own dead to get at the defending line. Scapula ordered two divisions to cross at two points on either flank, and Caratacus had no alternative but to divide his line to meet this twin threat. The Romans died by the dozens, by the hundreds, but gradually they forced their way up the far bank and at last the line of defenders began to retreat, foot by foot, but it was not until late afternoon that Scapula himself and the general staff were able to cross. Fighting with a savage desperation the defenders gave more and more ground. Scapula threw everything into a final frontal assault before darkness could intervene, and finally the line broke and the defenders fled back into the mountains leaving their dead and dying in their wake.

But of Caratacus there was no sign. The Romans found his wife and youngest brother among the prisoners, but Caratacus himself had escaped. Flavius could remember how Scapula had raged in a fury close to insanity but there was nothing he could do. The following morning when he brought his legion down the mountain he left a further 700 Roman dead behind him. Three days later they had arrived back at the fort at Viroconium to learn the news that the Roman forces in South Wales had been driven back across the Severn estuary and were licking their wounds at Glevum.

The Romans had won a battle, true, but after a campaign lasting two years Scapula found himself back exactly where he had started, with the additional specter of having to explain to the Emperor and the Senate in Rome a failure that had cost a total of over 2,000 Roman lives.

Flavius had been with Scapula throughout that entire two-year Welsh campaign, and had survived without a scratch though he had been in the thick of all the fighting. It was therefore bitterly ironic that he had now fallen prey to this lone woman.

"The stubborn resistance of the Welsh tribes," said Gilda, "is an example to the whole realm, and proof that you Romans are not invincible." She glanced up at the sky. "It is now time for we Druids to play a part in this matter."

Despite himself Flavius again felt a shiver of apprehension. "You are mistaken, Witch-Maiden," he said harshly, "if you think I am going to take part in any foul ritual of yours!"

She looked at him contemptuously. "You will have no choice," she said briefly. "Do you not already feel drowsy from the special herb I put in your food?"

He frowned, and a stab of fear lanced through him. He remembered the curious taste of the dried meat, and as he did so he felt his eyes grow heavy with fatigue. He struggled furiously against his bonds, but again his efforts were futile. "I will not sleep," he burst out, "and nothing you can do will make me!"

She gave a short laugh and did not reply. She took certain objects from her ox-hide carrying bag and arranged them in a semicircle so that the massive oak tree, and the boy himself, became the center of the circle. In the darkness of the forest night, despite the flickering firelight, he could not identify the objects, and was grimly thankful that he could not. Before he had left

Rome he had worried himself to the point of illness that he would not be able to bear himself with honor in the clash of battle, and so would disgrace his family, but after three years with Scapula he knew himself to have the courage demanded of a Roman legionary. This, however, was something different. What plans she had for him he did not know, except that they could bring his death, and his imagination conjured a hundred foul possibilities. He knew that he could bear with fortitude any acts made against his actual physical body—a Roman legionary was taught to withstand pain, even the agony of torture—but since she required him to sleep, then it was obvious that her intention was to command his very spirit in some obscene way, and a terror welled up in him at this dreadful prospect. At all costs he must remain awake.

"I will not sleep," he said aloud. "I will not sleep!" The priestess smiled to herself but said nothing. "I will not sleep!" he said again, but his eyes were growing heavier and heavier with every passing second.

Through his half-closed lids he watched her throw soil onto the fire until it was quite out, and in the increased darkness he could barely see her form at all. He was aware that she had come to stand at the edge of the circle, her arms flung wide, her face upturned to the night sky, and then came her voice pitched in such a vibrant, unearthly timbre that it sent a shock of sheer horror through every portion of his being. In his imagination it seemed to him that the whole forest had grown expectantly quiet at the sound of her voice, and that a thousand pairs of dreadful, unhuman eyes had turned menacingly in his direction.

"O Queen of Night, bringer of fear, thou who watches over the dark life of earth, I, Gilda, Mistress of the Oak, am thy Priestess! Answer unto me!"

As the invocation rang round the dark forest glade, Flavius was horrified to see the first shaft of moonlight come lancing down into the glade as though at her bidding and light up her dreadful face in an aura of unearthly silver.

His eyes closed, and then jerked open again. He tried to speak but his tongue would not form the words. Deep within him he could feel the tide of blackness welling up to engulf him.

And then came her voice again.

"O Queen of Night, I thy Priestess
    am filled with thy radiance!
Let thy power flow through me
    against those who know thee not,
Nor give unto thee that which is thine!

O Mistress of Belin, Queen of the Darkness,
Harken to me, thy Priestess!"

She stood for a moment, poised, her arms upraised, her face bathed in silver, and then she stepped within the circle and solemnly and ritually began to pace towards the offering at the center.

Flavius saw her coming. He tried desperately to keep his eyes open, to summon up every scrap of his willpower to defy her, but he knew that it was futile.

She came to a halt in front of him and flung out an arm and pointed down at him commandingly.

"In the name of the Queen of Night," her voice rang out, "I command thee to sleep!" and in the darkness of a forest grove, beneath a Druid oak, far from his native land, the young Roman closed his eyes and did not open them again.

Gilda felt a shaft of compassion for this boy who had been chosen as the sacrifice without his knowledge or consent—his crime had been no greater than thousands of others of his race. That the sacrifice was necessary she had no doubt, but it was no small matter to risk a life no matter what the circumstances.

Carefully she laid herself on the ground within the semicircle, her head towards the center, her arms spread wide on the moonlit grass, and with an ease of long training she slipped from her body and rose above the grove. Waiting for her, as she knew they would be, were the astral figures of Cranog and Melvina, the High Priest and High Priestess, and also Kerrin, the Ceremoniarius, her seniors whose physical bodies at that moment sat in ritual trance in far-away Mona. She bowed to them in acknowledgement of their presence, and then turned to the scene below.

The physical bodies of herself and the Roman still lay where they had been left, bathed in moonlight. The astral of the Roman hovered over its physical body, bewildered, almost blind, groping around in an inner environment that was obviously totally unfamiliar to it. Here was a very young soul indeed.

Melvina, the High Priestess, stepped forward and raised her arms. With a curious circling motion of her hands she gathered up, as it were, the astral of the Roman in a swirl of force, and the grim-faced Druids moved away with their victim helplessly in tow.

A few moments later they hovered over the near-by Roman marching-camp. Most of the inhabitants were still awake. Some were idling the time away playing dice, some were polishing their weapons, and a conscientious few were tending their horses before retiring for the night. Half a dozen or so in the main hall, heated with wine, were engaged in a fierce argument that quickly developed into a drunken brawl. The majority of the officers were gathered in their own quarter discussing the Welsh resistance, and the veteran centurion commander sat alone in his room picking his way laboriously word for word through written orders that he had received that day from Scapula at Viroconium.

The Druid faces registered their distaste. They were aware that sooner or later the Romans would learn that the Druids were on the island of Mona. If battle-hardened Catuvellauni warriors had not been able to prevail against these barbarians, what hope would the priesthood have in the face of the inevitable onslaught that would follow? After eight years of observing Roman tactics and behavior, the Druid priesthood had become aware that the Roman success lay not only in their training and discipline, not only in the fact that the Roman legionary feared his officers more than he feared the enemy, but also in their arrogant belief in their own invincibility. If the Druids could destroy that belief, if they could instill a fear of Druidry in Roman hearts, then their discipline might crumble and render them more vulnerable to defeat.

The only way to instill that fear was to implant the suggestion in their Group Mind. The most effective way of doing that was to take one member of the group concerned, under ritual conditions, and force him to enact an astral scene depicting the Roman forces being horribly slaughtered by the Druid priests in battle—to thus create on the inner a giant thoughtform. The dreadful fear felt by the one member in that experience would not only ensoul the thoughtform and give it life, but would also be fed directly into the Group Mind of which he was a member.

Cranog turned and looked at the astral of the captured Roman. The danger was that this soul, denied any return to its physical body during the course of the ritual enactment, might seek to escape the fear by rising to a higher plane. The result would be its physical plane death. *That* would be murder, and the Druids concerned would have incurred a Karmic debt of some magnitude. The danger was so real that many of the senior Druids, Gilda included, believed that the victim's death was inevitable.

The High Priest turned again to the scene below. Once created and ensouled, the thoughtform would directly affect every member of the Group Mind of the Romans. Images would rise unbidden in their imagination, scenes of dead and dying Romans, terrifying visions of Druid power. Such scenes would instill a fear in their hearts, and that fear would feed the thoughtform and cause it to grow, and as it grew it would become stronger and so be more effective and thus engender yet more fear. As its strength increased the thoughtform would reach out to touch the minds of Romans in other camps, and before long it would be feeding on the fear in the minds of every Roman in Pretannia. The effect would be devastatingly cumulative.

The senior Druids waited with a patience born of long training for the camp below them to settle down for the night. The astrals of the Romans below them were not required to take part in the ritual enactment, but Cranog knew that the thoughtform would have a greater effect during their sleep than during their waking hours. Gradually, one by one, the Romans retired to their bunks for the night, and as they fell asleep their astrals began to emerge, each one as blind and helpless as the one the Druids had captured. Cranog shook his head. It was typical of such a barbaric race that not one of the entities below gave any indication of a spiritual development beyond the most crude and primitive level.

The High Priest turned to his companions. "It is time," he said briefly. They nodded and moved away to take up their positions at the four cardinal points, Cranog in the East, Kerrin in the West, Melvina in the South, and Gilda in the North. The astral of the captured Roman remained at the center, peering brutishly and suspiciously about it.

When all were in their positions Cranog made the deosil circumambulations to "set the place," and opened the ritual with the usual cardinal invocations. When the preliminaries had been completed Cranog said powerfully and vibrantly: "Brethren, I invite you to join me in this our sacred rite. Therefore with will and purpose create the scenes described!"

He paused for a moment, and then went on: "We are standing now on the shore of the territory of the Ordovices gazing out across the open sea. It is dawn on a clear, fine day. Across the sea we can see the rounded lines of the hills on the island of Mona. The sea is calm. A soft breeze is blowing, and the early morning sun glitters on the surface of the water."

As he spoke, Cranog and the senior Druids began to create the scene described. On the physical plane they would have built the scene in their imagination, but here on the astral plane they were able to work directly on the substance of the plane itself. As they built the scene in their consciousness so it began to grow up around them until they were indeed standing in such a place with all the reality as though it were the physical plane itself. Also it was immediately apparent that the astral of the captured Roman was beginning to see the scene as it was being built around him, and was apparent that he, too, could hear the voice of the Magus.

"On the beach," said Cranog, "stands the solitary figure of a Roman legionary in full battle armor."

As he spoke the Druids saw the astral draw itself up to its full height and indeed become clothed in armor as described. The bewilderment and the blind groping had gone. The figure stood there on the astral as it would have stood in the parallel scene on the physical plane—young, tall, and arrogant in its strength and seeming invincibility.

"Soon other Romans arrive," intoned Cranog, "his companions in battle, and soon the beach is crowded with nearly a full legion."

As he spoke the figures indeed appeared suddenly in the scene, thousands of them, officers, legionaries, and horses, and drawn up on the beach were hundreds of flat-bottomed boats. The other Roman figures were not the astrals of those in the camp below but thousands of simulacra created by the Druids themselves. The Druids were aware, however, that the astrals in the Roman camp below could see the scene being built, as it were, above their heads, and more and more of them paused in their helpless groping to stare in wonderment at the incredible sight.

So real had the scene become to Flavius that he now took an active part, speaking to his friends, caressing the neck of his horse, waiting for orders from his centurion. This day had been a long time coming. For eight years the Romans had been seeking the Druids, and now they were found, trapped on that island there with no means of escape. He looked up at the clear sky—ideal for a sea-borne invasion.

"Not long now!" one of his friends shouted. "How many will *you* kill?"

Flavius laughed with the joy of impending battle. "A good deal more than you, Pontius!" he shouted. "I'll wager three skins of wine that my tally is greater than yours!"

"That's a wager, by Zeus!" the man laughed.

"Shut your mouth and get down to the boats," a centurion bellowed. "You are holding up the embarkation!"

Two hours later the invasion fleet crossed the Menai Straits towards the island of Mona. As they came within a hundred yards of the beach many of the Roman soldiers began to glance at each other nervously. The scene on the beach was like nothing they had ever seen before. A horde of a thousand priests and more were milling along the water's edge, demented, screaming like fiends from the underworld, their hair streaming in the wind, brandishing swords. Among them were groups of women, seemingly insane, yelling, tearing their breasts, the veritable Furies themselves. And on top of the earthworks were the senior Druid magician-priests, their arms upraised to the sky calling down curses on the approaching fleet. It was the most nightmarish scene that the Romans had ever witnessed —it was like a scene from Hades itself.

The officers bellowed their orders and the fleet moved in. Suddenly, for no reason that any could see, two of the leading boats began to sink, flinging their occupants into deep water. On the right flank three more boats began to founder, and to the left three more. Favius looked ahead to where the horrifying figure of the Druid High Priest stood athwart the earthworks pointing down again and again at the Roman fleet, and each time he pointed a boat began to sink. Flavius jerked his eyes away and watched in horror as hundreds and hundreds of Roman legionaries threshed about in the water, dragged down by the weight of their breastplates, disappearing one by one beneath the waves. It was impossible that boats could be struck down by a pointing finger hundreds of yards away. Such things could not be. No mind could conceive the horror of such magic and remain in balance. From deep within himself Flavius could feel a bubbling terror well up; a blind terror that pushed him to the edge of a screaming insanity.

But the Roman officers, horrified beyond human measure but still in command, bellowed their orders and the fleet moved in to the beach, but of the two hundred boats that had set sail, only one hundred reached the beach safely. Flavius saw the leading boats grind onto the beach and saw his companions, men he knew, begin to splash through the shallows to engage those shrieking demons that faced them. He watched in horror as Roman after Roman was cut down and trampled underfoot. In a matter of minutes the shallows ran red with Roman blood, and already five hundred Romans had died without being able to bring down so much as a single Druid priest or priestess.

The terror in Flavius was now so extreme that he could barely hoist his sword as his own boat ground into the beach. Somehow he struggled over the thwarts and splashed through the shallows towards that demented horde. Suddenly a huge Druid priest loomed in front of him. Flavius raised his sword in panic-stricken terror and struck, but somehow he missed, for the priest still stood. Again he struck, and again, but each time he missed—and to his utter horror he saw the Druid begin to smile at his futile efforts. Again Flavius raised his sword, and in a fresh wave of terror he saw the weapon in his own hand turn into a loathsome, wriggling serpent that struck at him again and again, burying its fangs in his face and arms.

The Druid priest laughed and seemed to grow in size, towering to the sky, looking down from his immense height to this insignificant creature that had dared to pit its puny strength against a Druid magician, and emanations of the most intense power began to radiate down towards the tiny Roman. Scream after scream of abject terror burst from Flavius' lips, and all control snapped and his soul fled shrieking from the scene, rising higher and higher in its terrible fear until it broke through the barrier of the upper astral and escaped into the sanctuary of a higher plane.

Cranog stepped forward and raised his Serpent Staff, and instantly the scene dissolved. He could see the astrals of the Romans in the camp below huddled together by the force of the intense fear, but of the astral of their captive there was no trace. Grim-faced and saddened he turned to his companions. "We have achieved our purpose," he said quietly. "There is now on the inner a created entity that is already pulsing waves of fear into the Roman Group Mind, but the life of the Chosen One is forfeit. He now lies dead in a forest glade, and we are responsible. This is no small matter, my brethren."

He raised his arms to the sky. "We, the senior Druids in earth, in the presence of the Great Ones who command all, do hereby acknowledge our debt to the soul of the Chosen One, and do vow that we shall in a future life repay that debt in full measure. Let this our vow be recorded!"

And the Druids turned and sped through the half-world back to their physical bodies on the far-away island of Mona

* * *

The veteran centurion commander stared down at the body still bound to the trunk of this massive Druid oak. The six legionaries with him fingered their swords nervously and stared about them. Flavius' eyes were wide open, and even in the frozen immobility of death they reflected an expression of abject terror. The centurion shivered inwardly. Parts of the nightmare that had given him such a troubled night kept flashing before his mind's eye. He shook his head and pushed the thought away. It was impossible for there to be any connection. It must be pure coincidence.

"The Druids will pay for this!" he growled softly.

The men glanced at him uneasily, not one of them willing to voice the doubts and fears that tugged at the edges of their minds.

chapter eight

"Who?"

"Queen Cartimandua and retinue," said the legate.

Scapula frowned in disbelief. "What in Zeus' name

is Cartimandua doing here at Viroconium? Oh, very well—show her in!"

The legate saluted and withdrew. A few moments later the guards escorted in the Queen and two disarmed Brigantian warriors. Scapula remained seated. He was a Roman governor and did not rise to any primitive barbarian, Queen or no Queen. "You are a long way from your home land, Cartimandua." He eyed the woman with distaste. Her robe did at least make some attempt at finery but it was ragged and somewhat dirty, even filthy. Her facial skin was hard and brown, though her eyes were sharp enough. Her hair hung like damp and dirty strands of rough rope to her waist. Scapula grimaced inwardly—even the lowest whore in Rome was more comely than she. "What brings you here?"

"To honor my treaty with Rome," she said briefly.

He raised his eyebrows. "A bit late, isn't it? You Brigantians have been giving me a great deal of trouble in your western marches, raiding across the border, attacking Roman patrols and outposts!"

"A few rebels—no more."

"Really! Yet rumor has it that your husband encourages such activities."

Queen Cartimandua shrugged. "Venutius is a hothead—he cannot see the long-term benefits to Brigantia in maintaining our treaty with you Romans. If he had his way he would lead the whole of our people in rebellion, but fortunately the majority still listen to me."

Scapula shook his head. It was incredible how some of these Pretannic women attempted to dictate policy to their husbands, and even sometimes succeeded —first Queen Boudicca against her husband, Prasutagus, and now Cartimandua against Venutius. How many more so-called "royal" families were similarly split? "Perhaps so," he growled, "but nevertheless Roman blood has been shed."

"For which I am here to make amends," she said calmly.

"How?"

She crossed to the embrasure and pointed down at the courtyard. "See there."

He hesitated and then rose to join her. In the courtyard, surrounded by Roman guards, were a dozen Brigantian warriors. In their midst was a huge fellow held prisoner by the others, his hands tied behind him, a hood over his head and shoulders to keep him blindfolded. "Who is that?"

"Command your guard to remove his hood and you will see," said Cartimandua. "You will recognize him, I assure you."

Scapula snapped his fingers and a guard left the chamber. A few moments later they saw him emerge into the courtyard and remove the blindfold. Scapula stared down at the prisoner, hardly able to believe his eyes. "Caratacus!" he said softly.

The Queen nodded. "You have been chasing him through all Wales for two years, I hear." She glanced at Scapula archly. "I now officially hand him over to you. Does that atone for the acts of some of my belligerent people?"

He nodded slowly. "Yes—it does." Scapula was already working out the possibilities in his mind. Caratacus was the most dangerous man in all Pretannia. Not even Aulus Plautius had been able to capture him. He would send him to Rome in chains—the Emperor Claudius would be particularly pleased. He could now rewrite his report. Instead of failure, his two-year Welsh campaign could now be justified—it was now all made worthwhile by the capture of this red-haired giant who had become a living symbol of anti-Roman resistance. He turned to the Queen. "Does your husband know of this?"

She shook her head. "No, Venutius was in the western marches when Caratacus arrived." She curled her lip disdainfully. "That Catuvellauni fool thought to join Venutius and persuade him to rouse the whole of Brigantia against you!"

Scapula nodded. "Then I am indeed indebted to you. However, I feel that you will have trouble in plenty when Venutius hears of this. This could split Brigantia right down the middle with you on one side and Venutius on the other."

"I can handle it."

"Maybe, but if you need help then send word to me." Scapula was delighted at the possibilities. With Cartimandua so obviously pro-Roman he need have no further worry about the north. At worst he might have to dispatch Legio IX at Lindum into Brigantia to help quell Venutius, but certainly Legio XIV here at Viroconium would be free to concentrate wholly on Wales. "Come," he said. "Let us go down—I want to hear what he has to say."

In the courtyard Caratacus smiled grimly as he saw the Roman approach with that Brigantian bitch. By the Lord Belin, he would give his right arm for just five minutes alone with her—Brigantia would then have to bury its Queen if there was anything left of her to bury!

Scapula came to stand in front of him. "Well, Caratacus?"

The Catuvellauni made no reply at first. He stared slowly and insolently from one to the other. "For the rest of your life, Scapula," he said softly, "you will have to live with the knowledge that a woman traitor had to do what you could not! All Rome will laugh at you!"

The Roman smiled. "I think not—anyway you will soon experience Rome's reaction personally!" He snapped his fingers for the guard. "Take him away. See to it that he is strongly guarded day and night."

Six months later Caratacus was dragged in chains behind a chariot along the last stretch of the Appian Way and into the mighty city of Rome itself. The sheer size of it stunned him. No one in Pretannia could possibly even begin to imagine the beauty and the colossal size of the buildings that stretched along the banks of the Tiber.

The Emperor Claudius and the tribune C. Gavius Silvanus watched the roaring crowd taunt the bewildered prisoner. "Only when a s . . . s . . . s . . . savage comes to Rome," said Claudius, "does he realize that he is indeed a savage!"

Four days later the prisoner was taken before the Senate for questioning. In all that time he had not been permitted to bathe or even wash himself. His tunic of animal skins was torn and filthy, his hair was matted, his face lined with grime, and the white-robed patrician Romans could smell him from yards away. Several of the older senators felt a pang of compassion. The man was a savage, a barbarian, and yet there was an air of dignity about him.

The guards removed his chains and stepped back. Caratacus rubbed his wrists and stared around him. He moved slowly across the well of the chamber. The guards made as if to go after him but several senators waved them away—they wanted to see what he would do.

Caratacus, King of the Catuvellauni, drew himself up to his full, enormous height and paced slowly round the circular well looking up into the face of each senator in turn. When he had completed the circle he came to a halt. He stared up at the lavishly carved roof, the gleaming white pillars, and then down at the incredibly beautiful marble floor. He then looked at the entire Roman Senate and shook his head as though saddened at the mischievous behavior of children. He spread his hands wide in a gesture of hurt bewilderment.

"Why do you," he cried loudly and passionately, "with all these great possessions, still covet our poor huts?"

His voice echoed and re-echoed round the Senate chamber but no one gave him reply—they just stared down at him as though at some captured wild animal.

* * *

Cranog and Kerrin came across from Mona in a flat-bottomed boat to the mainland in response to an urgent message from Venutius. As they came ashore they saw the party of Brigantian warriors come down to meet them. "Greetings, Venutius," the Arch-Mage said.

"Greetings. I am sorry to have summoned you here in so abrupt a manner, but I really cannot afford to be away from my home territory any longer than is absolutely necessary, so I sent a messenger on ahead. I meant no disrespect."

Cranog waved the apology away. "It is of little importance—I presume you have some urgent news."

"I have indeed, unless you have already heard. Tell me, what is your latest information concerning Scapula?"

Cranog raised his shoulders a trifle. "Nothing very new. It has been nearly a year since your wife handed Caratacus over to the Romans and in all that time Scapula has been trying to penetrate further into Silurian territory but thankfully without success."

"Yes, those Silurians are grim warriors—I would not like to have to face them myself!"

"So what is the latest situation then?" said Kerrin patiently.

Venutius smiled grimly. "Scapula is dead!" he said softly.

The two Druids were indeed surprised. "In battle?" said Cranog.

"No, apparently not. Admittedly he has been fighting a non-stop campaign for three years against the Silurians and the Ordovices but as far as I can make out he became increasingly worn out, to the point of utter exhaustion, and just simply died—like an old man, though he wasn't aged by any means."

Cranog nodded slowly. "As a priest I am saddened by any death that occurs in less than peaceful circumstances—but undoubtedly it is good news for Pretannia. We thank you for coming all this way to tell us."

"Ah, but there is more yet. Apparently he died nearly two months ago, and taking advantage of the Roman lack of leadership Arviragus and the Silurian crossed the estuary of the Usk and met the Twentieth legion in full battle and beat them resoundingly. The Roman losses were enormous and the Silurians chased the survivors all the way back to the River Severn. The Romans made a stand with their backs to the river, but again they were beaten and the remnants were forced to flee back across the Severn and all the way to their fortress at Gloucester—Glevum, the Romans call it—and there they are now, licking their wounds behind barred gates, leaving Arviragus free to rampage at will!"

"Beaten in a set battle?" said the Arch-Mage, quite clearly astonished.

"Apparently—and the odds were about even too, I understand. Maybe the Romans are weary after so long a campaign—they landed at Richboro nearly nine years ago and they still haven't beaten the Welsh, or we Brigantians. Perhaps the tide is turning at long last."

"Maybe, but I doubt it."

"Anyway, the idea that the Romans are invincible in a set battle will have to be reviewed."

"Yes, but we must keep the matter in perspective. It is the only battle that the Romans have lost in nine years. I still say that the correct strategy is the ambush and the running skirmish."

"How goes your own campaign?" said Kerrin.

"Well enough. I still hold about half the Brigantian territory and my ex-wife holds the other half."

They were silent for a moment, and then Cranog said softly: "Your ex-wife Cartimandua has much to answer for."

Venutius frowned. "There is no need to be diplomatic, Cranog. Cartimandua is a traitor and we all know it! I will not rest until she is dead!"

"And the Deceangli?"

The King shrugged. "They were demoralized by their earlier defeats, but now they are beginning to recover. Many of them march with me."

"Good," said Cranog. "The Deceangli territory is quite vital. Any news on whom Rome will send to replace Scapula?"

"No, none as yet. I will inform you if I hear. And now we must go." He nodded to his warriors and they wheeled their horses around. "Ah yes, there is one more piece of news," he called out. "The Romans now know that you Druids have gathered at Mona— Cartimandua must have told them."

Cranog raised his eyebrows. "It had to happen sooner or later. We are as prepared as we can be."

Venutius raised his sword in salute. "Take care,

Cranog. The Romans believe that you Druids, more than any others, are responsible for fomenting all the anti-Roman resistance. They will destroy you if they can. Farewell!"

Cranog and Kerrin remained on the shoreline until the Brigantian party could be seen no more. "The thoughtform is doing its work," said Cranog softly. "Already the Romans are not as invincible as they were."

"Good," said Kerrin. "Let us hope that their confidence is eroded still further before they get to us. What now, Cranog? Back to Mona?"

"Yes, to make preparations for a journey. It is time I visited Glaeston again to see how the Culdees are getting on. With Scapula dead and the Twentieth legion in virtual siege at Gloucester the journey should be safe enough."

* * *

Cranog sat by the old Chalybeate Well in the early morning sun and stared around him. The Druids had left Glaeston only a few short years ago and yet already it was difficult even for him to tell exactly where Glaeston College had been. The stoneworkers had done their work well, not even a solitary piece of stone had been left on the old site, even the foundations had been prized up and removed. At Cranog's insistence the entire site had been dug over to a depth of two or three feet and all artifacts removed. His policy had been more than justified for now the entire site was covered in grass and bushes, and there were even saplings of elm and oak beginning to rise above the undergrowth. The Chalybeate Well was still there, of course, but that could so easily be a wayside well. Of Glaeston College there was no trace whatsoever.

A youngish man came slowly across the mounds and hillocks, and Cranog rose to greet him. "Josue!" he said softly. "It is good to see you again!"

The Culdee smiled. "I heard that you were here. Did you travel alone?"

"No, I came with Morgana and Gilda. It is forgotten by most, and sometimes even by me, that Gilda is daughter to Morgana and I. For too long our relationship has been that of priest and priestess, the Druid way of life demands it—it was good to travel as a family." He pointed to the west. "Our camp is close by—you will see them later. We brought two of the young Bards to do the hunting for us. I came on ahead."

Josue swept his arm around to indicate the old site. "A pilgrimage?" he said quietly.

Cranog nodded. "Partly." He looked down at the ground. "This very spot where we are now standing was where the great gates used to be—at least I think so. It is difficult to tell any more."

The Culdee pointed to the top of the Green Hill. "Do you notice anything?"

Cranog shaded his eyes against the sun and stared up at the plateau on the hill. "No, I . . . oh yes!" He shook his head and laughed softly. "I must be getting old not to have noticed!" The standing stone circle and the tower in the western quadrant that had been a landmark for untold centuries were gone. The Green Hill was now as naked as any other hill. "When did that happen?"

"We took the tower down during the first year after your departure. It was bad enough bringing it *down* the hill—how your ancestors managed to get it *up* there in the first place is quite beyond me."

Cranog nodded. "The old Wessex folk in the days of their early glory were a quite remarkable people."

"They must have been. The smaller stones of the circle we took down during the following year. They are heaped alongside the stones from your College. We covered the whole thing with a thin layer of earth and scattered grass seed. It now looks like a long grass mound. It would not defy a determined investigation but it will keep the stones hidden from casual observation. Later, when the Romans have gone, we will uncover them and build the abbey that you suggested."

Cranog looked at the Judaean. "Why did you dismantle the circle?"

Josue shrugged. "Several reasons. To remove

the last traces of your presence in this area so that the Romans would not ask awkward questions . . ."

"And because your people had a superstitious fear of them because of the rituals we Druids used to perform up there."

The Culdee smiled. "Yes, there was an element of that in it."

"Inspired by Zaacheus, no doubt."

"True, but it was his last command—he died even while the work was in progress. Some of our people were convinced that the demons of the hill killed Zaacheus in revenge for the desecration."

Cranog sighed. "If there were any demons, they were Zaacheus' own creation."

"Perhaps so."

The Arch-Mage looked up at the hill. "Drucius died up there—do you remember?"

"Yes, I remember—he was a fine old man."

"More so than you can even begin to know. Did you know, for example, that he knew you Culdees were coming to Pretannia thirty years before you actually arrived."

The Judaean frowned a little. He did not wish to be rude, but . . . "How can you *know* that, Cranog?" he said softly. "Tales become distorted with the years."

The Arch-Mage chuckled. "Ah, the splendid arrogance of youth! I am nearly sixty years of age, Josue. I was a young man of seventeen, only recently initiated into the senior Order of the White, when your father, Joseph, first brought Jesus of Nazareth to Pretannia. That was forty-two years ago and Jesus was a young boy, eight years old. When the party arrived at Glaeston Drucius spoke alone with the boy for some hours. The following day Drucius gathered the members of the White together and told us that although we Druids had borne the Light with honor for many centuries the time had come when we had to withdraw. He told us that a new era was about to begin, that your anointed one was a Star Logos, that the seedbearers to the new age would soon arrive, and that it was our task to see to it that you were made welcome and given every help in our power to establish the new priesthood. He did

not know your name but he knew you would come,
and he hinted as such to your father on that same day
forty-two years ago. Drucius was an old man even then,
but he clung to life desperately year after year so that
he would be here when you arrived." He smiled at the
young Culdee. "I *know*, Josue, because I was here and
heard his very words."

They were silent for some time, and then the
Judaean said: "I am sorry, Cranog—I did not know.
But tell me, how did he know?"

Cranog smiled. "He was a great priest. He could
recognize inner plane causes and be aware of what was
needed to bring them to fruition on earth."

"My people will have difficulty in believing all
this."

"It is not necessary that they do—it is not even
necessary that you tell them."

"And what will happen to you Druids?"

Cranog shrugged. "The Romans know that we are
at Mona. Sooner or later they will seek us out and then
Druidry will cease to exist."

"You could disband your Order now—burn your
robes and live as ordinary men."

The Arch-Mage seemed indignant at the suggestion. "Certainly not! I have worn the robe of Druidry
all my life—I do not intend to forsake it now!"

Josue bowed slightly. "I apologize—I did not intend to insult you. You spoke just now of the pilgrimage to Glaeston as being only part of your reason for
coming. What other reason had you?"

"Well, since the dissolution of Druidry is necessary in order to make way for the new priesthood, it is
not unreasonable that we should have some mild interest in your physical and spiritual welfare."

"Checking up on us?"

The Druid smiled. "If you like."

"Then come, visit our church—we owe you that at
least."

At that moment Morgana and Gilda came across
the grasslands. As they drew near Josue bowed low.
"Greetings," he said softly.

Morgana raised an eyebrow. "Take care, Culdee,"

she retorted, "you are beginning to sound like a Druid!"

"A courtesy, Morgana," he murmured, "because it is good to see you again."

"Yes, you once saw a very great deal of me," she said pointedly, "in fact all there is to see! You were much troubled by the sight, as I remember."

"Who would not be troubled at the sudden sight of too much beauty?"

Her eyebrows rose even further. "Time seems to have been a great teacher," she said. "You were not so courteous the last time we met."

"I was young then and inexperienced."

"And now you are older and no longer disturbed by the sight of a naked woman! Shall I disrobe and put your new-found maturity to the test?"

"Don't tease the man!" said Cranog irritably. Morgana was still a magnificent specimen of a woman, but the loss of youth and the appearance of the first lines of imminent old age had made her a trifle too tart for easy companionship. "At this moment he is showing more courtesy than you!"

Morgana hesitated, and then smiled apologetically. "You are right," she said. "I suppose a woman, even a priestess, never ever really forgets or forgives having been called a whore!"

"You must remember, Morgana," said the Judae-an, "it was not I who called you that harsh name but some of our womenfolk, because of your effect on their men. It was said in a moment of anger."

"Well, anyway," she said briskly, "they no longer have any cause to anger. I am long past the age when I could stir men's loins!"

"Really?" he murmured. "I find that difficult to be-lieve."

She laughed outright and turned to Gilda. "Be warned, my daughter, here is a boy who seems to have become a man!"

Gilda had inherited the magnificent beauty of her mother—her copper-hued hair fell in waves of reddish gold to her waist, and strange, compelling lights flick-ered in the green depths of her eyes—but there the in-heritance ended. She walked a lone path through the priesthood—no man, priest or otherwise, had ever lain with her. Her way was the wild way of the woods at night. She was a tree with eerie moonlight in her branches—a wolf on the trail, a bat that flutters in the glades at night—she was a creature of the darkness, not the darkness of evil but the darkness and secretiveness of the inner soul of Nature.

It seemed to Cranog that Gilda flinched away from her mother, though she made no move. Morgana could at times be almost totally insensitive to the moods and feelings of others. Gilda was in that stage of her development whereby to her the world of Nature so perfectly manifested the will of the Great One that mankind, by comparison, had become repugnant to her.

"Are you the one they call the witch-maiden?" said Josue softly.

"The superstitious sometimes call me that," she said briefly.

"The description is not accurate?"

"I am the Mistress of the Woods, and the superstitious fear the forest at night. I go where the wild wolves go and dance with the oaks until dawn." She glanced at him, almost contemptuously, and smiled thinly and briefly. "Would you come with me into the forest at night, Culdee, and see for yourself the truth of what I am?"

"Not where the wolves go!" he said feelingly.

"You would be safe with me—they are my friends. You could learn a lot from a wolf."

"The lesson of bestial savagery? Thank you, but my people have learned that lesson already from the Romans."

"Savagery? Truly, man is indeed more savage than the wolf. No, Culdee, there are other lessons to learn. The wolf mates but does not lust. He kills but not for pleasure. Can you say the same of your fellow man?"

"Maybe not, but a man for all his faults is of the same essential nature as God."

"And who is to say that a wolf is not?"

"But he is still an animal."

"Indeed yes, but if you have the courage to walk with me through the forest ways at night I will show you the very face of God himself!"

They were silent for some time. Morgana made as if to speak but Cranog waved her to be quiet. He wanted to hear the Culdee's answer. His reply might tell him all he wanted to know of the Culdee priesthood.

"I think," said Josue slowly, "that a man can see the face of God anywhere he looks if he has the eyes to see. But only a very advanced soul can see him everywhere—we lesser beings can only see him in those areas that are akin to our particular temperament. You have seen him in the woods, Gilda, and I am glad for you. I would see naught in the forest but the savagery of the natural law of kill or be killed—you must permit me to look elsewhere. It is sad that I cannot see him in the woods, and sad that you cannot see him anywhere else. We both have much to learn."

Cranog nodded. "That was the answer of a true priest, Josue. I am glad that the priesthood is in such good hands." He then changed the subject abruptly on to less dangerous ground. "Tell me, did the Romans ever come to Glaeston?"

"Yes, but not for two years after your departure —they were kept pretty busy in the south, and still are for that matter. Even when they did get here it was only a scouting party headed by a not too intelligent centurion. By that time the raw earth had been covered by grass, and similarly the mound of stone. They did not seem to see anything unusual."

"They presumably questioned you about we Druids."

"Yes, they had heard that there were Druids at Glaeston. I told them that you were only a small group and that you had moved away for fear of being involved in the fighting. I said that I had no idea where you had gone except that it was towards the north somewhere."

"Good." Inwardly Cranog sighed with relief. In Judaea the Romans sought to destroy Christianity because they saw the cult as a rallying point for anti-

Roman nationalism. In Pretannia the Romans would undoubtedly seek to destroy Druidry for the very same reason. If there was no obvious connection between Druidry and the Culdee Church then there was a fair chance that the Christians in Pretannia would be left in peace, and it was for this reason more than any other that Cranog had withdrawn the Druids to Mona. The Culdees had enough problems as it was without inviting the additional burden of Roman persecution because of their friendship with Druidry.

He smiled at the Culdee. "And now I would like to accept that invitation to visit your church."

The Druids remained for three full days with the Culdees at Glaeston and Cranog was more than satisfied with everything he saw and heard. The atmosphere in the Culdee community was far happier and far more relaxed under the leadership of Josue than it had been under the poisonous, guilt-ridden suspicions of old Zaacheus. The Druids were treated with reserve at first, particularly Morgana, but Cranog's gentle persuasiveness soon won them over and by the third day the Culdees were quite happy to chatter freely with their guests.

The Culdee church, though still a somewhat crude wattle and daub structure, had been considerably enlarged, and the thriving community were all housed in peasant-style cottages rather than the tents that Cranog remembered. The Holy Thorn still thrived, but the Cup had been withdrawn from the altar to a place of safety away from the possible desecration by a chance Roman patrol. Cranog was pleased to hear that plans had been drawn up already for the new church that they would build with the Druid stone once the Romans had gone.

The two aspects of Culdee life that impressed Cranog more than any other were marriage and church membership. When the Culdees had first arrived in Pretannia they had with them nearly two dozen children. Many of these had arrived at maturity and a good half of them had married outside the Culdee community, and already there were nine children from these mixed marriages with more to come. "It was essential that inter-community marriage be encouraged," Josue said. "Our group was too small to survive by marrying within our own ranks, and anyway it is necessary for use to integrate fully into Pretannic life." The same philosophy applied to church membership. Anyone could become a member by learning a simple catechism and by offering a declaration of faith and good intent. Because of the influx of non-Culdees, the church was already being referred to as the Christian Church rather than the Culdee Church. Cranog was amused by the initiation ritual—a crude affair by Druid standards, consisting of ducking the aspirant in the River Parrett.

Apart from the many differences in philosophy and practice between Druidry and Christianity, the great fundamental difference was that Christianity was a religion for the common people whereas Druidry was a religion for the elite. The Christian Church actively encouraged everyone to become a Christian, whereas Druidry in effect actively discouraged membership by the severity of their training, their examinations, and their initiation rituals. Druidry took only the very best —Christianity took everyone. In Druidry everyone was a priest or priestess—in Christianity only the few functioned as priests while the remainder formed the congregation. Cranog had the gravest doubts as to the wisdom of the Christian method—it seemed to him that ritual and spiritual standards must of necessity be far lower—but he did not interfere. This was the new priesthood—their ways were different.

On the third day the Culdees held a special service to pray for the welfare of the Druids at Mona. Cranog was quite touched by the gesture though he doubted whether any real protection would result. These Christians had a touching, childlike faith in the efficacy of prayer, as though all the world's problems could be solved simply by asking—the sooner they learned that it was the responsibility of humanity in earth to solve the problems in earth the more meaningful their religion would be.

During the prayer Cranog was moved to make a symbolic gesture of his own. He rose quietly and went to the altar. He removed the Druid symbol from around his neck, the Serpent entwined round a Pillar of Rock, and laid it on the altar cloth. He then knelt for a few moments and visualized the inner Lodge. In his visualization he removed the Druid symbol from the inner altar and replaced it with a Christian cross. On the inner the symbolism was unmistakable. The Culdees could not know of his action on the inner but they did appreciate his gesture on the outer.

On the morning of the fourth day the Druids departed amidst scenes of some emotion, which touched the Druids more than they cared to admit. Finally the two Bards and the two priestesses walked on ahead and the Culdees withdrew to their church, leaving Cranog and Josue alone.

Cranog took the younger man's hands in his own. "Farewell, Josue. I am glad that I came. The Light is now safely in your hands—guard it well."

"We will, with help from the inner as you would say. But what of the Druids?"

Cranog smiled. "We will wait at Mona for whatever destiny awaits us."

Josue was obviously troubled. "It may mean your deaths, all of you!"

The Arch-Mage nodded. "Perhaps, but if so then we accept it. The importance of death lies not in the death itself but in the manner of dying and in the new life that springs from the ashes of the old."

The younger man nodded. "Farewell then, Cranog, we will remember you in our prayers."

Three days later the Druids were clear of the lowlands and well into the mountain forests of Siluria on their way back to Mona. It was late autumn and there in the mountains they could feel the first faint heralds of winter. The previous night they had heard the wolves howl in the high timber ahead of them. The young Bards had shivered in apprehension but Cranog had seen Gilda smile with anticipation.

The full moon was already sinking behind the ridge when Cranog awoke—the night was nearly over. The Druids were camped at the beginning of a mountain pass at the head of a valley through which they had come. The way ahead promised a steep but clear rocky trail, an easier path than the twisting, narrow forest trail that they had left behind. Something had awakened him. He rose quietly and stared around. The fire was still burning, though low. In the moonlight he could see the sleeping forms of the two Bards and Morgana—but not Gilda. Not only had she gone but had taken her blanket-skins and her ox-hide carrying-skin with her. He nodded to himself, having half expected this possibility. A few moments later he caught a glimpse of her a fair distance back down the trail where it entered the forest. He hesitated, looked back at the sleeping forms, and then slipped quietly from the camp to follow her.

Because of the moonlight he was able to cover the first few hundred yards down the rocky trail quite rapidly, but when he entered the forest he could barely see the trail at all and had to almost feel his way step by step. He had a shrewd idea where Gilda was going. About a mile into the forest was a small glade, and when they had passed through it yesterday Gilda had been quite taken by its quiet beauty and particularly by the majesty of the giant oak that dominated it. But a mile in such darkness through such a narrow forest trail would take a long time, and he was no longer a young man. He took the trail slowly and cautiously, with patience, and it was only when he saw the glade ahead made visible through the trees by the half-light of pre-dawn did he realize just how much time the journey had taken. He covered the last few yards even more cautiously and stopped at the very edge of the clearing.

Gilda stood facing the oak, quite naked, her discarded robe flung aside. She held her arms together upraised above her bowed head, and although he could not hear her words he knew that she was intoning the Ritual of the Sacred Oak. He kept silent, not wishing to interrupt. Now more than ever he regretted that Druidry over the centuries had neglected the old Moon worship in favor of the more male-orientated Sun rituals— Gilda had always been in effect a Priestess of the Moon and as such had been outside the mainstream of Druid philosophy and practice.

The title of the ritual that she was using, and its actual wording, was Druid, but it had been rewritten by Druids from a much older source. The essence of the ritual pre-dated Druidry and even pre-dated the ancient Wessex folk who had built Cor Gaur and the other stone circles, and legend had it that it even pre-dated the arrival of the emigration from Atlantis ten thousand years ago. Its real source, according to the legend, arose in the far misty past from a time when the national religion, as it were, was a female cult which did not permit membership to males. In those far-off days the males ruled the physical social life of the community, the Hunter and the Warrior, but the females ruled the Mysteries—an era of priestesses but no priests. Legend spoke of how the virile males were from time to time summoned to the Temple for the ritual mating, but for century upon century, even millenia upon millenia, the males did not connect that act to the subsequent appearance of a child, an event that was always considered by the males to be the most awe-inspiring secret of the Mysteries of the Temple. Knowledge of the female moon-cycle, procreation, and childbirth was the most closely guarded secret of the Mysteries, and kept secret from the males by the doom of the most dreadful death to be inflicted on those who even tried to penetrate that secret.

Cranog had long thought it a possibility that Gilda had incarnated during that period and its influence was overshadowing her present life. It would go some way towards understanding Gilda's seemingly unnatural antipathy towards Morgana, her mother, whose natural freedom of sexual expression with many a different male, though permissible and natural under Druid custom, would seem the part of Gilda's inner self to be the most gross betrayal of Temple secrets. Cranog sighed. True or not there was little that he could do about it— Gilda would have to find her own path of spiritual evolution out of her present difficulties.

Gilda lowered her arms and Cranog stepped into

the clearing. She turned and regarded him silently. She then picked up her robe and drew it round her shoulders.

"Were you leaving without farewell?" he said quietly.

She smiled faintly. "Farewells would have meant explanations."

"Not to me."

She drew the robe around herself and tied the cord. "No, probably not. You alone in all Druidry know that I am not a true Druid at heart and never have been—and what is more you know why. My place is here in the forest with the Oak and the Moon—the sun rituals are not for me. It was bearable at Glaeston because I could slip away into the forest when the need was on me, but at Mona I was stifled."

"Yes, I know that."

"I would have seen you on the inner when next you slept, my father," she said gently.

He sighed. "I know, but I would not have questioned your action—you could have said farewell to me."

She nodded. "To you, yes—but to my mother?"

He had to admit to himself that she was right— Morgana would not have understood, and certainly she would refuse to understand when he broke the news. "I will explain it to her as best I can."

"Tell her I will see her on the inner, and I will visit you at Mona from time to time."

"You will be welcome," he said simply.

She hesitated, and then said: "There will be some who will think me afraid to stand with Druidry against the Romans, but you know the truth of that—try not to let them speak ill of me."

"You have my word." He stepped closer and took her in his arms. "Farewell, my daughter," he whispered. "May you find what you need."

She clung to him fiercely for a moment, and then broke away. "Farewell," she said quietly and calmly, but there was a slight catch in her voice that revealed her feelings. "Try not to . . ."

At that precise moment, in a rush of silent feet, a

score of wolves streamed into the glade and formed a half-circle around them, leaving the giant oak at their backs. In sudden shock Cranog began to back away but Gilda stopped him. "Stand perfectly still!" she commanded. "Or else they will tear you to pieces. Perfectly still!"

Cranog could not remember ever having experienced such a rush of terror that now gripped him, and it was only by the most severe exercise of willpower that prevented him from running in blind panic. But gradually he mastered the fear—he could not dismiss it entirely but he did manage to regain control, though he could feel the sweat running in rivulets from his face and down his chest.

There were a dozen full-grown males in the pack, half a dozen yearlings, and two old she-wolves. The other females were presumably in the pack-lairs with this year's cubs, and since this was presumably the end of a night's hunting those dens would be close by, probably in the rock-caves above the tree-line.

"Stand perfectly still!" she said again, and then began to speak softly to the pack, soothingly, her voice rising and falling melodiously almost as though she was singing to them. The words she used were unimportant, the intonation and timbre of her voice was all-important.

Cranog had not realized how large a wolf could be. The big one slightly in front of the others, presumably the pack-leader, was six feet from snout to rump, and the silent snarl and dripping fangs were for Cranog the very embodiment of bestial ferocity.

How long they stood there Cranog never knew, it could easily have been thirty full minutes, and in all that time Gilda's soothing voice never ceased. Gradually, one by one, their hackles fell and their snarls vanished until finally the entire pack were sat on their haunches, their tongues lolling, their heads cocked to one side listening to the Mistress.

Suddenly her voice stopped, and the silence crackled with tension. Slowly, unhurriedly, Gilda took two paces forward. Instantly a dozen or more, including the leader, came to their feet. Again she began to speak to them, and again gradually they quietened down. Again her voice stopped and she held out her hand. For some minutes she remained thus, poised, and then the big leader came forward slowly, stiff-legged, lips wrinkled in that silent snarl of dreadful warning, and sniffed the outstretched hand. Having satisfied himself, he then lowered his head and still snarling silently he sniffed her feet. He then drew back and walked stiff-legged around her and came to Cranog. It needed the utmost surge of willpower to stand still under that inspection but the wolf seemed satisfied and turned once more to sniff at Gilda as though to reaffirm his first impression. There then occurred something that Cranog would not have thought possible. The big leader came to stand facing the pack with Gilda at his rear, her robe touching his rump, and even to the human mind the gesture was quite plain—the leader had accepted the strange beings and was now challenging the pack to do the same.

For a long time nothing happened, the tableau held as though frozen, and then one of the males came stiff-legged from the line to face his pack-leader. What happened then occurred so fast that Cranog could barely believe that he had actually seen it. Without the slightest warning the challenger drove straight for the leader's throat. The bigger wolf dropped, twisted, and as the challenger rushed past he raked his fangs along his flank and opened a deep gash through fur and flesh. The challenger staggered under the blow and sprang sideways and brushed past Gilda leaving a smear of blood on her robe. He then drew back, snarling hideously. But gradually his hackles fell and then he walked stiff-legged back into the ranks. The big leader waited but no other challenger came forward. He then turned, sniffed once more at Gilda, again at Cranog, and then trotted away. The line still remained, though one or two of them broke away to examine the far side of the glade.

"It is over," she said quietly. "But stay still and I will put it to the test." Slowly, cautiously, she moved forward into the middle of the glade, stopped and then retraced her steps. "Yes, we are now safe providing you make no sudden move."

He wiped the back of his hand across his brow. "I have never seen anything like that!" he said feelingly. "You are truly a Priestess of the Woods!"

She smiled at him. "There are not many who could have endured that as you did. You have much courage, my father."

"And much fear, believe me!"

She laughed softly. "You will live to tell the tale a hundred times." She looked up at the sky. The dawn had come and gone and they had not even noticed. "The others will be awake now. You must go. Tread slowly until you are well on the trail. They will not harm you." She took his hands in hers. "Farewell."

He nodded and began to move away across the glade. The fear welled up in him as several of the wolves sniffed at him as he went by, but their demeanor was now one of curiosity instead of menace. At the far side of the glade he stopped and looked back. The big leader had returned to Gilda, and unbelievably she was actually stroking his ears.

He shook his head in wonderment and turned to the trail.

chapter nine

The new governor arrived in Pretannia in the year 52, and it was Kerrin who brought the news to Cranog. "His name," said the dark one, "is Aulus Didius Gallus. Do you remember him?"

Cranog nodded. "Indeed I do! He was the general in command of cavalry under Plautius when the Romans first landed at Richboro nine years ago in 43. It was his commander of cavalry, Hosidius Geta, and the legate of the Twentieth legion, Vespasian, in command of the infantry, who forced their way across the River Med and put Caratacus and the Catuvellauni to flight."

"And since then," said Kerrin," he has apparently served with distinction in the Crimea and rose to the proconsulate of Asia. He is now both very distinguished and very senior."

Cranog raised his eyebrows. "I suppose we should be flattered that Claudius deems us sufficiently important to warrant the appointment of such an august personage!" His eyes clouded and the lines of worry creased his forehead. "I suppose this means," he sighed, "that we can expect a renewal of the campaign against the Silurians and the Ordovices—they will want to revenge the defeat that Arviragus inflicted on the Twentieth legion."

"Undoubtedly," said Kerrin. "It is going to be a bloody time for all of us."

But in this the Druids were wrong. Aulus Didius Gallus arrived to find the Silurians raiding far and wide with that one victory against Legio XX already to their credit, but Gallus had received very precise instructions from Claudius *not* to renew the war against the Welsh, nor to attempt an invasion of Brigantia, but simply to maintain the existing frontier. "Too many Roman lives have been lost already," he had said. "Let us be satisfied with what we have. Perhaps in a few years their fear and distrust of us will have abated sufficiently to give an opportunity for a more peaceful expansion." Gallus doubted it—these people were too fierce and too full of pride ever to give up dominion over their territory without a fight—but certainly there was no harm in waiting a few years.

However, apart from that troublesome Welsh frontier and the civil strife in Brigantia, the remainder of lowland Pretannia was already settling down as a normal Roman province with Londinium beginning to develop as a strategic port and the civilian municipium of Verulamium already founded and thriving. Scapula may have had little success against the Welsh but in Gallus' opinion the establishment of Verulamium was probably the single most important contribution since the original invasion. If the success of Verulamium could be repeated in a score of other major Pretannic towns, then it would form a foundation from which Rome could rule Pretannia perhaps for hundreds of years. There were some in Rome who considered Scapula's governorship to have been a failure, but Gallus could appreciate just how much had been achieved in the nine years since his last visit.

Gallus had brought replacements with him to cover the Roman losses. Legion XX was still equally divided between Camulodunum and Glevum and he now brought each up to full half-legion strength. Legio IX at Lindum was also brought up to strength plus two additional auxiliary cohorts. Legio II in the south was still spread thinly along a score of forts along the south coast. Resistance in the south was still felt, and felt strongly, but there were signs that it was at long last beginning to diminish. Gallus dispatched replacements to the south plus three additional auxiliary cohorts to help ease the burden. The second legion were vociferous in their complaints—they referred to themselves bitterly as the forgotten legion—and Gallus was at pains to reassure them that in keeping the whole southern territory quiescent they were making an invaluable contribution.

The remainder of the replacements were used to bring Legio XIV at Viroconium up to full legion strength and it was there at Wroxeter, as the natives called it, that he established his command headquarters as Scapula had done before him. During the next six months, in a series of lightning sorties using both Legio XX at Glevum and Legio XIV at Viroconium, he drove Arviragus and the Silurians out of the client-kingdoms of the Dobunni and the Cornovii, back over the River Severn to their own land. The frontier was now established again and he turned his attention to Brigantia.

He had strict instructions not to invade Brigantia, and yet at the same time he needed to keep the peace. The struggle between the pro-Roman Cartimandua and her anti-Roman husband, Venutius, had grown more intense to a point where he felt that he had to interfere

—he could not afford to let Venutius grow too strong, otherwise there was a chance that he could enflame the whole of northern Pretannia against the Roman invader. In the year 53 Gallus was forced to send in three auxiliary cohorts to help Cartimandua and in a running skirmish Venutius was heavily defeated at Templeboro. Throughout the long winter that followed, Brigantia, if not actually at peace, did enjoy a cessation of hostilities, but in the spring Venutius emerged from the western marches stronger than ever and again marched against Cartimandua. This time Gallus dispatched the entire Legio IX from Lindum into Brigantia to help Cartimandua. Again Venutius was defeated but again he was not beaten. He withdrew his forces into the western marshlands round the estuary of the river Mer and from there he carried on a campaign of lightning strikes against Cartimandua's forces with a military skill that evoked a grudging respect and even admiration from the Roman governor.

In the year 54 came news from Rome. Claudius had got rid of Messalina long ago on the grounds that her behavior did not befit an Empress of Rome, and he had subsequently married Agrippina. His choice for his second wife was even more tragic than his first. Agrippina's reputation was that of a voracious and coldly venomous woman, and apparently she had more than lived up to her reputation by having Claudius murdered, by poison. The already infamous Claudius Caesar Nero now wore the purple. Gallus received the news with some equanimity. Of the last five emperors three had been murdered—Julius, Caligula, and now Claudius. He was, however, a little concerned that he might now be withdrawn from the governorship of Pretannia by the new Emperor and returned to Rome, and this was not a pleasant prospect. A commander of his stature would inevitably be drawn into the struggle of power politics that always followed the succession of a new Emperor as the lesser lights fought among themselves for positions in the new power alignment, and Aulus Didius Gallus considered such petty scramblings to be beneath his dignity. But as the months went by it became apparent that the new

Emperor, Nero, was not yet concerned with foreign policy—he had enough problems in Rome itself—and that Gallus would be left in peace to run the full term of his Office.

The struggle in Brigantia continued, but like the Silurians in Wales Venutius avoided any further direct confrontations in set battles, preferring to maintain the policy of the raiding party and the running skirmish. He had learned the lesson of his two defeats that nothing could be successfully achieved against Cartimandua while the Roman legions were free to interfere. He bided his moment waiting for the time that would inevitably come when Legio IX at Lincoln and Legio XIV at Wroxeter would be busy elsewhere. When that time came he would then exact justice against Cartimandua for her treachery.

In 57 Aulus Didius Gallus completed his term of Office and returned to Rome to a reasonably cordial if not spectacular welcome. Nero, whose psychotic madness had established himself as the absolute demigod master of Rome with an insane ferocity that even surpassed the earlier rule of Caligula, now took the opportunity to turn his eyes in the direction of Britannia. The previous Claudian policy of holding the lowlands only was revoked and Nero became determined on complete conquest. He appointed Q. Veranius as the new governor, a relatively young man at forty-five who had held the consulship some eight years earlier and who had won an immense military reputation in his early thirties in Asia Minor against hill tribes similar to the Silurians of Wales. Aulus Didius Gallus, and P. Ostorius Scapula before him, had been political administrators as much as military commanders, but Veranius was a soldier who understood foreign policy only in terms of blood and the sword.

Veranius wasted no time at all on his arrival in Pretannia. Within weeks Legio XX at Glevum and Legio XIV at Viroconium drove deep into Silurian territory in the same pincer movement that Scapula had used earlier. Without the military skill of Caractacus the Silurians found themselves outmaneuvered at every turn. Arviragus was not even permitted the winter months to regroup his forces, for Veranius mercilessly drove the legions through the harsh mountain winter in an almost frenzied pursuit of the fleeing Silurians. By the spring of 58 the two arms of the Roman pincer met and held the entire central territory, and the Silurians and the Ordovices had been driven westward into the coastal territories of the peaceful Demetae tribe.

But Veranius paid the price of his own ruthlessness. His health, already weakened by diseases contracted in his earlier campaigns in Asia Minor, deteriorated rapidly in the harsh Welsh winter. Had he waited out the winter in a semi-permanent march camp he might have lived to complete the campaign, but a winter spent in driving rain and snow, nights spent coughing his lungs up in wet tents, and days spent in forced marches through harsh terrain, and bloody fighting, took their toll and in the spring of 58 he died.

His replacement was C. Suetonius Paullinus. Like his predecessor Paullinus had earned a great military reputation, in his case in Mauretania where he had successfully fought a series of mountain campaigns—and like his predecessor he was a ruthless military commander with little patience for the niceties of civilian administration. Like Veranius he was a man of the sword and he too wasted little time on his arrival in Pretannia. He joined Legio XX and Legio XIV in central Wales and immediately expanded west and south and in two years, by the spring of 61, he had overrun the whole of Wales. The Silurians and the Ordovices were not totally defeated but they were driven into the high mountains and there eked out a precarious existence utterly helpless against the scores of Roman marching camps and forts that sprang up all over south, west, and central Wales manned by 10,000 legionaries commanded by the ruthless C. Suetonius Paullinus.

In 61 Paullinus turned his attention to North Wales, and in particular to the island of Mona. Not only did Mona house the granaries of the Ordovices, the destruction of which would finally crush the stubborn Welsh, but there too were the Druids the arch-instigators of anti-Roman resistance throughout all Pretannia.

"This abomination called Druidry," he said to his commanders, "will be crushed—annihilated." He eyed them bleakly and grimly. "There will be *no* prisoners whatsoever. You will see to it, each of you, that every priest and priestess is put to the sword such that none remain alive to tell the tale or to spread the poison of their evil elsewhere. They are to be obliterated from the face of the earth!"

* * *

King Prasutagus of the Iceni was dead and laid to rest. The Pretannic nobility who had gathered to the feast in his honor were now gone. The great hall of the King's palace at Lynn was silent. Only the young King Cori of the Coritani had remained behind.

"My fellow kings," he said bitterly, "and those so-called nobles of Pretannia would not listen to me! But how much longer can we afford to tolerate the Roman presence in our land? Are we so poor in heart that we now merely shrug and spread our hands in helpless resignation?"

Queen Boudicca shook her head. "You bear the same name as your dead father, and the same impetuous nature. Your tongue will be your death one day."

"Maybe it will, but I would sooner die fighting the Romans like my father than live in their bondage!"

"Hush now, Cori—I have just buried my husband, a King! Have you no respect?"

The young king grunted. "You don't fool me, Boudicca. Prasutagus was a good man, but you showed as much impatience as any of us with his policy of appeasement, his attitude of peace at any price. Look at that ridiculous will of his! He may have been the wealthiest king in all Pretannia but he was by no means the most intelligent."

Boudicca sighed. "I gave him three daughters but no son. Since there is no son to inherit, then our treaty with Rome is no longer operative, and as such the

Iceni territory instead of being a client-kingdom will now be incorporated as part of the Roman province of Pretannia—and I will cease to be a queen!"

"But did Prasutagus really believe that making the Emperor Nero his part-heir would preserve the kingdom for you and your daughters? If he did, then he must have been even more naive than we thought."

"Anyway, he is dead now, Cori. The matter is done and cannot be undone. Let us leave him in peace. Slaves from the procuratorial office at Camulodunum will be here within the next few days to claim the Iceni kingdom, and there is nothing that I can do about that."

He slammed his fist on the table. "But there is. The Romans have no more than forty thousand men in all Pretannia. Ten thousand of those are in the south spread along the entire coast—ten thousand are in the north at Lindum—and fifteen thousand, maybe more, with Paullinus himself in the west. At the very most there cannot be more than five thousand at Camulodunum. The Iceni, the Coritani, the Trinovantes, and the Catuvellauni could raise three hundred thousand! We could wipe Camulodunum off the face of the earth if we wanted to."

"Caratacus tried it, and so did your father, and look what happened to them! And anyway, the other tribes would not follow me into war."

The young king leaned forward in his chair and spread his hands on the table. "You are a powerful woman, Boudicca, and much respected. The Coritani would march alongside the Iceni, that I guarantee, and so too would the Catuvellauni, they have an old score to settle as well as more recent grievances—and look what is happening to the Trinovantian territory around Camulodunum, the Trinovantes have grievance enough, believe me! This so-called 'colonia' that Scapula introduced is bleeding the very life out of the Trinovantes. Under this system any Roman soldier who reaches retiring age and who wishes to remain in Pretannia is given a grant of land on which to settle, regardless of who it might have belonged to before—half a hide for a common soldier, I believe, a hide for a centurion, and so on. This is bad enough but such is their greed that they are grabbing ten and twenty times the amount of their grant. There is one ruffian of a centurion who laid claim to an entire valley five miles long and drove out the Trinovantian families who had been living there for centuries! And what happens when the Trinovantians complain to the military—nothing! The authorities turn a blind eye because they know that when they too reach retiring age they can do likewise."

Boudicca made as if to speak but she could not stop the angry young king in full flight. "And it's all-right for you wealthy Iceni," he went on, "but look what is happening to the rest of us! The Romans told us that if we cooperated in the so-called Romanization of Pretannia, we would all make vast profits from trade, but instead we are all hopelessly in debt to the Roman moneylenders. In anticipation of these mythical profits we were encouraged to borrow vast sums of gold to build new towns for our people and new Roman-style villas for ourselves. Beautiful and luxurious they may be—I live in a style that no previous king of the Coritani would have thought possible—but I have no way of repaying my debt if I live to be a hundred years old, I can barely keep up the payments on the interest. And all the families of the nobility that I know are in the same position!"

"Who is your moneylender?"

"Seneca, the philosopher, at Camulodunum—used to be Nero's tutor, I believe. Most of us go to him. He's the biggest but he is by no means the only one. Catus Deccianus himself, the procurator, is calling in huge amounts of gold. He said that the subsidies that Claudius gave us to secure our cooperation were loans, not gifts, and so we have to go to Seneca for yet more gold to pay off Deccianus. And in addition to all this they have tricked us into financing this wretched Imperial Cult. The Temple that we built for them at Camulodunum was supposed to have been dedicated to both the Emperor *and* to Rome, but it was dedicated to Nero only."

"To his Numen, I believe," said Boudicca, "the divine force that supposedly guides the Emperor, not the Emperor's person itself."

"Well, whatever it's dedicated to; we paid for it! They set up a provincial council to serve the cult, and each town, or civitas as they call it, has to send delegates to this council, and the annual priesthood of the province is elected from these delgates. We welcomed it at first because we thought that at least the priests of the Roman cult would be Pretannic, but it was not until after we had gone through all this did we discover that it was the priesthood who were required to bear the cost of the cult, including the cost of building the Temple—so once more we had to borrow from the Roman moneylenders!"

Queen Boudicca rose and faced the young king. "I listened with patience when you said all this to my guests, even though they had come to honor my dead husband, not to listen to your tirade. And now patiently I have listened to it all again. But enough is enough, Cori! If you want a rebellion then raise one yourself!"

His face was set with anger. "I cannot do so without the Iceni, and you know it," he said bitterly. "And what is more, a combined army would follow you, Boudicca, but they would not follow me. Without you there cannot possibly be a rebellion!"

"Then so be it," she said angrily. "I am tired of war and tired of intrigue. Leave me in peace!"

He rose and threw his cloak around his shoulders and buckled his sword. "Peace," he said acidly. "There can be no peace under Roman rule!" He strode for the door. "Very well, Boudicca—if you wish to skulk in hiding in your widow's robes and leave your kingdom to be ravaged by these bloody-handed barbarians, then do so. The day will come when you will remember my words and regret that you paid them no heed. When that day comes you know where to find me!"

Three days later the slaves from the procuratorial office arrived at Lynn and arrogantly demanded the surrender of the kingdom. Boudicca, imperious as she was, endeavored to accede to their demands with dignity, but they, being slaves, delighted in having a queen at their mercy. "Since you are no longer a queen," said one of them sneeringly, "you will have no further need of this," and he plucked the jeweled crown from her head and tucked it inside his robe. She tried to snatch it back but he pushed her away so violently that she staggered and fell to the ground. They laughed and pricked her with swords, and then warming to their game they stripped her robe and flogged her naked body, laughing and shouting obscene jests as she tried to cover her aging breasts. Attracted by her cries her three daughters came running and the slaves' eyes grew red at this more comely prospect. They bound Boudicca naked to a stone pillar and in front of her eyes they stripped and raped her daughters repeatedly and commited foul and obscene acts.

Some time later, after the slaves had gone, the terrified servants crept from hiding and released the queen and sent messengers hurrying to carry the news to the Iceni nobles. Within the hour a dozen arrived at the palace and were admitted to the great hall to find the still naked Boudicca tenderly washing the blood and the filth from her daughters' ravaged bodies. She rose to greet them. "My Lords," she said with great dignity, "I, your Queen, and the princesses royal stand naked before you so that you may see what shame the Romans have brought upon our House and upon our people!"

The elder noble stepped forward and gently laid his own cloak around the Queen's shoulders, and at a signal the servants led the weeping princesses away. "Your majesty," he said softly, "this outrage will be revenged even though my life and that of my sons be forfeit in so doing!"

For two days the rioting raged in the streets of the Iceni capital of Lynn, and the detachment of Roman soldiers made many arrests in retaliation. At the end of that time the whole Iceni warrior force arose and put to death every Roman at Lynn. The slaves who had outraged their Queen were castrated and dismembered, and their armless and legless torsos were hoisted onto the city walls to die.

That night messengers went thundering through the land to the Coritani, the Catuvellauni, and the Trinovantes, and seven days later one hundred thousand warriors marched on Camulodunum, their numbers swelling with every mile they marched. Lulled into a sense of security by Iceni sympathizers, the Roman garrison at Camulodunum was taken completely by surprise. When the rebels arrived they found the town open, undefended, with no emergency ramparts built, and neither had the non-combatants been evacuated. The procurator, Catus Deccianus, was not at Camulodunum but in Londinium to the south. The garrison commander sent messengers to Londinium for help but Deccianus could only spare two hundred men, and even these arrived too late. Camulodunum, the Roman town of half-timbered houses, was burnt to the ground, the garrison was massacred, and the remnants of the Roman forces who withdrew into the Temple to make a last stand were overwhelmed in two days.

News of the uprising reached Petillius Cerialis, the legate of Legio IX entrenched in two major fortresses on the River Trent in the north on the Brigantian frontier. Cerialis marched with half a legion, a vexillation of some 2,500 infantry, plus cavalry. As he hurried south to the rescue he was ambushed, his infantry massacred, and he himself and his cavalry had to retreat hastily back to his fortress at Longthorpe.

Four thousand Romans had died, and three days later the grim news reached Paullinus in the west, but by that time two hundred and thirty thousand Pretannic warriors, flushed with the greatest victory in their history, were marching on Verulamium.

The news reached Paullinus just as he was returning to the mainland from the island of Mona where he had settled the Druid question once and for all. It was therefore with a grim satisfaction, and a renewed confidence in his own ability, that he now turned his attention to the east to face this other threat. He knew that he could not reach the Catuvellauni capital in time. He had no alternative but to abandon Verulamium to its fate and concentrate his forces at Londinium. He sent messengers racing south to Legio II at Isca Dumnoniorum, or Exeter as the natives called it, to command them to withdraw with all speed to Londinium. He himself, his general staff and cavalry divisions, left North Wales to head southeast at full speed to arrive there before them, leaving his infantry to follow at forced-march pace. With the cavalry from Legio XIV at Viroconium, Legio XX at Glevum, and Legio II at Isca Dumnoniorum, he should be able to hold Londinium until all three sets of infantry arrived.

The legate of Legio II in Exeter was absent, on leave in Rome, when Paullinus' message arrived. Poenius Postumus held temporary command. He simply did not believe the message he received—it seemed too incredible that Camulodunum was lost and that half of Legio IX at Lindum had been massacred. There must be some dreadful mistake somewhere—and anyway, how by Zeus was he supposed to march the legion to Londinium when they were spread out in dozens of marching camps along the whole south coast? It would take weeks to round them up into one coherent force— and what would happen to the entire southern region if he abandoned it now? The only proper course for him to pursue was to remain precisely where he was, and he sent a message to this effect to Paullinus at Londinium.

When Paullinus arrived at Londinium he found that the procurator, Catus Deccianus, had fled from Pretannia to Gaul, and there were simply too few troops to defend the town. His only hope was the cavalry from Legio II, with their infantry to follow. Three days later the message from Postumus arrived and Paullinus vowed there and then that when this was over he would personally see to it that Postumus never held a command rank ever again.

By this time further messengers arrived with the news that the Pretannic horde had sacked Verulamium, massacred the garrison, and even now were pouring south to Londinium. Paullinus had no alternative but to abandon the town and take the garrison troops with him back up Watling Street to rejoin the infantry battalions of Legio XIV and XX who were hurrying down it. They met at a valley just north of Towcester, and there they paused to take stock of their situation. Two days later the message arrived that Londinium had gone the way of Camulodunum and Verulamium. Adding the figures up Paullinus grimly estimated that in the destruction of the three towns, plus the defeat of Legio IX, nearly ten thousand Roman legionaries had died and no fewer than sixty thousand Romanized Pretannic citizens and allies. The figures were hardly believable.

Paullinus had ten thousand men at Towcester, and ranged against him were two hundred and thirty thousand of Boudicca's horde—odds of 23 to 1. Roman forces were quite used to fighting against odds of 5 to 1, but to reduce the odds to that figure he would need another thirty-six thousand men, nearly four full legions brigaded with auxiliary cohorts. He knew that it would be pointless to appeal to Rome for such reinforcements, Rome was having its own problems in the east where Armenia had been lost and where the Romans were almost powerless to take counter-measures owing to the total demoralization of their troops. If there were any legions to spare they would be sent to Armenia, not to Britannia. Advising the Senate in Rome too early as to the situation in Pretannia would throw them into a panic, coming as it would on top of the disastrous Armenian situation. He must deal with this local matter himself with the few resources at his command. There would be time enough to advise Rome when the rebellion had been put down. If he failed . . . but Paullinus refused to even consider such a possibility. Since there was no possibility in obtaining reinforcements from Rome, his general staff were vociferous in their advice that he had no alternative but to abandon the whole of central, west, and north Pretannia to Boudicca, and withdraw Legios XX, XIV, and IX to the south to join Legio II. From that strengthened position they could then begin the task of re-conquest. By all military standards their advice was correct, but he knew that such re-conquest could take five, even ten years—and he further knew that he himself would be withdrawn in disgrace from the governorship, and Paullinus was not a man to submit to such defeat too easily.

For three days Paullinus listened quietly and calmly to the arguments and urgings from his officers, but at the end of that time he shook his head and said firmly: "Gentlemen, I have never run from an enemy in my life and I do not intend to start now. The Fourteenth

Legion is at full strength of ten thousand men—6,000 Roman legionaries and 4,000 in auxiliary cohorts. We are here at Towcester and here we will remain. Flushed with victory Boudicca will undoubtedly seek us out, but we have several days at least in which to choose our ground carefully. They will attack us as an ill-disciplined rabble and will impale themselves on our defensive wall. Are there any questions?"

There was a stunned silence. It had been a possibility, true, but they had not dreamed that he would match their tiny force against Boudicca's horde. The infantry commander cleared his throat. "The odds are 23 to 1—it is impossible!"

"We will choose our ground carefully," said Paullinus icily, "such that they will only be able to bring a fraction of their force against us at any one time—thus the odds are reduced to normal proportions."

The cavalry commander shook his head vehemently. "It is suicide! The Senate would not approve!"

"If we succeed," said Paullinus sarcastically, "the Senate will approve wholeheartedly."

"And if we fail," the infantry commander retorted, "there will be none of us left to face their anger!"

"Good. I see that you understand the situation," he said briskly. Paullinus rose and donned his cloak. "I will leave you to your deliberations, but this I tell you —whether you like it or not the Fourteenth Legion will meet Boudicca here at Towcester, and that is final!"

The following day Paullinus sent scouts out to the east in three directions to give early warning of the approaching horde, while he and his sullen general staff toured the area for suitable ground on which to make their stand. In a small, narrow valley to the northwest of the hamlet of Towcester they found the near perfect conditions they wanted. The head of the valley and the sides were steep-to and thickly wooded. It would be impossible for any force to attack the rear or flanks down those tangled slopes in any serious numbers. The mouth of the valley was an open plain but very narrow, no more than seventy yards across. Paullinus nodded to himself in satisfaction—he doubted that anyone could attack across that plain with any more than five thousand at a time, and therefore at the actual front line of the battle the odds would be about even, since he could only use half his own force at a time. Also the valley was so boxed-in that the Roman legionaries would not be able to escape—they would have no alternative but to stand and fight, a point that did not escape his general staff. Wisely he chose not to move the full legion to the valley until Boudicca's horde was actually sighted—he did not want the legionaries to appreciate the same point until it was too late.

Paullinus noted with evident satisfaction that the rebels did not arrive as one compact army group but in dribs and drabs in bands of a hundred or less—evidence of their obvious lack of discipline and organization. The legion moved into the valley in the late afternoon, watched by the early arrivals who were grouped on a nearby hill. Trees were felled and dragged across the plain to form a wall across the front, but low enough to be leapt at full gallop by their own cavalry if necessary. Camp fires were lit at strategic points and an unusual number of guards were posted to watch through the night hours.

The main body of the rebel army arrived during the afternoon of the following day. Young Cori, King of the Coritani, was delighted with the situation. "They are trapped," he gloated. "We will massacre them to the last man!"

Boudicca was doubtful. "They had plenty of time and plenty of warning. Why have they chosen such a position? Paullinus is no fool."

"Because obviously he does not trust his troops not to run. Now they have no choice but to fight—and that suits us very well. If you agree we will attack at dawn, and with two hundred and thirty thousand against a mere ten thousand there will not be a Roman left alive by noon!"

So confident were the rebels that before dawn they brought up their supply wagons, emptied them, lined them up across the plain, and used them as observation platforms for their excited women and youngsters to watch the coming battle. The warriors themselves milled around in one vast sea of bodies, eager to fight but under no control or discipline whatsoever, waiting for Queen Boudicca herself to give the signal for the attack.

The Romans, by contrast, were drawn up in a rigidly disciplined formation across the entire width of the valley behind the wall of felled trees, going back rank upon rank with the cavalry at the rear and with Paullinus and the general staff in the center.

Corio and Boudicca, on horseback, watched the scene from a slight rise in the ground to one side of the plain. Corio was grinning hugely with suppressed excitement. "It is time, Boudicca—give the signal!"

She nodded and raised her sword high. She waited a few seconds and then brought it down—and with a vast animal roar the horde broke into a run straight at the Roman lines.

Of all the warrior-kings throughout Pretannic history only Cunobelin and after him his son, Caratacus, had any experience of directing the battle of a huge army—inter-tribal warfare was usually conducted with no more than a few thousand on either side. It was not until the rebel army began to bear down on the Roman lines did Corio begin to appreciate how huge the army was and how narrow the valley. Too late he realized that he should have sent the army to the attack in successive waves instead of one vast sea of screaming men.

The first to arrive had to pause to negotiate the line of tree-trunks, but those following behind, not understanding what was happening at the front, pressed on, pushing and shoving in their eagerness to get at the Romans. Those at the front, with the pressure of nearly a quarter of a million men behind them, and given no room in the press to adequately wield their swords, found themselves jammed against the logs unable to move.

The Roman front rank were kneeling behind their shields, their spears embedded in the ground, points forward. It was their task not to fight but to maintain a living barricade behind and through which the second and third ranks could wield their swords and spears. The second rank, also kneeling, now rose at a barked command and in a single flowing movement hurled their spears into the thick of the rebel warriors. The second rank dropped again to a kneeling position and the third rank, on command, also hurled their spears into the thick of struggling bodies. The second rank rose again and a further rain of death fell on the rebel army—and then the third rank, and then the second— eight times the rain of spears flashed across the narrow gap, four from each rank. The second and third ranks, now spearless, grasped their swords in anticipation of the next command. Along the line of tree-trunks over five hundred Pretannic warriors lay dead or dying, transfixed by spears, and so far not a Roman life had been lost.

At a command the front rank turned their shields sideways and so created gaps between the row of spears embedded in the ground. At another command the second and third ranks trotted forward through the line of spears and engaged the enemy with swords at the line of tree-logs. Paullinus, watching the fierce hand-to-hand struggle, allowed the action to continue for a full fifteen minutes and then nodded to the legate. A further command rang out and the Romans broke off the engagement and retreated back through the front rank, who promptly shifted their shields and closed the wall. The second and third ranks did not pause but continued right through the Roman ranks to the rear. What had been the fourth and fifth ranks now trotted forward and became the new second and third ranks, and the whole maneuver was repeated. Again eight times the spears flashed across the gap, and again the Romans advanced to engage with swords at the line of logs. The pile of Pretannic dead along the line was now so high that those who pressed behind could gain no ground whatsoever.

Up on the high rise Boudicca and Corio watched the slaughter in horror. The precision of the Roman maneuver was terrifying. The Pretannic dead already numbered close to a thousand and there could not be more than a dozen or so dead Romans along the line. "Get them out!" shouted Boudicca. "It is impossible this way. Get them out!"

Corio urged his horse forward and down the slope, bellowing commands as he rode. Because of the noise and daze of battle it took him a long time to make himself understood, and still the slaughter went on, but at last the army began to turn and move away to the rear.

Paullinus smiled coldly, waited until the rebel army was spread out over the whole plain, and then nodded to his cavalry commander. Two full cavalry divisions came thundering down the outside of both flanks at full gallop, leapt the line of logs and were into the retreating lines, swords flashing, and more and more Pretannic warriors were cut down. Goaded by this harrying the center turned at bay and spears began to whistle towards the galloping Romans. Two horses came crashing down, and three more, and the cavalry broke off the engagement and galloped back over the line of logs and back to the rear of the Roman formation, leaving the plain littered with dead.

But Corio at least had learned the lesson quickly. After a great deal of shouting he finally made himself understood and he sent in roughly 5,000 warriors only, the first two hundred of whom had very strict instructions. Protected by a wall of shields head-high they attached vine-ropes to the tree-trunks in the center of the line and dragged them clear. The Roman infantry commander turned to Paullinus. "Shall I send a detachment to close the gap?"

"No—we will use the fall-back-and-encircle maneuver. Make sure your timing is right."

A gap thirty yards wide had been opened and the five thousand began to pour through, but instead of maintaining their rigid front line the Roman formation suddenly altered. The entire middle portion from the front rank almost to the rear swiftly but calmly swung aside to each flank so that instead of a solid rectangle their formation was like an open-ended box. The inrushing rebel horde thus met no resistance but poured straight through into the box, with the Roman ranks now on either side of them facing the middle.

At precisely the right moment the two cavalry divisions again came thundering down the outside of the flanks, and when they reached the front they turned inwards and fought their way into the middle through the thick of Pretannic warriors, and thus cut the invading force almost exactly in half. The rear half of the Pretannic force now found themselves facing a solid line of Roman cavalry, whereas the leading half numbering two and a half thousand found themselves in the very middle of the Roman force surrounded on all sides. At a barked command the Roman ranks advanced towards the middle with the odds in their favor of 2 to 1 while the cavalry pushed forward and drove the rear half back across the plain. Of the two and a half thousand inside the Roman formation not one survived. Of the two and a half thousand fleeing before the cavalry charge only two hundred made it safely back to their own lines.

From the two actions over seven thousand Pretannic warriors lay dead and dying, whereas the Romans had lost barely a hundred men.

A fierce argument broke out between Corio and Boudicca. The Iceni queen wanted to withdraw, to abandon the battle altogether. "Too many have died already," she said fiercely. "Too many, Corio!" But the young king was furiously adamant. "We must expect losses—we cannot stop now. We must overwhelm them by sheer weight of numbers!"

Again he sent in a force of five thousand, the leading few hundred protected by a wall of shields, and this time they dragged the entire line of tree-trunks clear so that the two armies now faced each other unimpeded. The Romans formed their rectangle again, and the front rank dug their spears in the ground points-forward, and knelt behind their shields to await the onslaught.

"This will be their last attack," said Paullinus calmly. "When we have beaten them off the battle will have been won."

The infantry and cavalry commanders looked at each other. There was still two hundred and twenty thousand against their own ten thousand—the chances were still remote.

The entire Pretannic force now began to move towards the Roman defensive wall, but it was noticeable that their earlier eagerness to fight was considerably diminished. Young Corio, on horseback, led the advance, but his heart sank as he looked along the line of his warriors. Despite their numerical superiority their expressions were doubtful, fearful, and they moved forward slowly, reluctantly—their seven thousand dead companions did not inspire confidence. As they drew near the Roman lines a rain of spears again flew out to meet them, and again, and again, and the rebel warriors began to die. Corio, bellowing encouragement, tried to urge them forward more swiftly but if anything the pace slowed even further.

The rebel army came up against the Roman formation in a ponderous, slow-moving, massive wave. Had they gone forward at full charge their sheer weight might have broken the Roman line, but as it was the line absorbed the initial shock and remained firm. The second rank of Roman legionaries, standing virtually astride their kneeling comrades of the front rank, stabbed and slashed through the wall of shields at the mass of living bodies that pressed up against the line of embedded spears. Hundreds of Pretannic warriors were dying every second along the entire seventy-yard front line in that first clash, and as the number of dead grew they formed a natural barrier against those who pressed from behind. At several points the Roman front line collapsed as the kneeling legionaries were cut down, but as each one fell another from behind took his place.

The Roman rear ranks, with terrifying precision and regularity, hurled a flight of spears once every minute over the heads of their comrades, aiming at a line twenty yards back in the Pretannic mass. The rebels along that line could do nothing but endure the hail of spears as they pressed forward to take their place at the front.

Corio, his sword held high, bellowing commands, took a Roman spear in his lower chest. For a moment he remained rigidly upright, and then blood gushed from his mouth and he toppled sideways and fell into the sea of struggling bodies. The horse, freed of control, reared in panic, lashing out with his hooves, until a spear thudded into his throat, and he fell across the wall of dead warriors, his legs kicking feebly as his life's blood pumped from his torn throat to stain the ground.

Again the cavalry came thundering down the outside flanks and attacked the rebel army on either side, sweeping along their flanks, cutting and slashing down at the rebel warriors.

During a brief lull, as the rebel army hesitated, Paullinus took the opportunity to move the Roman forces forward beyond the line of Pretannic dead, and gained fifteen yards before establishing again the front-rank living barricade. Unemcumbered by the dead the two front lines could now engage more fully, and a second line of dead began to grow.

For two hours the slaughter went on. Every so often the Romans would advance ten or fifteen yards, exchanging their front ranks for their rear ranks in order that no legionary remained for too long in the thick of the front line fighting. Boudicca, watching in silent horror from the high rise, could scarcely believe the carnage below her. Between five and six hundred of her warriors were being hacked to death every single minute, and still the battle dragged on interminably. Incredible though it seemed, it was obvious that those at the rear of the Pretannic army had no idea of the slaughter taking place at the front, and still they pressed forward giving no chance for their comrades to retreat. Those at the front had no alternative but to stand and be butchered.

But finally, though it took two hours, those at the rear began to realize that instead of pressing forward it was they who were gradually being pushed back yard by yard. With this realization some of them began to move away, and then more followed suit until finally Boudicca knew with an odd mixture of shame and relief that the battle was over. As the rear ranks began to stream away the pressure was relieved on those in the forward ranks, who now began to retreat more rapidly until finally they were able to turn and run. Within minutes the entire rebel army was in full flight.

The Roman infantry commander kept a tight control on his men. It would be disastrous if the Roman formation was abandoned in the excitement of pursuit —they were still incredibly and overwhelmingly outnumbered, but he did push forward faster and faster though maintaining their same rigid pattern. On the flanks the cavalry swept along the edges of the fleeing army cutting them down as easily as scything wheat.

The supply wagons were directly in the path of the routed army and soon were engulfed in the sea of panic-stricken warriors. Wagons were tipped over and women fell screaming to the ground, dozens and dozens of them being trampled underfoot as the rebel army fled away from the terrible Roman machine advancing across the plain at their backs.

The rebel army was in full flight, and after pursuing them for a mile or more Paullinus called a halt and pulled his forces back into the valley to make camp. He and his general staff rode to the high-rise to survey the scene. Across the entire plain from side to side, from front to rear, was a carpet of Pretannic dead, and the eye had to search hard to find a Roman tunic in that sea of death.

Paullinus was totally unmoved by the scene of carnage. "Gentlemen," he said coldly and calmly, "that which you said was impossible has been accomplished. I do not think I need comment further on your capacity for military assessment!"

A centurion came towards them carrying the body of a woman across his shoulder. As he drew near he bent and laid her on the grass. "Queen Boudicca," he said briefly.

"There are no wounds that I can see," said Paullinus. "How came she to die?"

"Poison—by her own hand apparently," the man said laconically.

The Roman commander stared down contemptuously at the woman who had raised the largest army in all Pretannic history, and the army that had suffered the most humiliating defeat. "Throw her body with the rest!" he said curtly. "Bury our own Roman dead but leave the rest. Bring me a tally within the hour." The man saluted and withdrew.

"Gentlemen," said Paullinus, "we will camp here tonight and march for Camulodunum tomorrow. Believe me, today's events are only a taste of the revenge that I shall inflict upon these wretched people!"

An hour later the tally had been completed and the infantry commander brought the figures to Paullinus. "A total of close to 70,000 Pretannic dead!" he said gleefully.

The other commanders exchanged delighted glances. Seventy thousand! It seemed impossible.

"And the Roman tally?" said Paullinus.

The legate smiled. "Just over 400!"

Paullinus was silent and they wondered what sour remark their cold commander would make. He did, however, surprise them all. "The Fourteenth Legion, including you its officers," he said quietly, "has conducted itself with unprecedented courage in the face of overwhelming odds. Today's action must rank as one of the most resounding victories in the whole history of the Roman army. I shall prevail upon the Emperor to grant Legio XIV Gemina the title of 'Martia Victrix.'"

The legate grinned delightedly. *Legio XIV gemina martia victrix!* An honor that could only reflect favourably on the careers of those officers who had brought such distinction to their legion.

Three days later the news of Boudicca's incredible defeat reached Legio II at Exeter. Poenius Postumus, still in temporary command, knew that it was only a matter of time before he would be brought to trial and disgraced for his refusal to go to the governor's aid. He knew what had to be done and fell on his sword and died in agony. When the news of his suicide reached Paullinus in Camulodunum he said coldly and curtly: "A fitting end, I think—certainly a better decision than his earlier one," and then refused to discuss the matter further.

Alone later that night Paullinus permitted himself the luxury of an entire wineskin. From a situation a few days earlier when it seemed that he would have to abandon half of Pretannia, and probably would have been recalled to Rome in disgrace, he had achieved glorious distinction for himself and had probably ensured Roman rule in these savage barbaric islands for hundreds of years to come. There was no doubt in his mind that great honor, wealth, and high position waited for him in Rome when his present term of Office came to an end—and he owed it all to Boudicca.

He raised the wineskin and drank deeply. "To Boudicca!" he said aloud and grinned. "My favorite woman!" He was not displeased with the turn of events —not displeased at all.

On the island of Mona and in the valley at Towcester the dead bodies of the slain began to decompose. Already the dead eyes had been torn from their sockets by carrion crows, and already the maggots were busy at their grisly work.

The smell of death hung over the land and rode with the winds far and wide. Those who had not marched with Boudicca at Towcester shut fast their doors and ventured not abroad. Huddled by their hearths they trembled with fear of what this omen might portend. Soon the survivors of the slaughter began to straggle through the hamlets on their way back to their own homelands, and the tale was told and retold. As the dreadful news spread further and further the people knew in their hearts that they were beaten and that never again could they lift their courage and their resolve to challenge the might of Rome.

Pretannia was at last truly conquered.

chapter ten

Gilda, Mistress of the Oak, paddled slowly across the Menai Straits towards the island of Mona dreading what she might find. Nobody had been able to tell her what Paullinus and the Fourteenth Legion had been doing in the west before having to turn eastwards to deal with the ill-advised Boudiccan rebellion. Ten days *be-*

fore the slaughter at Towcester, in her forest camp near Glaeston, she had tried to contact Cranog on the inner and had failed. She had tried again the following day, and every day since, but each time her vision had been clouded with waves of impenetrable darkness that had stunk of terror and of death. For ten days, as she had hurried northwards along the deep forest trails, she had lived with the torment of not knowing what had happened. Deep within her very being she feared that the actuality of what she would find would be even more unutterable than any scene her imagination could conjure.

As she drew near the beach her worst fears began to be realized, and by the time she drew the boat up onto the sand she was already in a state of shock. Slowly and dazedly she began to walk along the shoreline staring around her at the scene of indescribable horror. The state of shock protected her in part from too great an impact, but when she climbed the earthworks and found her father she broke down completely, and for a full hour she sat beside him, the tears streaming silently down her face.

When the reaction subsided she roused herself and walked inland a little to the ring of stones that Cranog and the seniors had been using for their rituals. She sat herself in the East and invoked the Guardians of the four Cardinal Points. The preliminaries completed she closed her eyes and rose to the inner plane Lodge. Once there she approached the altar and in a powerfully vibrant voice she invoked the presence of that inner plane being, the Keeper of the Akhasic Record, and by right of her seniority in the Druid order, and by right of her attainments on the inner level that none could deny, she asked to see the record of all that had transpired on the island of Mona that had brought the horror that she had just witnessed. The Keeper acknowledged her right, and the veils were withdrawn and she was permitted to see the dreadful scenes unfold themselves again.

She was drawn, as it were, into the vision and became part of it. The inner plane Lodge faded away and she found herself hovering over the island. She was aware that far away in the east the inflamed Iceni nobles were calling to arms a vast rebellion to avenge their outraged Queen Boudicca, but they had not yet begun their march southwards to Camulodunum. She was also aware that Paullinus and half the Fourteenth Legion had just left their fort at Virconium and were marching westward towards the coast. Below her she could see the hive of activity as the Druid priesthood prepared themselves to accept their destiny, and on the beach she could see the figures of Cranog, Kerrin, and Melvina walking together deep in conversation.

She drifted lower to overhear their talk, dreading what she must see and hear.

* * *

Cranog, Kerrin, and Melvina walked along the shoreline staring across the sea to the mainland to the east. "Will it be long?" said Melvina softly.

The Arch-Mage shook his head. "No, the message was quite clear—half a legion, Legio XIV, I believe, is already on its way here. They should arrive tomorrow or the following day." He smiled wryly. "It took a full legion to beat Caratacus, a full legion to hold Venutius at bay, and a legion and a half to scatter the Silurians and the Ordovices. We apparently only rate half a legion!"

"We are the priesthood, not warriors," said Melvina.

"True."

"Priesthood we may be," growled Kerrin, "but there will be many a Roman who will leave his bones here on Mona!"

Cranog smiled. "But not from any deed of yours or mine," he said ruefully. "I am too old to even raise a sword, let alone wield it—and you are not the man you once were, Kerrin."

The dark one nodded. "True enough—it is a battle for the younger priests." He paused and scuffed his sandal across a mound of sand. "But I am glad that I am here." He looked at Cranog. "I have not spoken of this to anyone but there was a time when I seriously considered leaving Druidry and starting a small ritual group of my own—and there have been many times since," he added heavily, "when I wondered whether I had chosen correctly." He smiled. "But today there are no doubts at all—I would rather be here at this moment in history than anywhere else."

Cranog put his arm around his friend's shoulders. "I am glad," he said simply. "I knew of your doubts and rejoiced in your decision."

"You knew?" said Kerrin softly.

"Yes, the signs are always unmistakable. This type of choice in many differing disguises is put to a priest at every phase in his personal evolution. It is an oft-repeated crossroads at which you have to decide your future direction. It is a form of initiatory test for the next phase. One way or another it is always a choice as to whether you wish to follow your own will or the will of the Great One."

"What would have happened had I chosen to leave?" he said carefully.

"Who can say, but I suspect that you would have conducted yourself and your group with honor, dedication, and sincerity—at least to begin with. But because you would have been following your own human will in spiritual matters, you would have undoubtedly attracted influences that would have led you away from your high ideals, and from there it would have been a short step to becoming a servant of the dark forces, and it would have taken you many lives to find your way back onto your true path."

Kerrin was silent for a moment and then said: "Why didn't you warn me?"

"Because each priest has to face the choice alone. There are some moments of truth that each of us has to face alone. Melvina here is faced with such a moment now." He looked at the High Priestess sadly. "I would not have mentioned it but for the fact that you were about to speak of it anyway."

She laughed ruefully, but her voice was strained. "You are right," she said. "A moment of truth indeed." She hesitated, and then said: "It concerns courage."

The two priests remained silent, waiting for her to

continue. "I already know of the problem," said Cranog gently. "It is a matter that you have to face alone, but you can speak of it to us if it will help."

She stared at the ground. "In all my many lives," she said quietly, "I do not think that I have ever died a violent death, and the thought terrifies me. I have lost count of the number of times I have dreamed of a Roman sword being plunged into my body—the pain and blood of it—I do not think that I can face that agony. I would do anything rather than face that appalling prospect!"

"You are living with the terror now," said Cranog. "The actual death itself will be as nothing by comparison. But let Kerrin speak of the matter, he has a greater experience of these matters than I."

Kerrin sighed. "Yes, I have died a violent death many times, and I can assure you, Melvina, of my own personal knowledge and memory that such a death itself is far less horrible than the dreadful anticipation of it. There is no pain, no agony in such a swift death —the shock of the impact mercifully numbs the body. It is true that you are thus flung into the inner like a spear, but it is all over so quickly that there is no time to even register any pain. What you are living through now is far worse."

"I hope you are right," she said, "but you will forgive me, I know, when I say that I am not convinced."

"We understand," said Cranog. "A few words can bring comfort but they are no substitute for a memory of actual experience. However, now that we have spoken of the matter I can now ask a service of you that will help both you and others." He shaded his eyes against the evening sun. "If you, the High Priestess, have these fears you can be sure that they are shared by many of our brethren. Like you they will not speak of it, thinking it a shameful thing to know fear. Move among them, speak to them, let them know that they are not alone in their fear, tell them what Kerrin has just told us. Your words will not allay the fear but they might make it more endurable."

"I will," she said. "And thank you."

She bowed and moved away, and Cranog turned to Kerrin. "It's the waiting that breeds these fears," he said sadly. "I will speak to the brethren at this evening's ritual—it may be our last. Is all in readiness?"

"Yes—one or two small details only to attend to." He hesitated and then said: "Do you have no fears, Cranog?"

"Of death itself, no—like you I have died a warior's death before now. My fear is of the wisdom of submitting all Druidry to death by the sword."

Kerrin shook his head. "It has been decreed by the inner that the days of Druidry are over. Would you go against the inner?"

"No, of course not—but have I really interpreted inner plane wishes correctly? I have no illusions about myself, Kerrin," he said quietly. "In any other age of Druidry I would have been a good ritual officer, but no more. I am not of the stature to be a true Arch-Mage of all Druidry." He waved Kerrin silent. "Don't deny the truth, my friend, it is unpriestlike. I am nowhere near the stage of advancement that Drucius had reached—and compared to the great Arch-Mages of the past, like the almost legendary Druthin, I am a mere neophyte."

"That may be true, but there is no shame in that."

"Indeed, but my fear is that my lack of understanding, my inadequate rapport with the inner, may be causing me to lead the whole of Druidry to an unnecessary death."

"But Drucius himself spoke of the coming dissolution of Druidry."

"Dissolution, yes, but he did not speak of death. Josue, the Culdee, might be right. Maybe I should have simply disbanded Druidry and left it to each member to decide whether to return to their various tribes or join the Christian Church."

They were silent for some while and then Kerrin said: "I cannot answer the question except to say that I believe that what we are doing is correct and in accordance with inner plane wishes."

"I hope you are right, for if not then I will have led a thousand men, women, and children to their deaths—unnecessarily and against inner plane wishes—and I will be remembered as the most cursed Druid in all history!"

* * *

Gilda, still hovering on the inner, moved away across the sea to the mainland. Moving forward a day and a half in time she drifted down to hover over the Fourteenth Legion that had now arrived on the western coastline.

* * *

Paullinus and his commanders walked slowly along the shoreline staring across the sea to the island in the west. "How many Druids are there?" said Paullinus.

"A thousand by all accounts, no more—and some of them are women."

"Then it should be easy. When will the boats be ready?"

"The rafts for the men, by dusk tomorrow. The cavalry can swim their horses, it isn't far."

"Very well, we will cross at dawn on the day after tomorrow."

"You will speak to the men?"

Paullinus frowned and stared hard at his commander. "You think it necessary?"

The man hesitated. "Roman legionaries are noted for their superstitious fears."

"What fears?"

"They say that the Druids are magicians and that they will cause us to drown long before we reach the island—or if we do reach the shore then each man's sword will become a serpent in his hand that will turn and strike him, filling his body with a loathsome poison."

Paullinus raised his eyebrows. "I had no idea," he said drily, "that a common soldier had so much imagination. Do you also have such beliefs, Commander?"

Again the man hesitated—and then shrugged.

"The Druids are indeed famed for their magic—who can estimate their capabilities?"

The silence hung between them. "It is axiomatic in the Roman army," said Paullinus, slowly and dangerously, "that the legionaries fear their officers more than they fear the enemy." He looked at the commander bleakly. "You will personally ensure that Legio XIV are aware that any man who refuses to embark on the boats, or who refuses to engage the enemy on landing, will be charged with treason against Rome, cowardice on the field of battle, and will be executed. Do I make myself clear?"

The man swallowed nervously. "Yes—I understand."

"And Commander," Paullinus added quietly, "I hold you personally responsible. If you are unable to make the matter clear to them I will replace you with someone who can!" His eyes swept the circle of officers. "I will not tolerate disobedience from anyone at any level. The Fourteenth Legion will embark at dawn on the day after tomorrow and they will put to the sword every Druid priest and priestess on the island. That is not a request—it is a command—see to it that it is carried out!"

* * *

On the island of Mona the Druids were assembled around the small stone circle. For some ten long minutes the group had remained silent, deep in meditation. Then Kerrin stroked the gong three times, softly, and their eyes came awake. Cranog rose and walked to the center and stepped up onto the altar stone.

"From those who see the Light of the Great One face to face," he cried powerfully, "I bring you greetings!"

"Greetings!" came the response in a thousand voices.

"To us who as yet are bound by the plane of physical matter they give the assurance that whence they come we may go, if we be found worthy. It is their duty and privilege to stand by us in this our darkest hour, to remind us that death is a gateway of tears and grief, and sometimes of pain, through which we pass to stand in our own true place alongside our brethren of the inner."

He looked round the circle. "In the coming enactment of our destiny none of you shall stand alone. I say unto you that each and every one of you shall feel the comforting hand of an elder brother on the inner, and when you pass through that dark gate you will be welcomed with joy and shall have justly earned a place of honor among our companions in spirit—for I tell you of my own true knowledge that there is no finer deed than the act of laying down your life in the service of all that we hold holy!"

He paused for some long moments, and then he drew himself up. "Brethren of the Order of the White," he thundered, "are you all resolved to share our coming destiny?"

The senior priest of the White stepped forward and bowed low to the Arch-Mage. "We are resolved!" he cried.

Cranog bowed in response, and then straightened. "Brethren of the Order of the Green—are you also similarly resolved?"

The green-robed senior Ovate Druid stepped forward and bowed. "We also are resolved!" he cried in a firm voice.

"Brethren of the Order of the Blue," cried Cranog, "are you similarly resolved?"

A young blue-robed Bard, no more than thirteen years of age, stepped forward and solemnly bowed as his seniors had done before him. "We too are equally resolved!" he cried in his high, boyish voice.

Cranog's eyes softened into deep pools of joy and compassion. "To those of the Bardic Degree who share our destiny," he said softly, "comes a special honor. I say unto you before this assembly of priests and priestesses of the Light that I, Cranog, Arch-Mage of all Druidry, consider it a deep privilege to be numbered among such company," and he spread his hands wide and bowed low in deep obeisance.

He then straightened and raised his arms high,

his face upturned to the evening sky. "We the incarnated Priesthood of the Light are thus resolved!" he thundered. "Let therefore our destiny be fulfilled!"

As his voice rolled through the ancient stone circle the assembly broke softly into the ages-old Sun Chant of the Fourth Degree from the rituals of old Atlantis.

> Helios, helios, quanto rhopantanek,
> Quanto rhopantanek, helioun.
> Waft thou my soul down the River of Naradek,
> Bring it to Light, and to Life, and to Love.

* * *

In the gray half-light of predawn the sea was calm. Four thousand Roman officers and men of Legio XIV in two hundred flat-bottomed raft-type boats paddled slowly across the Menai Straits. In the center of the fleet, surrounded by boats so that the horses were guided in the right direction, swam one hundred cavalry, the men swimming beside their mounts, one hand on the pommel. Paullinus did not hurry—slow and easy—he wanted the legion to arrive together. He glanced at the sky and smiled. The gods were in his favor today—had there been even the slightest turbulence he would have had a problem in launching the clumsy boats at all, let alone keep them so perfectly grouped—and certainly he would have had to leave the cavalry behind. It was a pleasant feeling to be so obviously in favor. He glanced behind him and saw that the sun would be above the horizon in a very few minutes —his timing had been perfect.

As they drew near the island he could see that the beach was crowded with figures. "A warm reception awaits us, I think," said Paullinus. "That high mound that runs the entire length of the beach is obviously some sort of earthworks."

"No problem," said the commander of infantry. "If necessary the cavalry can clear the top of defenders in minutes. They are only priests—I don't suppose they have the slightest concept of group formations in battle."

As they came within a hundred yards of the beach many of the Roman soldiers began to glance at each other nervously. The scene on the beach was like nothing they had ever seen before. A horde of a thousand priests and more milled along the water's edge, demented, screaming like fiends from the underworld, their hair streaming in the wind, brandishing swords. Among them were groups of women, seemingly insane, yelling, tearing their breasts, the veritable Furies themselves. And on top of the earthworks were the senior Druid magician-priests, their arms upraised to the sky calling down curses on the approaching fleet. It was the most nightmarish scene that Paullinus had ever witnessed—it was like a scene from Hades itself.

Some of the Roman soldiers stopped paddling, staring in horror at the scene ahead. The leading line of boats began to waver, and some of them lost way and threatened the formation of the second and third lines of boats behind them. A few more seconds of this and the Roman fleet would be thrown into confusion.

The infantry commander glanced at Paullinus and then stepped forward. He raised his spear and hurled it at the next boat in line which had come to a halt. The spear, carefully aimed, thudded into the wooden cross-beam among the terrified legionaries. "The next spear," he bellowed, "will kill the man who is not paddling!" Some of them grabbed their paddles again and thrust into the water, but some were still staring stupidly at the island ahead. The infantry commander barked an order to his own men and three spears flashed across the gap between the two boats. Two legionaries fell overboard, their blood reddening the water, and a third collapsed across the thwarts writhing in agony, clutching the spear embedded in his bowels. The crew needed no second demonstration. The remaining paddlers worked furiously and brought the craft into line again. Thirty yards along the leading line another boat had come to a halt, but the centurion in command followed the example of his commander and two more legionaries hit the water transfixed by spears. This was enough, and gradually the Roman fleet came into line again and forged ahead.

The infantry commander turned to Paullinus. "Five dead," he reported.

"A small price," said Paullinus indifferently.

A few minutes later the leading line of boats hit the beach, their flat-bottomed structure enabling them to go right in where the water was only a few inches deep, and the infantry began to pour ashore, splashing through the last few yards of shallows.

The resistance was more fierce than they had dreamed possible. The Druids were horribly demented, screaming as though in the very last transports of agony, and such was the ferocity of their seeming insanity that the first wave of Romans staggered under the impact of the onslaught. In the first few seconds a score of Romans lay dead and dying in the shallows, and with them a dozen Druids.

Cerdic, son of the dead Drucius, lay on his back in the shallows, a short Roman knife embedded six inches into his lower chest, the blade lying close alongside his heart. The ripples of a gentle sea stirred the hair of the dying priest and washed the redness from his skin. A half-smile of minor triumph played along his lips. He, Cerdic, the unassuming nonentity, kept so long under the blinding dazzle of the priestly reverence accorded to his dead sire, had at last made his own small gift to Druid history, for by his side, face down as though in shame, lay the bodies of two dead Romans dispatched to the inner by Cerdic's hand.

Kerrin, in command of the beach forces, shook his head helplessly. The demented screaming that had been deliberately used to strike fear into the hearts of the Romans, was having an even greater demoralizing effect on their own forces. Instead of the ordered formation of defenders that they had so carefully planned and rehearsed, the Druids were now indeed a milling horde with no discipline whatsoever. The sheer weight of numbers had caused havoc among the first Romans to land—there were more Roman dead in the water than Druid—but as more and more boats arrived the legionaries quickly formed themselves into disciplined groups and steadily advanced up the beach, shields up, swords slashing a path through Druid bodies. In the first few minutes the Romans lost over a hundred men, but as the battle raged more and more Druids began to die—a hundred, two hundred, their bodies began to litter the beach and the sand ran red with their blood.

Some Druids died hard, their hands frozen in terror, their swords useless, just standing there waiting to be cut down. Others died fiercely, contesting everything thrown at them. One giant Ovate Druid whose name Kerrin was ashamed to have forgotten—his headdress gone, his robe more red than green, his breast torn open by a spear, a score of weeping wounds crying blood, his sword wrenched from his hand—nevertheless, unarmed as he was, took three Roman legionaries crashing to the sand with him and broke the neck of the first and strangled the second even as the third stabbed at him again and again and again until he could move no more.

A Roman centurion, sent staggering aside from his group by a glancing blow from a thrown spear, was dragged to the ground by half a dozen screaming priestesses. Gentle priestesses who had but yesterday sung the Helios Chant with reverence and hope and faith now clawed at the Romans with truly demented hands. Dazed he did nothing to defend himself. Fingers raked his cheeks, nails dug frantically and insanely into his eyes and blood spurted from the sockets. Blinded he tried to rise but they held him down, stabbing with their short knives at every inch of flesh they could see. No single thrust took his life—weakened by a hundred cuts and stabs, his eyes weeping streams of blood, his soul fled shrieking from the scene, and still they shrieked their terror over his dead body, still stabbing and cutting until the tide of battle rolled over them and they themselves died in a sea of wounds.

A young Bard, no more than ten years old, separated from the rest, carefully and calmly grasped the hem of his robe and drew the garment up over his head and cast it aside as unhurriedly and peacefully as though he was undressing for bed. In sheer horror Kerrin watched the boy's puzzled expression as he stared down at the coils of thick tubing that hung down to the sand from his open abdomen. The boy bent and tried to gather the coils and push them back inside himself, but they kept slipping from his hands. He sank to his knees in the sand and looked up at the sky as though seeking an answer to his problem, but mercifully the question froze in his eyes, an answer no longer needed.

Kerrin shook himself and rushed bellowing into the thick of the fighting. Without even striking a blow he died in precisely three seconds, his head almost severed from his neck. Kerrin, the dark one, whose whole life had been spent mostly in doubt had no doubt at death—Druid he had lived and Druid he died.

Up on top of the earthworks Cranog watched in helpless horror, silent, unable to utter a single word as his brethren were slaughtered before his eyes. By his side, equally silent, was Melvina, her hands clutching and unclutching continually. No more than ten minutes had passed since the first Roman raft had landed and already five hundred Druids lay dead and dying.

The remnants of the beach forces were now fleeing back to the earthworks, clambering frantically up the steep slope. The Roman infantry followed more slowly but more disciplined. The cavalry was now ashore and forming into two groups which cantered to opposite ends of the beach and gained the top of the earthworks at the two flanks. Once at the top they turned inwards and came galloping along the defense line towards the center, scattering the defenders as they came. Still without speaking Melvina waited until the cavalry was almost on them and then she simply stepped out in front of the leading horse. Her body was picked up and thrown by the flying hooves, and through the swirling clouds of dust Cranog could see the body being smashed and trampled as the troop passed. Miraculously unscathed, Cranog rushed over to her as the last horse thundered by and knelt by her side. Her face was almost unrecognizable. The jawbone was smashed into a dozen separate pieces, and slivers of white bone protruded through her cheeks. Her skull was curiously dented at one side and there was blood seeping from one ear. Her robe was in tatters and one breast had been so cruelly trampled that it hung to one side attached to her chest by a single strip of skin. Her chest on that side was one huge open wound, and one gleaming white rib protruded into the air. It was incredible that she was still alive. Her eyes were open. Her hands clutched his robe. She tried to speak but couldn't. She shook her head resignedly and blood gushed from her mouth and stained his robe.

Cranog rose calmly and quietly. Driven beyond the capacity to feel any further horror he just stood there watching the scenes of slaughter almost dispassionately. Of the thousand Druid priests and priestesses who had met the invasion just fifteen minutes earlier, only a handful now survived. He watched calmly as Morgana, his companion in earth, mother of his daughter Gilda, was dragged to one side by a dozen blood-spattered legionaries and stripped and laid naked on her back. The soldiers were clearly intent on rape but a centurion strode over to the group and spoke harshly to them. One of the men shrugged and placed the point of his sword between her breasts and just simply rammed it home. Even the bestial shriek of agony that burst from her lips caused no reaction in the Arch-Mage.

When the spear hit him he was merely puzzled as to why he could not feel any pain. It had come from behind him, pierced his side at the back and protruded from his lower chest. He sank to his knees and toppled over onto his side. As his eyes closed he could only feel an overwhelming gladness that it was all over.

Paullinus waited on the beach for his officers to report. There did not seem to be a Druid left alive. His staff-tribune pointed back across the sea. "A boat, Commander." Unseen in the heat of battle a small fishing vessel under a single clumsy mainsail had indeed beaten its way into the bay. A figure in Roman uniform stood in the prow. "A centurion, I think," said the tribune. "Probably a messenger. It must be urgent for him to have commandeered a vessel so quickly and to have followed us here."

"Very well. Bring him to me immediately he lands."

The officers came to report. "One hundred and forty-three Roman dead," said the infantry commander, "including the five during the crossing. No officers."

"And the Druids?"

"There are a dozen survivors, no more, who fled inland. My men are hunting them down."

"Good. So much for the vaunted magic of these so-called priests!" He turned to look at the incoming boat. "I will issue the necessary further orders when I hear what that messenger has to say."

Fifteen minutes later the centurion came splashing through the shallows and conferred alone with Paullinus. The officers could see the expression of astonishment on their commander's face as he questioned the man; a look that changed to one of deep anger and grim determination.

Finally Paullinus came back to the group. "You have until midday to clear up matters here. Bury our own dead but leave the Druid bodies to rot. Hunt down those survivors and destroy them—I don't want even a single Druid left alive on this island. We sail at noon. I want to be back on the mainland by this evening. We will rest there overnight, and then we march at dawn!"

"But where to?" said the infantry commander.

"Eastwards," said Paullinus grimly, "to see a queen!"

* * *

Gilda came back into her body with a jerk, and opened her eyes. She rose numbly, closed the ritual, and then retraced her path to the shore. She took a helmet that lay on one of the Roman graves and filled it with sea-water and carried it to where her father lay. She carefully removed the spear that still transfixed him and gently began to wash his bloodstained body. When she had finished she rose and saluted him gravely.

"To Cranog and those who stood with him," she said softly, "who died in order that the Light shall shine more abundantly. Let those who now bear the lamp take heed to bear themselves with equal honor!"

She raised her arms to the sky. "Let not these things be forgotten!" she cried passionately, and her voice echoed and re-echoed along the empty shoreline of Mona.

epilogue

The two horses nibbled peacefully at the dawn grass. The light wind, chilled by the promise of winter, stirred their manes. Across the back of one of the horses, roped securely, was a long, still bundle wrapped in animal skins. The hill-stream gurgled pleasantly as it ran from the high forest behind them down through the rough meadow to the lake villages of Glaeston below. Here, where the horses were tethered, a double loop in the stream's course had formed a deep pool where the water paused to meander quietly for a few yards before continuing its downward plunge. A huge willow drooped lazily over the pool, and on the far bank a cluster of reeds stirred in the wind. Gilda the Witch-Maiden, silent as a tree, sat by the water's edge deep in contemplation. Presently she rose and nodded to herself in satisfaction as she saw a figure robed in white climbing the slope. She waited patiently until he finally forded the stream below the pool and came towards her.

"I received your message," said Josue quietly, "and came alone as you asked." He glanced towards the horses. "The news reached us a week ago concerning the massacre at Mona," he said gently. "My people are grief-stricken at such horror, and no words of mine can adequately express our feelings."

She nodded calmly. "I was far away in the forest on the mainland when the Romans went to Mona. When they had gone I crossed the straits and searched a thousand dead to find my father. I have treated his body with oils to preserve it for the journey and so brought it here to you."

He shook his head in wonderment trying to imagine the horror of such a self-imposed task. "And what seek you with me?"

"There are no Druids left alive to give him Druid burial according to the old ways," she said quietly. "Will you give him burial according to the rites of your Christian cult?"

He nodded. "Yes, and gladly, and we will erect a stone to mark his resting place."

"It is enough," she said. "He would have asked for no more." She went over to the horses and stared at the still bundle for a few moments. She then untethered the other horse and swung up onto its back. "Farewell, Josue. Honor my father—he was more of a friend to you Christians than you still realize," and she touched the horse's flanks with her heels and rode away.

After she had gone he untethered the other horse with its sad load and started back down the slope to Glaeston—the priest of the new age and the dead priest of the old.

Waft thou my soul down the River of Naradek.
Bring it to Light, and to Life, and to Love!

ABOUT THE AUTHOR

PETER VALENTINE TIMLETT was born in 1933. A former jazz musician, Mr. Timlett has traveled widely, living for several years in Australia. At present he works for a large British publishing house and lives in Bedfordshire, England. His first novel, *The Seedbearers*, was prompted by his interest in the occult. *The Power of the Serpent* and *Twilight of the Serpent* are his second and third novels in this fantasy trilogy.